MW00918096

WE THE FUTURE

CLIFF LEWIS

CLIFF LEWIS

Mendota Heights, Minnesota

First Edition
First Printing, 2023

Book design by Cynthia Della-Rovere
Cover design by Cynthia Della-Rovere
Cover illustration by Carl Pearce (Beehive Illustration)

Jolly Fish Press, an imprint of North Star Editions, Inc.

Library of Congress Cataloging-in-Publication Data (pending)
978-1-63163-696-7

Jolly Fish Press
North Star Editions, Inc.
2297 Waters Drive
Mendota Heights, MN 55120
www.jollyfishpress.com

Printed in Canada

For the future,
otherwise known as
Jack and Lucy

PLAN A:

ACTIVATION

STEP 1:

RUN FOR YOUR LIFE

My chest, like the future, was burning.

Still, I ran up the mountain trail. Even with the sun so low, with daylight running out, the birds went on chirping like they had all the time in the world. Nobody'd told them it wouldn't last. I wheezed and ran on. Once I reached the mountaintop, I gave myself permission to catch my breath—only a little. The inhaler in my pocket could open my lungs, flood me with sweet, cool oxygen. But not yet. I reached for the other pocket instead. Mom's phone.

1-9-8-5—Invalid PIN.

1-2-3-4—Invalid PIN.

1-0-2-7—my birthday. I'm in.

I opened YouTube and hit *record*.

"I know how the world ends," I panted. "Just ran up Martic Pinnacle in Carbon Hill, Pennsylvania . . . but I'm not supposed to run this much. Because an asthma attack . . . like the one I'm having now . . . could kill me."

I pointed Mom's phone over the mountain's edge, toward the coal-burning power plant in the distance.

"Those smokestacks . . . are the reason I need this." I reached into my pocket and pulled out the inhaler, a blue plastic thing that looked like a cross between a PEZ dispenser and a prescription pill bottle. "But my medicine . . . can't protect me forever."

I mic-dropped the inhaler for dramatic effect. With struggling lungs, I told YouTube all the terrible things I'd learned about the climate apocalypse, a looming disaster the coal plant had already started. I wheezed and rattled off the hundred ways that ordinary people were speeding themselves to the brink of destruction. The vehicles, the vacations, the stuff in their grocery carts—all the "harmless" little choices that would bring on the end of the world as we know it.

"If the storms don't get you, something else will. The weather is just the beginning. One breakdown will set off a hundred others. A drought makes a war makes a plague. This is a chain reaction. So when the world breaks down, and my inhalers run out, it won't be the weather that kills me. It's gonna be the asthma," I gasped. "We are running. Out. Of time."

DONE.

I hit *publish* and dropped to my knees, scrambling for the inhaler. But it was gone—bounced right off the mountaintop. So much for dramatic effect. My lungs shrank and my panic grew, which made my lungs shrink even more. A chain reaction.

A cruel thought sparked in my skull and combusted somewhere deep in my stomach:

I could die up here.

Was I seriously about to clock out of this world with "Pretending to be a Climate Influencer" on my death certificate? In a way, it was almost funny, if it wasn't for the one thing that made it unbearably sad: Mom.

I punched three numbers into her phone and waited for an answer:

"9-1-1, what's your emergency?"

Too many to count, I thought, already unable to speak.

My throat tightened. My thoughts drifted. Would anyone come to save me? Probably not. But had it been worth it? Had my wheezing, ninety-second video been enough to save the world? I'd probably never find out.

I lay flat and watched the overlook a few paces off. It crossed my mind that the last thing I'd ever see might be this golden, deepening sunset. I could do worse.

Then the web of filthy lights around the distant coal plant flickered on. Ew.

Fossil fuels: 1

Jonah: 0

Why even *try* to fight back when an army of smokestacks and tailpipes had all taken dead aim at one Jonah Kaminski? First, it was the asthma. Then, less than an hour ago, it was the fuel tanker. That gas truck ran Mom's Prius straight off the road on our way home from what might've become our final round of miniature golf. No one got hurt. Not even the Prius. But the irony was more than I could take. I'd felt so angry—so brave—when I grabbed Mom's phone and made a run for Martic Pinnacle. As if I could take down the entire carbon empire with a single video upload. But the empire had time on its side and was always a hundred steps ahead of me.

My head was feeling carbonated now, a prickly wave of tingles scattering out across my body. The world went speckly. Everything in front of me bent, warped like the surface of a giant soap bubble. Until the bubble popped, and everything snapped right back to normal.

Normal, except for the pink astronaut.

The astronaut planted an American flag, Neil Armstrong–style, straight into the mountaintop dirt.

I had to be hallucinating. Dying will do that.

The pink mirage picked up Mom's phone, ended the 9-1-1 call, and knelt beside me.

A voice crackled out from the pink helmet, high and carefree. "Jonah Kaminski?"

I nodded, my desperate face reflected in her visor.

She handed me something small and silver: an inhaler.

"I'm from the future," she said. "We need you."

STEP 2:

PREPARE FOR THE WORST

I wasn't always such an apocalypse-hater. In fact, I used to be a pretty big fan.

It all started with zombies. In fifth grade, on the day Dad walked out, I saw my first zombie movie. Mom let me watch one of the old black-and-white ones, where the corpses all lumbered around like reasonable dead people. By sixth grade, I'd worked my way up to the newer ones, where zombies can sprint like Olympic gold medalists and humans can produce unlimited quantities of CGI blood. But it wasn't the gore that pulled me in. It was the planning.

I had this collection of retro composition notebooks. Each contained a handwritten zombie survival guide, complete with inventories, maps, and step-by-step instructions on what to do when the living dead start running the world. I filled seven notebooks with seven plans, each starting with the same two questions:

1. Where am I?

2. Where is Mom?

One notebook was labeled "ME @ SCHOOL + MOM @ WORK." Another was "ME @ HOME + MOM @ WORK." You get the idea. Most of them had Mom at work because . . . well, most of the time, Mom was at work.

My favorite notebook was "ME @ HOME + MOM @ HOME."

It went a little something like this: We'd fight our way out to the car with kitchen knives and head straight out for supplies. But we wouldn't go to the Superstore or Guns 'N' Ammo—not unless we wanted to crowd-surf over a zombie flash mob. Instead, we'd go to Home Run Sporting Goods, Carbon Hill's best-kept secret for all your apocalypse-shopping needs.

I had the shopping list all worked out:

✓ Baseball bats

✓ Protein bars

✓ Flares

✓ Solar generator

✓ Hunting gear

✓ Tylenol

✓ Cheetos

The hunting gear was for Mom, who'd learned how to shoot during her brief stint in the military before I was born. The Tylenol was also for Mom, who'd lost a foot during that same stint and dealt with bouts of knee pain ever since. The Cheetos were for me. I couldn't bear to live in a world without orange powdered cheese.

After Home Run Sporting Goods, we'd take the back roads to Uncle Mark's bunker in Stewart County. The way I figured it, if the United States Congress were just a swarm of zombies wandering the National Mall, then Mom and Uncle Mark wouldn't have any politics to argue about.

Nothing brings out the impossible like the end of the world.

Zombies made the world feel simple. They kept my mind off the tougher stuff, like Dad's new family, and Mom's long hours, and bills piled up on the kitchen counter. If I was deep in a good survival guide,

I didn't have to worry about Mom spending too much on Christmas again this year. Fake zombie apocalypses were much more relaxing than real-life problems. I didn't become an apocalypse-hater until the end of sixth grade, the day I went to the hospital and learned about the *real* apocalypse—the one that grown-ups had already started. That's when the end of the world stopped being fun.

But you don't wanna hear about that. Who in their right mind would? I, for one, know exactly how the world will come to an end, and I can promise you this: the pink astronaut is a lot more interesting.

I sat up and watched the pink astronaut turn to face the horizon. She unlocked her helmet and shook loose a shower of glossy black braids before taking one small step toward the edge of Martic Pinnacle.

I had just finished taking another puff from her silver inhaler when I heard the astronaut breathe in the hot September air—not fast like she was out of breath, but slowly, like she was taking a drink.

"You alright?" Her voice sounded breezy, and far younger than I'd expect from a seasoned astronaut.

I nodded, even though she wasn't looking back. "Who are you?"

She turned to face me, backlit by the orange clouds. Her face was dark brown, and her eyes were sun bright. She smiled with tears on her cheeks. "Call me Sunny."

"Sssssunny," I stammered. The astronaut was a girl. And by a girl, I mean a kid—she couldn't have been much older than me.

The girl called Sunny slung off a pink backpack that looked rugged enough to survive a nuclear blast. She dug out a dog-eared, spiral-bound pad with big block letters running across its cover. "LESSON PLANNER," it said, like something straight off a teacher's desk. Sunny kissed the book. She turned a few scrapbook-looking pages of handwritten diagrams until she found it: an old sheet of newspaper, which she unfolded over the gravel beside me.

I peered around her shoulder. The paper looked a hundred years old, yellow and brittle, but its header—oddly enough—displayed tomorrow's date. And that wasn't even the weirdest part: This ancient-looking newspaper featured a photo of *me*. It was the one from last year's picture day with a small-but-not-unnoticeable spot of Nutella on my cheek.

The headline read:

LOCAL BOY DIES ON MARTIC PINNACLE

I gulped, suddenly wondering if pink astronauts carried emergency barf bags. Here I was, reading the announcement of something that *almost* happened minutes earlier, before this astronaut appeared in this exact spot at this exact moment in time:

I. Almost. Died.

Before this fact could sink in, I watched a brand-new headline sink itself into the front page of the *Carbon Hill Gazette*. The text faded, shifted, rewrote itself:

LOCAL BOY GOES—

Sunny yanked the paper out of view and balled it up before I could finish reading.

"It worked," she whispered.

This was probably when I should've said thanks. But if you've ever had a pink astronaut materialize right in front of you just to undo your regularly scheduled death, you'll know that in times like these, your mind is not flooded with gratitude. It's flooded with questions. Why me, out of every "local boy" on Planet Earth? And what was my new headline? *LOCAL BOY GOES* where? How exactly had my future changed? I opened my mouth to ask, but I couldn't get a word out. The questions were still coming in.

Sunny stowed her Lesson Planner and rose to face the horizon. She put on a pair of pink-rimmed glasses and admired the still-magnificent sunset.

"It really is the 2020s now, isn't it?" she whispered.

"Of course," I managed to reply while climbing to my feet. Joining Sunny, I let the sunset wash over me and finally felt a trickle of gratitude seep in. The colors unfolded so vivid and free, like fireworks in slow motion. It was beautiful.

Sunny sighed. "It's the most hideous thing I have ever seen in my life."

I gave her a puzzled look, wondering if she needed a new prescription on those pink-rimmed glasses—until she pointed below the horizon to the Allister Energy Plant.

"There's no smoke," she said through gritted teeth. "I always thought there'd be smoke."

"It's just invisible," I muttered, mostly to myself. "That's part of the problem."

I was well aware that the poison from those smokestacks could not be seen, even though the death that it caused was quite visible all over Earth. This coal plant, and thousands like it, were doing their best to kill the world—just like they were trying to kill me.

This kind of lung disease rarely strikes a person so hard all at once, but my first asthma attack almost took me out. If it had, I would've spent my last moments watching Tony Torricelli pretend not to pick his nose at the edge of the athletic field.

Our gym teacher, Ms. Pain (her actual legal name), had saved our annual fitness exam for the last week of school, which kinda felt like an early punishment for all the hours we'd spend on screens over the summer. She had us run a single mile without stopping. It seemed easy enough until halfway through my second lap, when I collapsed behind a bush near the edge of the schoolyard. Tony Torricelli had already finished his mile and lounged a couple bushes away, delicately cleaning his left nasal passage.

Lucky for me, Tony checked to see if anyone was watching. What he found was me, flat on the grass, clutching my chest for dear life.

Tony called Ms. Pain, who called Nurse Lulu, who called an ambulance. I'm not sure who called Mom. Maybe Mom just knew.

The doctor told us that my asthma must've been there awhile, but it finally flared up now. Probably some combination of the day's unusually high humidity and Carbon Hill's unusually low air quality. Apparently, they'd been seeing more asthma patients than usual that week.

I couldn't fall asleep in the hospital bed that night. For a while, Mom and I tried watching TV, but the hospital didn't have Netflix—just back-to-back episodes of a reality show about "X-treme" corporate executives. I was oddly fascinated by the cringe factor of HeTV's *PunkWork with Smash Kelly*, but only for the first hour.

Before Mom fell asleep on the recliner, I borrowed her phone and hunkered down for a YouTube zombie binge. But the first video was a bait and switch: "Ten Reasons Why the Climate Apocalypse Is the REAL Zombie Apocalypse." It was one of those animated explainers that are supposed to make science seem interesting to kids. No "real" zombies about it. But before I switched it off, Reason #10 caught my attention:

The Climate Apocalypse Is Making Us Sick.

A cartoon zombie gave the highlights. Every time people burn fossil fuels—the gas in our cars, the coal in our power plants—those cars and power plants burp out all kinds of poisonous gases, like sulfur dioxide (SO_2) and nitrogen dioxide (NO_2), which can trigger breathing-related illnesses like . . . take a wild guess.

I stuck around for Reasons #9 though #1, bingeing all twenty minutes of the video. The YouTube recommendation algorithm took over after that.

Up next: "What the Coming Climate Apocalypse Means for Kids Born Today."

Up next: "The Disease-Carrying Insects of Climate Change."

Up next: "How the Climate Wars Might Send Us Back to the Stone Age."

Mom's phone battery died after less than an hour of climate-YouTube, but that was more than enough time to flood me with rage. Apparently, science can do that.

Ever hear of carbon dioxide (CO_2)? Well, CO_2 makes SO_2 and NO_2 look like a cool spring breeze. Too much of this gas isn't just a Jonah-killer; it's a full-blown Earth-killer. You see, whenever CO_2 spews out of the Allister Energy Plant, a lot of that gas gets stuck in Earth's atmosphere. After that, the CO_2 starts acting like those sheets of plastic Mom stuck to our windows to save on heating bills last winter. Carbon keeps the heat from getting out. That's why the world keeps getting hotter and hotter. Little by little. Year after year.

It's not just in your head.

Grown-ups call this "climate change"—the most boring possible name for the End of the World as We Know It. And not my doctor, not my science teacher, not a single grown-up had ever told me what "climate change" actually meant. Only YouTube had the guts to tell me that people my age would grow up with sick lungs and scorched forests and flooded towns and whole cities wiped away. Worst. Future. Ever. It was a future that couldn't promise me anything—not snow on Christmas, not sand on the beach, not safe roads, clean water, or breathable air.

I couldn't help but wonder: how could a guy who'd just nearly died of gym class survive in a world like that?

So, yeah, I might've freaked out a little. Let's just say it was a good thing they already had me in the hospital. That was the first night of my newfound obsession with the climate apocalypse, which kicked off the loneliest summer of all time. Cutting out CO_2 emissions from my life meant cutting my life out of the modern world. It meant saying no to AC, to beef, to dairy, to joyrides with Mom and visits with friends—not that I had any friends to begin with.

Once August came around, I'd hoped that school would brighten things up. It didn't. In sixth grade, I'd been awkward; now, in seventh grade, I was awkward, asthmatic, *and* climate obsessed. All through September, I looked perfectly timid on the outside, but inside, it was hurricane season. Each day swirled with new questions, new doubts, new fears. Knowing about the apocalypse had made life so miserable that, by the last Sunday of September, I couldn't stay quiet anymore. The tanker truck just gave me a little push. I "borrowed" Mom's phone, ran up Martic Pinnacle, captured a video, and ran out of oxygen.

That's how the coal plant tried to kill me—and how it certainly *would* have killed me if the pink astronaut hadn't shown up when she did.

STEP 3:

RAGE, RAGE, RAGE

"It's so much worse than you think," Sunny the pink astronaut said. She stared daggers off Martic Pinnacle, her eyes dead set on the Allister Energy Plant. I'd never seen anyone, apart from myself, take a building so personally. "So much greedier. More destructive than you could possibly imagine." She spat off the mountain.

It took a lot to break my attention from Sunny's righteous fury, but Mom's phone hadn't stopped buzzing and dinging for the last full minute. It was blowing up with notifications. I read the lock screen. No way. I blinked and read it again. Apparently, a big YouTuber had stumbled across my video and blasted it out to all her social channels. I'd already racked up 7,000 views. A Jonah Kaminski viral video felt about as believable as a time-traveling pink astronaut. But then again, there must've been some connection between these two impossibilities. Why else would someone have leapt across time *just* to rescue one very random Jonah Kaminski?

"*We need you*"—that was what she'd said. Sunny had saved me for a reason, and now I understood what that reason was.

"Sunny," I said, much too quiet. Even at a time like this, the awkwardness kept my mouth taped up like usual. I cleared my throat and tried again. "I know why you're here."

Sunny kept glaring at the power plant. "And why's that?"

"My video," I mumbled. "It's going viral. Right now. And who knows what could happen if I keep posting more?"

"Show me," Sunny said.

With quiet pride, I handed her Mom's phone.

Sunny flung it off the mountain. "No more videos."

A gale-force wind screeched out of my throat—sounding more like a sheep's bleat than a human shout.

Sunny strolled away from the pinnacle. "I'm starving. How's the food these days?"

Finally, I shaped my screeching into words: "That wasn't even my phone!"

"Pancakes would be good. Or chocolate. Or chocolate pancakes." She scooped her helmet off the ground and made for the walking trail.

"What are you—" I leapt ahead and swiped the crumpled newspaper out of Sunny's hand. Just as I suspected: *LOCAL BOY GOES VIRAL WITH MARTIC PINNACLE VIDEO.* "Why would you want to *stop* me from making more videos?"

Did Sunny travel all the way back in time from who-knows-when just to cancel a newly trending online activist like me?

"I'll tell you why I tossed that phone." Sunny snatched back the newspaper and tore it to ribbons. "It's because *slacktivism* was one of the most destructive forces in the early twenty-first century. That's why."

"Slacktivism?"

"Lazy activism," Sunny said, now tearing the ribbons into confetti. "Hashtags. Online arguments. *Videos.* The problem wasn't that people didn't care about saving the world. It was that those people never built any real power to save it."

Sunny held out the pile of scraps. They fluttered off in the September breeze.

"It still doesn't make any sense," I replied. "Imagine what could happen if a million people heard my message."

"With all due respect, your message needs a little work," Sunny said, trudging off down the nature trail. "And besides, I don't need to *imagine* what would happen. I know the history."

I ran to catch up. "What do you mean 'the history'?"

"The history of your video," Sunny said. "Of the century. Of everything that happened after you died."

STEP 4:

Go Viral

Here's how history had gone without me, before Sunny went ahead and changed it:

On Sunday, September 25, I ran up Martic Pinnacle, posted my video, and died. Within twenty-four hours, the news of my untimely death boosted my YouTube count to 12 million views. Everybody knew my name. Even Smash Kelly from *PunkWork with Smash Kelly* posted a tribute. People held vigils and small protests in my honor. #ForJonah trended for two weeks straight.

Then the world met Chewbagoat.

On Sunday, October 9, a dad in Fort Lauderdale, Florida, uploaded a clip of his family pet, a fluffy brown goat, buckled into a car's passenger seat. "Chewie, hit the hyperdrive!" he shouted. The goat responded with a pitch-perfect Chewbacca roar. The video was nineteen seconds long. It came to be viewed 13 billion times. "Chewbagoat" became the most viral video in the history of the world.

By Christmas, everyone knew Chewbagoat, but no one remembered me. Carbon emissions rose that year, just as they redesigned the Fort Lauderdale Rainforest Café in Chewbagoat's honor. They called it "Chewbagoat's Cantina." In 2048, the Cantina flooded, along with the rest of Fort Lauderdale. By 2067, whole towns in southern

Florida had washed away. By 2074, acres of New England maple trees had died off, and the last of the Texas cattle had dropped dead in the desert heat. The amber waves of grain had thinned out. The fruited plains had dried up. In 2076, the United States of America celebrated its 300th anniversary by bitterly dividing into fifty separate nations.

After that came the wars.

One famine, two pandemics, and three superstorms later, a girl was born in 2087 in what used to be called Carbon Hill, Pennsylvania. Her parents named her Sunday Turner, but they always called her Sunny. Thirteen years later, that girl would find a way to get back to Carbon Hill in the early 2020s.

She traveled back in time with only two goals in mind:

1. Save my life.
2. Save the future.

All this Sunny told me over a plate of banana-chocolate waffles. And chocolate-chip pancakes. And a hot-fudge sundae. Basically, anything with chocolate on the Wayback Diner's twenty-four-hour menu.

For the life of me, I couldn't understand how she'd become so relaxed about all this, so carefree. Must've been the waffles.

"Have some," said Sunny. She was still wearing her astronaut suit with a matching pair of pink-rimmed glasses, her shiny black braids all bundled behind her head to keep them away from the syrup. She slid a plate across the table. "You know," she said, twirling her fork, "when I come from, chocolate's worth more than gold."

I pushed the waffles back. "I'm good."

I'd lost my appetite. You would, too. Just imagine hearing about the end of your own life and the end of life as you know it while "Earth Angel" streams on the fake digital jukebox. *Surprise, you're not dead! BTW, we're all gonna die.* I wasn't sure if I wanted to burst into tears or run for cover. On the bright side, Sunny's apocalyptic forecast had shocked the awkward right out of me, at least for the moment. This was the most time I'd spent conversing with another kid my age since . . . well, since Gideon.

"Honestly," I said, "I don't get how you can eat right now. I mean, you just delivered the worst news of the century."

Sunny straightened, as if my reaction were the last thing she'd expected to hear.

"The worst news?" She grinned. "Buddy, you're looking at the *best* news of the century right here."

I gestured at the timelines Sunny had sketched on napkins across our window-side booth. "The future is a nightmare. Where's the good news in that?"

"You're talking about the *old* future," Sunny said through a mouthful of waffle. With a sweep of her arm, she wiped all the napkins away. "Everything's on the table now, so eat up." She slid her plate back over to me, and I reluctantly took a bite.

"There's no time like the present," Sunny continued. "From here, anybody can change the future. Changing the past? Now, that's the hard part, but even so." She gestured to her pink astronaut suit. "Look out, Allister Energy."

"Fine," I said, mopping up the last of the chocolate sauce with a fluffy waffle chunk. "So we're gonna take on fossil fuels. Change the future. Save the world. Great. But how exactly are two kids going to do that?"

Sunny winked. "You tell me."

I nearly choked on the chocolaty waffle. "Now, wait a minute—" I needed a plan. Instead, I got a heart-attack-sized platter of home fries topped with gooey cheese and two fried eggs. The server left, and I nudged the plate toward Sunny. Before digging in, she bowed her head for the second time that evening.

"Sorry," I said, cutting into Sunny's prayer. "You're meaning to tell me that you traveled back in time to save the twenty-first century from a global climate apocalypse, but you don't even have a plan for how you're gonna do it?" I pressed my sweaty palms on the table and tried to breathe easy.

Sunny peered up, her hands still folded. "How 'bout we pray on it?"

"I'm not religious," I muttered.

"I'm not seeing your point." Sunny grabbed the Cholula. "Look, Jonah. What part of 'good news' don't you understand?" She sprinkled hot sauce onto her plate. "The dead are raised, and a pink astronaut just traveled back in time to stop the climate apocalypse. All things are possible." To emphasize her final point, Sunny picked up a wad of fries and chomped.

"And that's all you can tell me."

"In a way"—Sunny wrinkled her nose—"it's the only thing I'll ever be able to tell you."

I rested my head on the table. "So you've got no plan whatsoever except to save one guy's life and eat breakfast for dinner?"

"I never said there wasn't a plan." Sunny rested her hand on the

Lesson Planner scrapbook and smiled as the server dropped off the check. "What I *said* was I'd pray on it. And I will. Every single day I'm here."

"So there *is* a plan?" I said. "Then let's hear it." Clearly, people from the future had a problem with getting to the point.

"For starters," Sunny replied, "I want you to round up your Crew." She slapped two twenty-dollar bills on the table.

"My what?"

"Your friends," Sunny said. "But only your closest."

I gulped. If there was anything more impossible than time-travel, it was the idea of me, Jonah Kaminski, the friendless wonder, rounding up my "friends."

Desperate to change the subject, I grabbed one of Sunny's twenty-dollar bills. "Your money is wrong. These are supposed to have Andrew Jackson on them, not Harriet Tubman."

Sunny grabbed the Tubman twenties and rolled her eyes. "What's *wrong* is having Andrew Jackson on US currency. Evil dude. But you're right. These Tubmans are a few years too early." She pulled out some ones and fives from an envelope in her Lesson Planner.

Outside our window, a police cruiser blazed across the highway—lights flaring, sirens blaring. Then another. Then two more. All of them headed toward my side of town.

I shot to my feet. "Gotta get home," I choked, suddenly remembering Mom.

I hadn't seen her since I'd grabbed her phone and run off to record a near-fatal asthma attack at the top of Martic Pinnacle before hanging up on my own gasping 9-1-1 call only to go viral and disappear. She might be a little concerned.

"Sunny, I appreciate you saving my life. Obviously." I stepped away from the booth. "And it's not that I don't believe you can change history. I mean, if you'd asked me this afternoon whether a few kids can change the world, I would've called it impossible. But everyone always told me that time-travel was impossible, too, so who knows? Here's what I do know: I'm not the kid to help you do it. Because, honestly, I don't have any friends to round up."

I went for the exit and pushed into the late September heat wave. The distant sirens and unseasonable crickets swirled together in a symphony that sounded like the end of the world.

The Wayback's door jingled open behind me.

Sunny's space suit glittered like magic in front of the chrome-plated diner. She eyed me from the stoop, looking even more determined than she had at her landing site on Martic Pinnacle. Sunny had a mission.

"Let's talk about friends."

STEP 5:

TRY NOT TO SCREAM FOR ICE CREAM

Once upon a time, I had a friend.

Even then, I wasn't exactly what you'd call a social butterfly. More of a social turtle, really. It probably had something to do with how quiet my house had always been. Mom worked long hours, and my dad worked long nights. Most days, I hardly saw the guy. So I learned to do things on my own. I could start the laundry by myself, vacuum the carpets by myself, and microwave the ramen by myself. Most days, Jonah Kaminski was a party of one, a lone wolf. Or a lone turtle, I guess.

I had only one friend, but he was a good one. Gideon.

One night in third grade, Gideon and I stayed up until 2:00 a.m. crafting homemade Pokémon cards over sleeping bags in my living room. We were making Gideon a set, since he was never allowed to buy them. His mom insisted that *Pokémon* meant "Finger demons" in Japanese, and she held to this belief no matter how many times Gideon googled it for her. I knew this because Gideon told me. Because we talked. All the time.

But two years back, in fifth grade, the talking stopped. That was the year Gideon's father passed away unexpectedly. That same year my dad moved out—also unexpectedly.

You'd think we'd have a lot more in common after that, both of us losing a dad, but to me, our stories couldn't have been more different. At Gideon's house, you'd see sympathy cards, flowers, quilts made from his dad's shirts. My dad took all his shirts with him. And it's a well-documented fact that when your father packs up and leaves town for no good reason, nobody sends you a sympathy card.

Whenever I tried to stop over, Gideon would be gone. There seemed to be an infinite train of well-wishers waiting to whisk him off to a county fair, or an ice-cream shop, or the trampoline park. Was I jealous? A little. But mostly, I felt useless. I mean, what could I do to make Gideon feel better? It's not like I could drive him to Bounce-O-Zone.

Slowly but surely, I forgot how to talk to Gideon. What could we talk about, anyway? I wouldn't dare bring up my own problems. I mean, life at home was hard, but it's not like anyone had died. Gideon's life was different, his world was different, and I had no place in it now. So, I quit. Our friendship faded into silence. And when a social turtle like me gives up his only good friend, he's not exactly racing to find a new one. I liked my shell just fine.

That's how I became Creekside Middle's leading expert in Not Making Friends.

Life hacks for maximizing your friendlessness:

✓ Stop taking the bus and walk to school alone.

✓ Work on survival guides at desk before class (head down).

✓ Never sit at the same lunch table two days in a row.

I became so skilled at Not Making Friends that I forgot how to talk to anyone but Mom. Whenever I tried, my mouth went dry. Then my back went prickly. Then my heart rate went for the gold. And all that came *before* asthma joined the party. Now, according to my doctor, those feelings of anxiety can trigger my asthma attacks, which can trigger more anxiety. The whole thing is a terrible chain reaction—a feedback loop. If I don't keep an inhaler handy, my awkwardness is a life-threatening medical condition.

But there I was, telling Sunny the whole sad story. Don't ask me why, but apparently walking home to the sound of sirens after a near-death experience is a pretty good way to make me unload my emotional baggage. Also, it felt good to say these things to someone other than Mom, to say anything this raw to a person my age. Talking to Sunny was like using an inhaler that relieved something so much deeper than my lungs.

All Sunny had to do was listen. It wasn't until we'd reached Ocean Avenue that she said anything at all. She stopped me with a hand on my shoulder.

"Jonah. I'm sorry for your loss," she said, looking me dead in the eyes. "And I'm sorry you didn't hear that enough. But I've got something else you need to hear: Gideon is still your friend. Your dad might be long gone, but your friend never went anywhere."

Technically, she had a point. I could see Gideon's house even then, right from where we stood. If I ignored his stepdad's perfectly polished work truck on the roadside, I could easily imagine I'd gone four years back in time, to the days when I would hop that chain-link gate and pop in through the Baylors' front door without even knocking.

But I was no Sunny; time-travel was off the table for me.

I shook my head. "Gideon's still around, sure, but that friendship is shot. There's no bringing back the dead."

"Still wrong, resurrection boy," Sunny replied. "You're living proof that no one's ever too far gone. As a matter of fact," she said, with a little catch in her voice, "I'm counting on it."

Something chirped loudly. Sunny snapped to attention and pulled back her sleeve to check her wristwatch. The timepiece was thick, heavy looking, and gunmetal gray. It reminded me of a weapon. She whispered something into it and checked the watch face.

"I can't believe it," she sighed, her eyes lit by the tiny glowing screen. "They found me."

"What are you talking about?"

Sunny dragged me behind a parked car and pulled me low to the ground.

"Look," she whispered, showing me the notification on her watch: *JUMP DETECTED at 40.3267407/-78.9219698. ORIGIN: 2100 C.E.* She tapped the coordinates, which turned her display into a tiny map of my neighborhood, then pointed to a blinking dot. "How close is that?"

"Just a few blocks from here."

"Then stay down. I never expected them to use that piece of junk. Talk about a death wish." Sunny gave a nervous chuckle.

Even the pink astronaut was frightened. I could feel my heart thumping its way up my throat.

"Sunny," I whispered. "Who's 'they'?"

She covered my mouth. "Hear that?"

It played without words, but I knew the tune so well that I couldn't hear it without recalling the lyrics:

Oh, say can you see . . .

The electric melody got closer, and my heart beat faster.

. . . by the dawn's early light . . .

A boxy truck rounded the corner of the block, and with it came the music. It was an ice-cream truck—more beautiful than any I'd ever seen in Carbon Hill. Ours was a rusty, repainted thing that had probably spent a former life delivering US postage. This one was too pretty for a town like mine.

. . . the bombs bursting in air . . .

"Tell me, Jonah," Sunny whispered. "Have you ever seen a real, honest-to-goodness ice-cream truck with a name like that?"

The logo curled along the side of the vehicle in flowing, old-fashioned letters: *Ice-Cream Truck*.

"Feels off." Our usual truck was called Doctor Swirly, which sounded like the name of a toilet-based comic book villain, but that's what we got in Carbon Hill. "*Ice-Cream Truck* isn't even a name. Seems a little obvious."

"An obvious *disguise* is what it is," Sunny said as the truck steered off to the next street. She grabbed the Lesson Planner from her backpack and searched its scrapbook pages. "It's them, alright. I just never thought they'd be so reckless."

And I thought I was confused before. What exactly were we hiding from? Who were "they"? Why were they here? How were they reckless? I had all the questions, but I couldn't muster anything more than a stupefied, slack-jawed stare.

Sunny's finger landed on a small comment in the margins. "It's my fault. Missed a step. I was supposed to disable it." She let out a long, deflated sigh, leaking positive energy like a punctured weather balloon. Before I got a good look, she shut the Lesson Planner and packed it away. "I've gotta lay low. And get into something a little less . . . sparkly."

"Wha—"

"Meet me here tomorrow morning," Sunny said, taking me by the shoulders. "Nine thirty."

I managed to squeeze out a few words: "But I have school!"

"Nope," Sunny said. "No school tomorrow."

I knew for a fact that she was wrong. "Wanna see a calendar?"

"Wanna argue dates with a time-traveler? Nine thirty sharp." Sunny broke away, and my first real question finally broke loose.

"Sunny!" And here was the question that drowned out all the others, the question that had quietly smoldered in the back of my brain since she'd first appeared:

"Why me?"

Sunny stopped.

"Out of all the people in the world," I blurted, "what's so important about me? You didn't even like my video."

Sunny threw up her arms. "It wasn't in the video, but there *was* something special the video showed us." She shrugged. "Just something about you."

"And what exactly was that?"

She slapped me on the shoulder. "You'll figure it out."

And with that, Sunny the pink astronaut launched herself into the night.

STEP 6:

Carry the Weight of the World

It looked like every emergency vehicle in Carbon Hill had stopped over for dinner. The entire place flickered in the colored lights of police cruisers, an ambulance, and even a couple of news trucks. Everyone was on the lookout for that asthmatic, internet-famous missing child.

The moment I reached the front yard, my mom tore a path through the gaggle of first responders, abandoning her cane at the stoop and limping toward me. She arrested me with the kind of hug that almost hurts.

"Hi, Mom."

She pulled back to inspect my face. My ears. My clothes. She frowned only to keep herself from bursting into tears. I could tell.

The officers and paramedics closed in:

"Did anyone harm you, son?"

"Are you breathing alright?"

I did my best to tell them the truth, or at least the time-travel-free version of it. They were satisfied enough. But the news crew wasn't so easily pleased. They crowded around as Mom shielded my face from their lights and asked for a little space. The reporters didn't hear so well.

"What's your full name?"

"Have you read the YouTube comments?"

"How does it feel to be an instant viral celebrity?"

When the Channel 8 microphone accidentally bopped me in the forehead, Mom snapped into active duty. She snatched the mic like she was disarming an enemy combatant, then put on her best news anchor impression.

"This is Jonah's mom reporting," she announced. "Under a 1995 court decision, I can legally sue this station for any emotional harm you bring my son with all these cameras in his face. And since your crew's currently standing on *my* private lawn, the state of Pennsylvania grants me the right to remove them with force. *Deadly* force if necessary."

Channel 8 took off faster than you can say "online law school." In her spare time, Mom had spent the last three years studying to become a public defense lawyer. It was always fun to watch Mom go legal on someone, but less fun when she had tears welling up in her eyes.

Before long, only Mom and I remained, sitting quietly together on the stoop.

It was time to tell her. Everything. But where would I start? My head swirled with apologies, explanations, stories, and sadness. Most of all, I couldn't shake the thought that some version of history had once existed where Mom would have been sitting right here on this very stoop, alone, waiting for a son who would never come home.

"Phone." Mom opened her hand.

I looked away.

"Dropped it," I answered. "Off Martic Pinnacle. Accidentally, I mean."

"You're joking." Mom laughed and shook her head. "I gotta say, Jonah"—she gave me a squeeze—"for such a quiet guy, you sure know how to make some noise. They told me you're up to 700,000 views. Gotta be the most interesting thing that's ever happened in this town."

Yeah, I thought, *except for that one time a girl from 2100 materialized on top of Martic Pinnacle.* It was time to come clean.

"Mom—" A retro electronic beep chimed in to cut me off. It was Mom's cordless phone from the early 2000s, the one she still kept for emergencies. She scooped the chunky handset from the stoop.

"This is Cassandra," Mom answered. "Yes. Okay . . . He's doing just fine . . . Yes . . . Only a few minutes ago . . . I'll tell him . . . Thank you so much, sir. Good night." Her voice was quiet by the end of the call. She set the phone down and let out a long, shuddering breath.

"Who was that?"

Mom stared for a second, then snapped out of her funk. "That was Richard Allister."

"*The* Richard Allister? As in, President-of-Allister-Energy Richard Allister? Richest-guy-in-Carbon-Hill Richard Allister?"

Mom nodded slowly.

"How does he even know who I am?"

She quit nodding.

"He saw my video." I knew it. She knew it. That's why her voice had gotten so small on the phone. Mom wasn't usually one to keep quiet, no matter who held the other end of the conversation. But talking to Richard Allister? Different story. This one man had total control of the Allister Energy Plant, which happened to be the one place where just about everyone in this town made a living. Everyone, including Mom.

Going to bed early had never felt so good—and that's saying a lot. I'd always been a pretty big fan of my bedroom. It used to be my parents', in the days before my dad moved out. He'd spent most of his time cooped up behind this very door. His room was his kingdom, the place where he'd sleep and watch old '90s movies between night shifts at the energy plant. Sometimes I would pace the hallway, hoping he'd notice the creaking floorboards and pop out the door, eager to come help me heat up dinner or hike up Martic Pinnacle. Instead, one day my dad popped out the door and never went back in.

The day he left, Mom cleared out the bedroom. She replaced the black-out window shades with bright yellow curtains that flooded my room with light by day. For the nights, she dotted the walls and ceiling with little speckles of glow-in-the-dark paint that looked like galaxies running in every possible direction. It was the best décor that a security guard's wages could buy.

Tonight, Mom insisted on tucking me in, which would've felt embarrassing on any night when I hadn't almost died. But after a day like this, a little coddling was fine with me.

Mom ruffled my overgrown hair. "Where'd you get the new one?" she asked, examining my silver inhaler from the year 2100.

I didn't answer, no longer sure how much I wanted her to know. About Sunny. About the future. About Sunny's plan to fix it, which I still barely understood. My feelings had changed, and for just one reason: Richard Allister.

Mom had handled so many impossible things in her life: Losing a foot. Losing a marriage. Getting a son with an expensive illness. It seemed like the only thing that had ever gone well for Mom was her job at Allister Energy.

The company put pictures of Mom all over the place—on brochures, websites, even a TV commercial once. You might think they did it because of Mom's military service and her Purple Heart medal. Or perhaps it was because Mom's cane and prosthetic foot made Allister Energy look like the kind of company that welcomed all kinds of people.

But I had a simpler explanation: Mom's smile was pure electricity.

Last year, Allister had awarded Mom the Starlight Hero Grant, which was paying for more than half of her law school bills. Sure, Allister Energy was bad for the world, but it was pretty good for Mom. If I intended to save the future, I'd have to do it without getting her fired—not until she finished her law degree, anyway.

"Earth to Jonah." Mom tapped on my forehead. "Where'd you get the inhaler?"

"Um." I faked a yawn. There was only one way to keep Mom out of trouble with Richard Allister. I would keep her out of this. Completely. The future was my burden to bear.

I pretended my eyes were drooping shut.

"Must've been one of those paramedics," Mom whispered as she switched off my bedside lamp. "'Night, Jonah. Love you."

I was pretending to sleep, so I didn't say anything back.

STEP 7:

MASTER THE ART OF THE CLAPBACK

Sunshine peeked over the housetops as I opened the front door. I took a puff from my futuristic inhaler, tightened my backpack straps, and stepped out into the light. Until now, I'd been free to pretend yesterday never happened. And with Mom already off working a double shift, pretending had been extra easy. I'd spent all morning alone, in perfect, busy bliss, crossing off tasks on my massive dry-erase kitchen calendar.

Unplug appliances: did it. Stir backyard compost: done. Prep dinner ingredients: *bon appétit* (the meatless, dairy-free tacos were basically just salads rolled into tortillas, so prepping was easy enough).

But now it was time to leave the stoop, to quit pretending and reenter the world as Jonah Kaminski, public freakout video star. It was time to walk to school.

I'd made it halfway down the block when I noticed a front door swing open across the street. A tall, sturdy kid moseyed out onto his own front porch. His shaggy hair was all messed up in the back, but he wore a chill expression that told you he really wasn't worried about it. Even though he stood taller than most seventh graders, he still walked with a fifth-grade pep in his step.

"Gideon . . ." the flat voice of his robotic stepdad called from inside. He bolted back into the house and reemerged with a lunchbox.

Gideon cracked open the gate to his chain-link fence and struggled to wriggle through without Einstein making a run for it. Einstein was a mustard-colored labradoodle who always needed a haircut. You could never see his eyes under the fluff, but his smile showed more than enough personality. Einstein had the whitest, toothiest grin—almost humanlike. The dog's smile grew the biggest whenever he escaped from Gideon's front yard, which for Einstein was a daily ambition.

Gideon shut the gate, shaking his head with a smirk. I smirked along with him. That is, until the two of us made eye contact for 1.21 nanoseconds. I turned my head as fast as my neck could carry it and locked my eyes on the sidewalk.

In general, I was pretty good at guessing people's thoughts. It felt like basic math, especially when it came to Gideon. Back in third grade, he couldn't figure out what he wanted for Christmas, so I told him: a HaptiGlow LED Laser Tag set. And I was right. Gideon put that toy at the top of his list and had the best dang Christmas of his life.

This mind-guessing ability of mine was a gift, but also a curse. Because this morning, there was just one thing I knew for sure: Gideon hated me. How could he not after being ghosted by his once-best friend?

So I kept my eyes dead ahead and made sure they never once strayed in Gideon's direction. There was plenty to look at on my side of Ocean Ave, thank you very much.

The closer I got to Creekside Middle, the better I saw that Sunny had been right: school was canceled. Student after jubilant student passed me by, every one of them walking away from school rather than toward it. Each time I braced for them to mention the video, but something else was going on—something a lot more interesting than Jonah's YouTube rant. I could've asked any one of them what was up, but that would've spoiled all the fun I was having not being noticed.

A stray elementary schooler tumbled into me. He gaped up like a lost puppy and clutched a half-empty yogurt pack in one hand. The other half had splattered onto his Smash Kelly T-shirt.

"No school!" The boy grinned, performed a miniature floss, and ran away.

"How come?" I called.

"No teachers!" he called back, hoisting a stick like a ten-foot lightsaber as he fled.

When I reached the school, I understood what the yogurt kid meant by "no teachers." Almost every adult from Creekside Middle flanked the building, marching in a stream of posters and picket signs. They wore matching purple shirts with tall white text that said CHSD TEACHERS UNION.

A few of them had megaphones, and all of them chanted:

"BETTER FUNDING! FAIR PAY! SHOULD'VE HAD 'EM YESTERDAY!"

This happened every couple of years. The only way our teachers ever got a decent raise was when they forced the district to give them one. So they'd go on strike, refusing to work until they'd gotten the deal they deserved.

I used to hate these strikes. After all, every day of strike meant one less day of summer vacation. But Mom never let me complain.

"Nobody would make a penny if we didn't have teachers," she would say. "Teachers should be the richest folks in town."

I'd never admit it, but our teachers looked strangely cool on the picket line—like an army, minus the weapons. It was enough of a spectacle to attract the local news. Lights and cameras framed the picket line like a Marvel movie set.

Things got less cool, however, when I accidentally locked eyes with Mr. Dinkle, the wackiest teacher in sixth grade. I'd never seen the guy without an outrageous tie or a funny smile. Watching him join an epic chant sent a wave of goose bumps across my arms, like I'd just wandered into the wrong corner of the multiverse.

"Hey, Jonah!" a voice called from behind me. I took a breath. For the first time since passing Gideon's house that morning, I allowed myself to face the opposite sidewalk.

No sign of Gideon. He'd probably had the sense to turn back well before Creekside Road. Instead of my former best friend, I found Lindsay Allister and her aggressively bright red hair. The richest kid in school waved me over from the front stoop of the Murder House. I crossed the street, checking my pocket for the inhaler.

The Murder House was that abandoned mansion where most students insisted some unspeakable crime had once gone down. They were wrong. According to Mom, all the houses on this street flooded when the Little Delaware Creek overflowed in 2001. Most of the properties were abandoned after that. It's probably why Lindsay's dad donated the land to Creekside Middle. Some things you just can't sell.

As I approached the haunted porch stoop, her gang gawked at me like I was infected with a zombie contagion. They were mostly eighth graders, even though Lindsay was in seventh. None of them had to guess why she'd called me over: As the only child of Richard Allister, Lindsay had to have seen my video from last night. Something told me she hadn't smashed that *like* button.

My palms moistened. My lungs stiffened. My mouth went dry.

After halfway dying in the last twenty-four hours, I could confidently say that there was one thing I feared even more than death: conversations.

"I saw your video," Lindsay said as I reached the stoop. Her gang broke into snorts and chuckles.

The tallest one, an eighth grader who looked like a twenty-six-year-old, pretended to cough: "*Faker.*"

Lindsay opened her mouth to speak, then rolled her eyes. She gazed back at her phone as a few others joined in the coughing chorus.

The tall guy—Deacon or Beacon or Bacon or something—lifted his phone for a selfie as he pretended to choke. "Agh! I'm dying! Save the whales!" Then he turned his phone to me, and I realized he was recording. "A thousand bucks he doesn't even have asthma."

Now Bacon had gotten me angry, and in my anger, I resolved to deck him with the most devastating clapback my big-league brain could produce. So here is what I actually, seriously, 100 percent literally said. On camera. In front of Bacon, Lindsay Allister, and all of Lindsay Allister's popular friends:

"PHONE HEAD!"

That was it. That was the clapback. Phone + head = phone head. As in, Bacon has a phone and Bacon has a head, and sometimes Bacon's phone appears beside his head. You know, like a "phone head."

Even I didn't get it.

Bacon fell on the ground laughing, and Lindsay went on acting like I didn't exist—even though she was the one who called me over in the first place. She let her friends do the dirty work, like bullies for hire. I clenched my fists, spun on my heel, and stormed away from the Murder House.

"Run home, faker!" Bacon yelled. "But not to mommy. She misses work, and Lindsay's dad'll give her the ax."

My throat clenched as I forced myself to keep walking, refusing to pull out the inhaler until Bacon and Lindsay were well out of eyeshot. I wouldn't give them the satisfaction, even if it meant risking another Martic Pinnacle moment. When I finally turned the corner, I whipped out my inhaler for a long, desperate puff.

Breathing is way underrated.

STEP 8:

RAISE THE DEAD

Perhaps it hadn't been such a bad move to avoid talking to other kids these last couple years. My run-in with Lindsay and her thugs had proved that I wasn't just asthmatic—I was deathly allergic to human interaction, too.

Prerecorded rants were easy, even if they wound up playing for thousands of people. You could always turn off the comments later. In conversations, however, the comments were always on, right in your face, popping up in real time like a YouTube Live. You had to think fast, improvise, stay cool—in other words, not be Jonah Kaminski.

Which brought me right back to my nagging question from the night before: why would Sunny choose me, a tongue-tied conver-phobic kid, to help her save the human race? The mission made zero sense.

With Bacon's laugh still ringing in my ears, I stomped down the block in a blind rage—so blind, in fact, that I nearly died of shock when a twenty-second-century girl popped out from behind an abandoned Land Rover. "Boo!"

"Sorry!" I shouted for no sensible reason.

". . . I forgive you?" It was Sunny, minus her pink space suit. Now I knew where she had gone after slipping into the shadows last night:

the Coal Valley Mall. She climbed onto the rusted-out car hood to model her outfit. Sunny wore bright yellow jeans and a bright pink T-shirt with a slogan printed in big block letters: THE FUTURE IS FEMALE. She spread her arms as if to welcome the incoming praise. "Do you like my 2020s disguise?"

I shrugged. "Wearing a shirt with the word *future* isn't exactly what I'd call a disguise."

Sunny blinked, the swagger frozen on her face, still waiting for the compliment.

"It's a cool outfit," I caved.

"Cool as a blork on ice!" Sunny clapped her hands for emphasis.

"What's a blork?" I was almost afraid to ask. Most of my classmates had spontaneously begun swearing the day we entered middle school, and I'd been hearing some new forbidden word almost every day since.

"You don't know the word *blork*?" Sunny's face was all puzzled like *I* was the weird one here. "Honestly, how do you people even talk?"

"Just good ol' English, I guess."

"Old English is right." Sunny strolled off toward Sil's Market at the end of the block. "What's bothering you today?"

So, she noticed.

"I'll tell you what's bothering me." I shoved my hands into my pockets and followed her into the store. "Lindsay Allister. She just got her friends to drag me for posting that video. Troll."

"Lindsay's not half-bad," Sunny said, petting the stray tabby cat that lived in Sil's shop. "Go easy on her."

"Ha!" My fake laugh sent the cat bolting. "Breaking news: Lindsay Allister is basically the princess of a fossil fuel kingdom. You might wanna brush up on your Carbon Hill history."

"I know my history, alright." Sunny collected one of each chocolate bar from the shelf. "And I'm telling you with absolute certainty: Lindsay Allister is not half-bad. Trust me on this."

"Look, if there's something you know about the future, just come out with it."

"Spoilers," Sunny sang. She pretended to zip her lips and headed for the checkout.

"Spoilers?!" I hounded her as we left the store. "Last night, you predicted that my teachers would go on strike. Wasn't *that* a 'spoiler'?"

"All I know is what I read in the papers," she replied, exaggerating a look of total innocence. She leaned against the *Carbon Hill Gazette* newspaper box. It was freshly stocked with brand-new editions of the brittle front page Sunny had pulled out the night before. This one carried the rewritten, death-free headline: *LOCAL BOY GOES VIRAL WITH MARTIC PINNACLE VIDEO.* The other top story was all about the strike.

"So, it's nine thirty on the dot." She checked her metal watch, the same device she'd used last night to detect the ice-cream truck's arrival. "Time to get started," Sunny said, breaking into a bold stride down the sidewalk.

I gave a firm, soldierly nod and did my best to keep up. With all the anger in my guts from that run-in with Lindsay and Bacon, I felt ready to tackle any mission Sunny had planned. "Whatever it takes," I said, "I'll do it."

"Only one task for today," Sunny said, still walking.

"Great." I cracked my knuckles.

"And only you can do it."

"Bring. It. On." With each word, I threw a punch into the air.

Sunny stopped and pointed straight across the street, to a tidy row house with green vinyl siding. The house where Gideon lived. "Round up your Crew," she said.

I felt like a colony of ants had crawled up the back of my shirt. "Um. Any other ideas for saving the world?"

"You can't save the world without people." Sunny pushed me toward the fence that, in third grade, Gideon and I had pretended was a Wakandan force field. "And you can't get *people* without talking. Besides, Jonah, I already told you: Gideon is still your friend."

I'd forgotten how much I'd told her on the long walk last night, before an ice-cream truck from the future cut us off. Sunny still owed me an explanation for that, come to think of it. But she was shoving me toward Gideon's fence too fast for me to change the subject.

"Look," I said, "I don't even know what I'm asking him for."

"It's simple. We need him to join our Crew." She threw open the gate to Gideon's force-field fence and pulled me toward the front porch where I'd once hawked lemon Kool-Aid to raise money for electric scooters. (We banked a grand total of $10 from a grand total of one customer, who may or may not have been Gideon's mom.)

The porch loomed in my vision like a ghost. *Breathe, Jonah,* I thought. *But not too much. And not too fast.*

I took a puff from my inhaler, then turned back to Sunny.

"Think of it from his perspective," I pleaded. "His best friend dumped him right after he'd lost his dad—the toughest time of his life. The guy probably hates me."

Sunny raised an eyebrow and tapped on her ear. "I don't think you're *listening*."

I finally noticed the guitar music wafting out from the house. The strumming got clearer as we stepped onto the porch. It sounded like a ukulele crossed with a banjo crossed with one of those rubber band guitars we used to make in third grade. I still felt anxious, but the sound of it drew me in. It was strangely comforting.

"Does that sound like a hateful person?" Sunny pointed toward the living room window.

There sat Gideon on a dining room chair, eyes shut, strumming on a too-small toy guitar. The purple plastic instrument was decorated with fat yellow lightning bolts and the words *ROCK OUT* in round bubble letters. I got the feeling he wouldn't want us to see this. Then Gideon started singing. It was an old folk song, and he hit the melody clear and high. I'd never known he had a voice like his dad's.

Sunny nudged me toward the front door.

I leaned away. "We shouldn't interrupt."

Ding-dong.

Thanks, Sunny.

I heard the guitar clunk to the floor. Panicking, I spun for the stairs, but Sunny blocked them. She turned me around and patted me on the back. Hard. Beyond the door, Einstein the labradoodle valiantly barked as the bolt unlatched. The door popped open.

Gideon screwed up his face, looking baffled to find us on his doorstep. "Jonah?"

We hadn't exchanged a word for years, but my name from his voice still sounded as natural as anything. Same old Gideon.

He maneuvered his legs to keep Einstein from slipping out the door. "Figured it was my stepbrothers. They forgot their key at home."

"Hey, man." I studied the floor. My mouth was open for business, but my brain wasn't in on the deal. Sure, this might be the same old Gideon, but I was far from the Jonah I used to be. What could I possibly say? "Um, did you, um, see my video?"

I couldn't have crafted a more random introduction if I'd tried. Sunny gave my shoulder a supportive squeeze.

"Your video!" Gideon replied, eagerly. He brought his enthusiasm down a notch. "Yeah, I saw it. Good stuff. I mean, I don't know much about the science, but it all sounded pretty smart, you know? Must be weird going viral like that." Einstein's snout poked out between Gideon's knees.

"For sure." I glanced over at Sunny. "It's been a weird couple of days."

Gideon shimmied his dog back away from the door.

"So, anyway," I went on. Or tried to. My small-talk database was experiencing a total system failure. Better cut to the chase. "Me and Sunny here are trying to start a club—group—thing?"

"A Crew." Sunny popped her head in front of mine.

"Yeah, a *Crew*, I mean, about climate—you know—all the stuff in the video?" Why was every sentence arriving in the form of a question? "Um. So. Wanna join?"

Gideon's face brightened, then dimmed. His arm slackened at the doorway. "I'm not sure I'd make such a good—STAY!" Einstein had wriggled through Gideon's legs and taken his shot.

Now the sandy floof was already out the door, already halfway across the yard—and Sunny and I had left the front gate hanging wide open.

I leapt from the porch to keep that fluffy bolt of lightning off the street.

Too late.

Einstein did not observe the rules of the road. He did not look both ways before crossing. He did not check for pizza delivery cars cruising much too fast for a quiet neighborhood.

"Einstein, NO!" I shouted, which only made him tumble-run faster as the car tore along its collision course.

We heard the screech of tires braking too late.

Ever notice how sometimes, right before something bad is about to happen, it feels like the world slows down, even stands still for a moment, before the table breaks or the foot slips or the bike tips over? Well, that's exactly how I felt as Einstein leapt in front of the speeding pizza delivery car. I froze in terror, and for a split second, it felt like everything around me had frozen, too. The car. The dog. The flock of migrating birds overhead.

The split second turned into a full second. Then into two.

"Hey, guys." Gideon's eyes looked wider than personal pan pizzas. He blinked and looked again. "Why is my dog . . . levitating?"

Einstein hung suspended in midair, frozen in front of the motionless car with a slobbery tongue floating at the side of his mouth.

"Sunny," I added, no less petrified than Gideon. "What. Is. Happening?"

"*Nothing* is happening," Sunny said. "When you stop time, that's kinda the point." She raised her gunmetal timepiece, tapped a button, then grabbed each of us by the arms. The world around us stretched outward. The car, the dog, the birds in the sky—all of them warped like a giant soap bubble.

My ears popped. Then the bubble did, too. Just like that, everything around us went back to normal. But this time, no pizza car.

"Where's my dog?" Gideon paced in a tiny circle.

"He's back in the house," Sunny explained. "Exactly where he'd been five minutes ago, which I guess would be *zero* minutes ago now."

Gideon froze again, this time with a hand to his ear. I heard it, too. Not far beyond the front porch, someone strummed on a toy guitar.

"Is that . . . ?" Gideon didn't bother finishing the question. We all knew the answer. The musician on the other side of those windows was Gideon himself, only a few minutes earlier.

"Are you meaning to tell me"—I took a puff from my silver inhaler—"that the three of us just traveled back in time?"

"By five minutes." Sunny checked her watch. "We'd better hide."

"From who?" Gideon looked as worried as he was confused.

"From ourselves." Sunny took us into the hollow of an overgrown rhododendron bush. "Our five-minutes-ago selves."

We ducked for cover just as past-Me and past-Sunny approached the house. We'd been talking about Gideon the whole time, which was now supremely awkward to relive with the Gideon of five minutes later crouching right beside me.

Past-Me and past-Sunny went through the front gate without shutting it behind us. Present-Gideon tutted disapprovingly. As soon as past-Me got distracted by a conversation with past-Gideon on the porch, present-Sunny left the bush and shut the gate, creeping low enough that none of our past selves seemed to notice. She hurried back to our spot.

"You just rewrote history," Gideon marveled. He was taking all of this remarkably well, now that his dog's future prospects had brightened.

Sunny flashed her winning smile.

"But how do we get back?" I asked.

"Like this." Sunny tapped her timepiece and took our hands.

The rhododendron bush warped and bubbled out around us, reminding me of how Gideon and I used to pretend this bush was our own secret portal to Asgard. My ears popped.

"Well." Gideon patted his arms, as if making sure he'd landed in one piece. "Guess that's how it feels to get around like Thor."

We left the bush to find a very confused-looking Einstein barking at the fence as a pizza delivery car screeched out of sight. This time, Einstein never made it into the street. This time, the gate was shut.

Gideon caught the furball in a wriggling hug and checked the dog for signs of damage. "That"—he offered Sunny a fist bump—"was epic."

I wondered how anyone could show such a pleasant reaction to emergency time-travel. But, looking at Gideon, I couldn't help but share some of the wonder I saw on his face. It reminded me of one reason I used to like being friends: Gideon's attitude was contagious.

"Next time you drag me through space-time, just give me a heads up, okay?" I joked.

Gideon laughed, but Sunny didn't. I soon realized why.

All three of us could hear it: the eerie national anthem of that ice-cream truck, driven by those people that Sunny called "they." I still had no idea who "they" were, but now "they" weren't far away.

STEP 9:

FETCH

Sunny plowed into Gideon and me, driving us both onto the porch and through the front door. She slammed it behind us.

The familiar smell hit me instantly. Powder detergent and kettle corn. In a split second, the smell took me back, like time-travel without all the tech. Memories raced through me. The countless dinners here when Mom was working late and my dad was sleeping through sundown. Sneak-watching zombie movies after 12:00 a.m. Getting caught but not getting in trouble. Malted chocolate milk.

"Mom doesn't let me bring peop—" Gideon's voice cut off under Sunny's hand.

"Get down." She dragged us into Gideon's living room. All three of us clutched the windowsill and peered into the street.

The national anthem got louder. Closer. Slower.

Finally, that old-time creamery on wheels crept into view. It rolled to a stop in front of Gideon's house. The music fell silent. The truck's back doors creaked open, and two people hopped out onto Ocean Ave: a tall, lanky woman and a short, stocky man.

"And you thought my *T-shirt* was a lousy disguise." Sunny poked me with her elbow. "At least it's from the right century."

The time-travelers looked as outlandish as their truck, wearing perfectly identical outfits: a bleachy-white suit with a white apron, a red candy-striped bow tie, and a white paper cap. It reminded me of that 1950s-style ice-cream shop Mom and I used to visit near the beach; the "soda jerks" who'd scooped our ice cream were uniformed a lot like this. And, as if they didn't look foolish enough, the man had waxed and curled his mustache, which made him look like something between a cartoon villain and the Pringles guy—only sweatier. They didn't exactly blend in.

"Who *are* they?" I whispered.

"The future"—Sunny stared at her watch—"catching up with me. Our time-jump must've sent them a ping."

We watched as the cartoon-mustache Soda Jerk used a pair of flashlight-like things to nervously scan the area around Gideon's chain-link fence. He pointed a finger at Einstein, who was still barking at the gate. In a frantic hurry, the tall woman scrambled to connect a gas pump–looking device into the side of their truck. She brought it near Einstein, afraid to step too close.

Gideon tried to stand up. "I won't let them hurt my dog."

Sunny pulled him back. "They won't."

"How do you know?" Gideon's voice cracked a little.

"Because they're not butchers." Sunny shut her eyes. "They're inventors."

"And what kind of invention is *that*?" Gideon pointed at the gangly gas pump contraption. The woman hauled it closer to Einstein and aimed it right at the dog. In an instant, Einstein froze in a bubble of atmosphere and faded out before our eyes. The dog had disappeared.

Gideon shot to his feet and leapt for the front door. Sunny tried to block him. I kept watching the Soda Jerks as they scrambled back into their seats and took off—not along the road, but away through time itself. The truck bubbled out before my eyes. Gone. For a second, it flickered back, now running in reverse to the sound of a backward national anthem, but just as soon as it reappeared, the ice-cream truck vanished yet again.

I snapped out of my stupor and followed Gideon and Sunny outside.

"You lied to me," Gideon was muttering with his hands covering his face. Even in a moment like this, Gideon didn't look angry—just terribly hurt.

"I had no idea this would happen." Sunny rested her hand on his back. "And besides, I said they wouldn't *hurt* Einstein, and so far, they haven't."

I cleared my throat. "Didn't they just, like, vaporize him?"

"No. All they did was move him. Probably back to their lab." She checked the notification on her timepiece. "In 2100."

My chest contracted with a sympathy pang. Based on Sunny's description, a visit to the future sounded like a fate worse than death.

"Why take him there?" Gideon said.

"They'll run a few tests. Get a few clues. Send him right back—I think." Sunny winced.

"You *think*?" I could hear the lump rising in Gideon's throat.

"Here's what I know." Sunny led us through the gate. "They didn't travel all the way to the 2020s just to play dogcatcher. They're here for a reason, and that reason is *me*."

"But wait!" I shot back, just before my words ran out. With so many urgent questions pressing around me, it was hard sticking to a single one: What was Sunny's master plan? Why did she choose to save me out of all the people she could have rescued the night before? Why was Lindsay Allister *not* the Actual Worst? But spotting the withered look on Gideon's face, I asked the question that seemed most important: "If it's not Einstein they want, then what are these people trying to get?"

"Their machine." Sunny stopped on the sidewalk, fidgeting with the gunmetal timepiece around her wrist. "I stole it."

STEP 10:

Confess to Your Crimes

Sunny had some explaining to do. And explain she did—all the way from Ocean Ave to the rundown strip malls along Route 30. Those two scientists had indeed invented time-travel, Sunny told us while we cut through the bargain grocery parking lot. But they did a lousy job of it. That glitchy truck was the best they could ever manage. So they found someone else to complete their design. A *genius*, Sunny insisted as we reached the Superstore. This person, like many of the world's geniuses, was poor—a thirty-something math teacher who knew her way around a line of code. They hired her as a temporary employee since no "temp" would have to get credit for fixing their faulty invention.

But the woman didn't just fix it. She perfected it. She created the timepiece, a more elegant, powerful device than they'd ever imagined possible. She even threw in a few features that the scientists didn't know about. But they got their invention. Tragically, the woman died young, and, no matter what they tried, those wannabe inventors couldn't replicate her handiwork. The timepiece would remain one of a kind.

"And now it's mine," Sunny concluded.

For the first time in the day and a half I'd known her, Sunny didn't seem to have much trouble spilling the details. Must've been a

Gideon thing. He had a way of making people feel comfortable, even as he mourned his own dog's unnatural disappearance. Sunny spent the rest of our walk around the Superstore catching Gideon up on everything I already knew.

" . . . so I handed Jonah that silver inhaler and said, 'I'm from the future. We need you.'" Sunny dropped a stack of composition books into her already-overloaded cart. "The rest is history. *Wait a minute.*" She came to a halt in the crafts aisle. Her mouth hung open in shock, like she'd just rediscovered the Wayback Diner dessert menu. "Does this store have . . . fruit?"

"Produce," I replied impatiently. "That way."

Sunny bolted. Gideon and I raced after her and almost got flattened by a cart full of detergent bottles.

What was so life-altering about the produce aisle? Just one question among 2,100 others. If Sunny threw me another riddle, my brain was going to overheat. I needed answers.

"The timepiece. You said you stole it . . ." I whispered the word *stole.*

"Mhmm." Sunny gawked in quiet wonder before bins of fruits and veggies. "These are extinct." She tossed an unripe banana bunch into the cart. Gideon replaced it with a ripe one.

But I wasn't here to inspect Sunny's fruit selection.

"Sunny." I stepped in front of her. "Why exactly does a kid *steal* a time machine?"

Sunny grabbed a package of strawberries and sighed. "Extinct," she repeated to herself before switching back to our discussion. "Well, of course, *only* a kid would do it. You think grown-ups are interested in changing history?"

Gideon and I shrugged in unison.

"I can think of a few exceptions, but most grown-ups," she said, "are obsessed with the way things are. They'll never save the world if it means they'll have to change it."

I laughed.

Sunny didn't. "It was their job to rebuild everything while we still had time. And what did they give us? Paper straws. Tote bags. Energy-efficient light bulbs. And that's about it." Sunny flung a sack of peaches into her cart. "*Ex-tinct!*"

Sunny was starting to remind me of Mom snatching up that Channel 8 microphone. When this girl went on a tear, you'd better duck for cover. She'd already attracted a few stares. I had to get Sunny away from all this rage-inducing fruit.

"Hey, look!" I searched for any distraction at the other end of the store. "Halloween stuff!"

Gideon and I forged ahead to the seasonal section. It was emptier here, more private. Sunny followed with her overflowing cart.

"So let me make sure I'm understanding this," Gideon said, leaning thoughtfully against a rack of plastic skeletons. "You stole their time machine."

"Correct."

"But they still have a spare?"

"A lousy one that might turn them into babies or land them in the wrong millennium, but yeah. The Soda Jerks still have a time machine."

Gideon raised a finger. "But isn't that weird? Why didn't they just use the truck to go back a few hours and stop you from stealing the timepiece?"

"Security," Sunny said, now brandishing a plastic sword and shield. "You can't time-jump into that facility. Only out of it."

"But still," I piped in, "couldn't they have gone outside, jumped back, and stopped you from sneaking in?"

"I'm sure they tried." Sunny cracked a smile. "But they wouldn't have known who to stop. You see, that math teacher they hired? She didn't just perfect an invention before she passed away. She hatched a plan. If it weren't for her, I wouldn't be here. She thought of everything—even the perfect night for someone to slip into that facility without being spotted: the annual Halloween masquerade ball. All I needed was her access card and a good way to hide my face." She pulled a toddler-sized astronaut suit off the rack.

"Wait a minute." I snatched up another. "Are you telling me that space suit was only a costume?"

"A very realistic costume. Pink, too."

I couldn't speak. Yesterday, when Sunny arrived in her glittering uniform, a silver inhaler in hand, I felt like history was finally getting under control. The professionals had arrived. I imagined some silvery, futuristic mission control center with a whole crew of pink astronauts ready to back Sunny up at any moment.

Now I knew the truth. There was no mission control, no backup, no crew. The pink astronaut was just another kid who'd seen how bad the future can get.

"So, tell me if I'm misunderstanding," Gideon said, rolling back into his interrogation about the mechanics of time-travel. Clearly he was digging for something, but I couldn't see what. "This watch thing was all you needed to travel backward in time, right?"

Sunny nodded.

"Can it go the other way?"

"Theoretically."

"That's great news!" Gideon rubbed his palms together. "So all we have to do is jump *ahead* to the year 2100 and break Einstein out of whatever ice-cream kennel they've got him locked up in. Easy-peasy."

"Is that a joke?" Sunny's cart ground to a halt at the wall of TVs. All of them ran the same footage of an insurance executive getting a neck tattoo—a *PunkWork with Smash Kelly* episode I still remembered from the hospital. Sunny rubbed her temples and shut her eyes. "Are you seriously asking to go *forward* in time?"

"Sure." His smile faded. "Why not?"

Sunny stared at the wall of screens and then down at her timepiece.

"See for yourself," she whispered. She tapped her device until every TV flickered in unison as one giant video wall, transforming the electronics section into a highlight reel of twenty-first-century devastation: A smoldering rain forest. A brown sky. A river of homeless families walking a desolate highway. My lungs ached—or maybe it was my heart.

Sunny planted herself in front of the footage and narrowed her watery eyes. "The air is poisoned, the water is worse, the food is terrible. Everybody's lost somebody they love. And I'm just talking about the everyday stuff. That's got nothing to do with what'll happen if they catch us in their facility."

"The ice-cream guys?" I asked, backing away from the 4K wall of devastation.

Sunny switched it off and took a breath. "The inventors would be the least of our worries. It's the people they work for. They're the real nightmare. That's why the Soda Jerks are so desperate to get their timepiece back. This timepiece is a one-way ticket to fame and fortune, and they're scared to death of what might happen if their employer finds out they lost it. Now just imagine how much trouble *we'd* be in."

"Poor Einstein." Gideon slouched. "It's hopeless."

Hopeless was the word, alright. I felt it myself, the weight of that whole terrible future sitting on top of my chest. Could it really be changed? Could one Jonah Kaminski do anything to un-burn a rain forest, un-pollute a sky, and re-home a highway of displaced people? Probably not. I'd been given one simple assignment—to recruit Gideon—and I hadn't even managed that.

But I could try.

"How about this?" I said, turning to Sunny and training my thoughts on the mission. "If you succeed, if we rewrite history and stop the climate apocalypse, are you heading back to the future after that?"

"It's home," Sunny answered. "Of course I'll go back."

"Good." I glanced at Gideon, then quickly away. "When you get there, would you be able to send Einstein home, too?"

"Absolutely." Sunny could see where I was going with this. She picked up what I was putting down. "If we can do this, Gideon, the first thing I'll do is find Einstein and get him sorted right back to his own little spot in the present."

"My front yard?"

"That's the idea." Sunny backed away. "Watch the cart for me, will you?" She hurried off toward the front of the store.

"Where are you going?" I called.

Sunny stopped in the middle of the aisle. "If you must know, I'm going to the bathroom. You do have those, right?"

"Oh, we've had 'em for like a hundred years, at least," Gideon answered.

Sunny shot gun fingers at Gideon and skipped away. Now it was only Gideon and me.

"So . . ." My voice came up short. I looked away, pretending to read the back label of a zombie makeup kit I'd randomly grabbed at the Halloween display.

It was one thing to talk with Gideon *and* Sunny, but me and Gideon alone was something else entirely. Like usual, the chain reaction started with my palms, which broke into a sweat. Then my heart rate picked up, too. It's not that I didn't want to talk. I did. But I could only *think* about wanting to talk. Actually talking? I'd have an easier time raising the dead.

If I asked him about his summer, he'd ask me about mine. I'd rather not recount my months as an eco-hermit. *Embarrassing.* If I asked him about his mom, it would only remind him of how badly I'd skipped out on his life. *Shameful.* If I asked him about something silly, like his always-hilarious labradoodle—well, Gideon's hilarious labradoodle was now trapped in a post-apocalyptic future thanks to me. *Awkward.*

I gripped the inhaler in my pocket.

Gideon was checking his phone. "I locked them out!" He slapped his forehead and made for the exit. "And they still don't even know about the dog. I gotta go. Look, Jonah, tell Sunny no hard feelings about Einstein. It's not her fault. We'll just have to bring him back, and I'll do whatever I can to help. Einstein was a good dog."

"He still is," I replied, too quiet for Gideon to hear as he barreled out of the store. I had to wonder: did he really need to leave just then, or was it my supreme awkwardness that sent him running?

"You have *got* to try these bathrooms!"

Sunny popped up behind me, and I held back a yelp. Now that I lived in a world with dognapping Soda Jerks on patrol, getting startled was a whole new experience.

"They've got hot water in the sink, and you can use all the soap you want!" Sunny looked around. "Where's Gideon?"

"Oh, right. Gideon." I tried to pretend I wasn't still cringing from our latest conversation—if you could even call it that. "He had to get home."

"We'll catch him later." The carefree Sunny stopped at a rack of decorative mirrors to check her braids. "I feel so bad about the dog, but I'm glad to have Gideon in the Crew. Seems like a good friend."

"Ex-friend," I said.

"Friend," Sunny insisted. "Wanna buy those?"

I was still clutching the tiny astronaut suit and the zombie makeup kit. "I'll take the kit."

STEP 11:

GET TO THE PLAN

All this walking had given me the limbs of a marionette puppet. I was the puppeteer pulling the strings, and somehow, miraculously, my body kept on moving. In one short day, I had walked to school, to Gideon's, to the Superstore, and then all the way to the Wayback Diner. (Sunny could not stop thinking about those waffles.) After that, we'd hit Home Run Sporting Goods for a camping-supply shopping spree before returning all the way to Creekside Middle. Full circle. Long day.

We approached the creek behind my school. Sunny was leading the way to "her place," as she put it. I had no idea why she'd picked a place so far from the edge of town. But at least she'd made the right call when she borrowed this cart from the Superstore. No way could we have hauled a thousand dollars' worth of camping gear and fruit all this way without it.

Sunny had spent all but $10 of her cash supply.

"What'll you do for money now?" I asked as we reached the long narrow footbridge. "No store's gonna take the Harriet Tubman bills—sorry to say."

Sunny shrugged. "I'll improvise."

"You seem to be doing a lot of that."

"*You* push." Sunny abandoned her cart at the threshold of the bridge and started across, calling back, "And I *did* come with a plan."

It wasn't the first time Sunny had mentioned her so-called plan, supposedly crafted by the same genius woman who'd helped create the timepiece. I knew that much, but it wasn't enough.

"Well, let's hear it." I leaned all my weight against the heavy cart just to get it rolling.

"The plan"—Sunny stopped at the center of the bridge and pointed past the water to the back of Creekside Middle—"is to follow their lead. We're gonna strike."

I could hear the union still chanting from their picket line. I considered Sunny's plan. It didn't sound big enough to alter the course of history, but at least it was doable. "You mean like when students walk out of school to protest a war or gun violence or something?"

"Sort of," Sunny said. "But I don't want just a handful of students to march out of their classrooms on a Friday afternoon. I want to strike like the teachers do. They've organized themselves into one big union so that, when they decide to walk out, the entire school shuts down. They make the news. The world listens up. It's called people power."

"That would take a lot of people." I let the cart slow down.

"Not *too* many." Sunny twiddled her finger in the air, running some invisible calculation. "Half the school oughta do it."

"That's 600 students!"

"Math wiz over here."

"Sunny." This time I abandoned the cart. I stared down into the speeding waters of the Little Delaware Creek. "There's 180 school days a year. If I convinced one student to join us every day for the rest of seventh grade, I wouldn't even be close."

"Don't have a stroke just yet." Sunny took the cart and continued across the bridge. "'Cause that's not even the hard part: You do not have 180 days to organize Creekside. You've got thirty-one."

Calmly, I drew a puff from my inhaler. Then I gave myself permission to freak out.

"A MONTH?!" My voice rang over the creek and bounced off the school. Sunny was asking the impossible. I couldn't organize a round of freeze-tag, much less a school-wide movement in thirty-one days. "It's not happening."

"It *has* to happen," Sunny shot back. "Not one day earlier. Not one day later. October twenty-eighth is Zero Hour."

"But why the twenty-eighth?" I asked. "And what do you mean by 'Zero Hour'?"

"You don't need to know that yet."

"Gahhh." I stomped across the bridge. I'd like to say that the two of us were having an argument, but only one of us was losing his cool. "You know the future, Sunny. So why won't you tell me anything about it?"

"I *am* telling you something." Sunny framed her hands for emphasis. "October. Twenty. Eighth. You'll need to recruit 600 Creekside students by that exact future day."

"Impossible," I said. "And I know what you're going to tell me. '*All* things are possible.' And it might be true—for you. But you saw me talking to Gideon. I could barely recruit *him*, and he's the one kid I know best around here. There's no way I'll be able to recruit 600 kids on my own in thirty-one days. I can't do it."

"Of course you can't!" Sunny took me by the shoulders and gave me a shake. "We need you to save the world, Jonah, but you'll never be able to do it alone."

I guess she had a point. Ever since the hospital, I'd been trying to fight the apocalypse alone. Last summer, I'd tried to fight it alone by starving myself of anything that caused carbon emissions. Yesterday, I'd tried to fight it alone with my near-fatal asthma vlog. And just now, when Sunny had mentioned recruiting 600 students, I'd imagined myself doing that alone, too.

I pushed Sunny's cart the rest of the way across the footbridge. "Well, if you can find more people to help you out, I won't stop you."

"Good." Sunny took over cart duty. "Because tomorrow, we're recruiting a campaign manager."

"But aren't *you* the manager of this whole thing?" We stopped before the Reservoir Park Wilderness Preserve entrance.

"If we fix the future," Sunny said, "I'm going home the first chance I get. So I won't be here forever. And besides, she can do a whole lot more than I can. This one's a real professional."

"Who is it?"

"Tomorrow, you'll see." Her smile went from warm to wicked. "One more door for the knocking."

My lungs tensed up at the thought of another doorstep recruitment. "If you say so."

"That's what I like to hear." Sunny motioned to the Wilderness Preserve sign. "Here's my stop."

"Wait—you're not sleeping *outside*, are you?"

Sunny patted the extra-large tent on the top of her loaded cart. "It's how I was raised. I can sleep like a baby anytime, anywhere—so long as I don't have four walls around me. And besides, these woods are so much nicer than the place where I grew up. Earth is still so young. And that smell . . ." Sunny took in a chestful of the September forest air.

Above her, the sky was turning purple. If Mom had gotten home by now, her panic level must've been off the charts after everything I'd put her through the night before. I drifted back toward the bridge. "See you tomorrow?"

"Nine thirty a.m.," Sunny answered. "Don't be late."

"Roger that." I waved bye before Sunny had a chance to reach out (I'm not a hugger) and raced across the footbridge over the Little Delaware Creek.

STEP 12:

Be Cool

I slogged home as fast as my exhausted legs would allow, which wasn't nearly fast enough. Coming home late after last night's near-death incident, I wouldn't have been surprised to find my front yard swarming with emergency vehicles again. Mom had probably called in the National Guard by now. But when I turned the corner to my block, I found no cop cars. No fire trucks. Just a single antique vehicle creeping its way down Ocean Ave.

. . . the bombs bursting in air . . .

An ice-cream truck. My heart rate doubled. Why hadn't I thought of this? Of course the Soda Jerks would be out patrolling the site of today's incident. Lucky for Gideon, his living room shades were down, and his mom's car was now parked out front. He was safe—not strolling through the middle of a time gun shooting range like me. This would've been a great time to break into a sprint, but these old lungs couldn't even manage a light jog. I had no choice but to stick with my Totally Convincing Casual Stroll.

The national anthem came to a stop just as the truck did. Right beside me.

The driver side window rolled down.

Be cool, I told myself. *You don't have what they're looking for. Just act natural.*

The short, round man with a waxed mustache smiled out from the driver seat. He glowed with a sheen of nervous sweat.

"Young man," he stammered gruffly, with an over-rehearsed stiffness in his voice. "Being the old, um, fool that I am, I seem to have misplaced my watch." He broke into a hacking cough.

"It's a family heirloom, you see," the woman croaked from the passenger seat. Her voice was even gruffer than the man's. They both sounded like heavy smokers, but perhaps that was just how all grown-ups sounded in their heavily polluted version of Planet Earth. The air must be awful. "Have you seen anything like this around town?"

The woman unfolded something like a road map and passed it to the man, who showed it to me. It was a blueprint of Sunny's timepiece and all its internal components. I stepped closer, and both inventors flinched. This must've been the closest they'd gotten to a real live person from the 2020s.

They were scared of me, but that didn't make me any less freaked out. Fearful people do all kinds of bizarre, deadly things, like swiping their mom's phone and sprinting up Martic Pinnacle to post a breathless YouTube video without using an inhaler. Desperate is dangerous. Nothing said that more loudly than the way the Soda Jerk woman now clutched at the gas pump–looking device—the same one that had sent Einstein into their sooty, smoggy, asthma attack of a future.

"Have you seen it or not?" The man glared suspiciously.

My mouth had dried out. I couldn't come up with a single word. All I could do was shake my head no, hoping my paralyzed look of terror might pass for common stupidity.

Apparently, it did. The man flung his blueprints back into the truck.

"Thank you," he grunted as the national anthem played on. He hit the gas, and the truck lurched ahead, screeching down Ocean Ave and careening around the corner.

Once they were gone, I bolted for the front door. My shaky hands fumbled with the house key until I got myself inside, now welcoming the thought of Mom's fiery lecture. At least I'd be home. But apparently, Mom wasn't. Our house was still dark. On ordinary days, Mom had a habit of switching on every lamp in the house as soon as she got back from work. It drove the conservationist in me up the wall, but that was Mom for you. The woman loved lighting things up.

But, for now, the house was dark and Mom-less. I consulted the wall-sized dry-erase calendar and remembered that today was a double shift.

Still exhausted, I collapsed on the living room rug and plunged into a swollen river of doubts. How could I possibly survive another door knocking tomorrow? And how would we even reach another door with those Soda Jerks on the hunt? The questions dragged me deep under the force of their muddy current, and I let them. Worrying was my most natural state, I thought, as the river pulled me out to sea.

"Jonah!"

The shriek jolted me awake, and I looked around, startled but happy to be free of that seafaring dog kennel I'd been dreaming about.

I found Mom at the front door, still dressed in her security uniform with a few sushi containers scattered around her feet.

"Hi, Mom." I yawned. "Just napping."

"Word to the wise, buddy: if you don't want a blood-curdling wake-up call, maybe try taking naps in your bed instead of playing dead on the living room floor." Mom kissed the top of my head like usual, then joined me on the carpet, took off her prosthetic foot, and unsheathed a set of chopsticks. "Eat."

We dined on the floor. Mom tried to set up an old iPhone while we enjoyed our drop-tested California rolls.

"Start thinking about your birthday." She spoke in that stern voice she used when urging me to treat myself. "Feels like I almost lost you twice this year. So I want number thirteen to be a special one."

I nodded politely. "I'll think about it."

"Good. How have you enjoyed your newfound celebrity status?" she asked while resetting her iCloud password for the third time.

I laughed. "Haven't heard much about it." It was true. The only time I felt mildly famous today was when I saw the newspaper headline about my viral video.

"They used to call it fifteen minutes of fame. Might be fifteen seconds these days." Mom rubbed a Q-tip on the dusty camera lens. "So, besides signing autographs, what have you been up to?"

I wanted to tell her everything, but that was impossible. I stopped up the words with a mouthful of shrimp nigiri and shrugged.

Mom shrugged back and waited for my answer.

I looked at the TV and pretended to take great interest in the episode of *PunkWork with Smash Kelly* that played on mute. The CEO of a cigarette company popped wheelies on his motocross bike as the painful silence swelled around me.

"Nothing much," I lied. A small lie, really. I just left out the part where I hung out with a girl from the future, traveled five minutes back in time, saved a dog's life, and walked the length of Carbon Hill once or twice.

"Nothing much?" Mom studied me like she knew I was holding back but wasn't sure how hard to push. "Well, you must've done *something* with your teachers on strike and a whole free day on your hands. Details, bud."

Of course, I couldn't give her details. Mom would get herself in deep the second she knew about Sunny. And getting her involved in an anti-coal campaign could risk her job at the coal-powered energy plant—along with the law school scholarship that Allister Energy provided. This whole future career that Mom had worked so hard to build—I couldn't let her lose all of that on my account.

"More details?" I started cooking up the most believable lie I could muster. "I rewatched *Night of the Living Dead*. And worked on a new survival plan."

"Wanna walk me through it?"

"No," I said, much too forcefully. "This one's just for me." I collected our empty takeout containers and stood up. "Still pretty tired. Think I'll read in bed for a while."

Mom handed me her napkin. "But isn't today the new *Deadwalk* episode?"

"I'm all apocalypsed-out for the day," I said. "Sorry."

"Don't forget to brush your teeth," she said, still searching my expression.

I nodded and backed away, leaving Mom alone on the living room rug.

I went up to my room and leaned back against the bedroom door. It hurt to shut Mom out. It physically hurt, a tight pain in my chest that no inhaler could possibly relieve.

But this was no time for relief. So I clenched my fists even tighter than the feeling in my chest. I could power through the pain. With a hardworking mom and a disappearing dad, I'd learned a long time ago how to do things on my own—prepping the dinner, running the dishwasher, cleaning the house. And now, if I really wanted to save the world, I'd have to do that on my own, too.

PLAN B:

ORGANIZATION

STEP 1:

WIN THE LOTTERY

Tuesday, September 27

31 days until Zero Hour

I awoke to the tune of a '90s grunge band building up to a wicked doorbell solo. Shielding my eyes from the blaring sunlight, I checked the time: 9:47 a.m. Dad's old clock radio had failed me again, this time softly playing a classic rock station instead of its noisy alarm.

The doorbell buzzed again. Sunny.

I tore off the covers, rushed downstairs, and went for the door.

Before turning the bolt, I experienced a brief moment of enlightenment. A boxer-brief moment, to be painfully specific: I'd forgotten my pants. Sunny knew too much about me already; she didn't need to know that I still wore Iron Man underwear. I ran upstairs and threw on the same outfit from yesterday, then charged my way back to the door.

I found Sunny on the stoop, glaring at me in her superhero pose. "Never leave a time-traveler waiting."

"I slept through my alarm," I said, just then realizing that my early morning ice-cream social with Nirvana was only a dream. "But don't blame me. Blame the zillion miles we walked all over Carbon Hill yesterday. I was beat."

"About that." Sunny clasped her hands. "Thought I'd give your legs a rest for today."

When she stepped aside, I had to wonder if I'd woken up after all.

I looked. I blinked. I looked again. "No. Way."

The SLYSR Model-Z was the Batmobile of scooters. Human hands had never fashioned a finer machine. The Model-Z had a 5400-watt engine and a lithium-ion battery that could carry you eighty miles on a single charge. Titanium frame. Stealth-black finish. Silicone-carbide grips. This was the birthday gift I would never dare tell Mom I wanted. At $1,899 a pop, just one of these beauties cost a couple hundred times what our old lemonade stand could've saved up.

Sunny had two.

"There's another with Gideon, but he's out for today." Her hands went into her pockets. "Got grounded for losing the dog."

"Ouch." My heart went out to him—especially when I looked at the SLYSRs glinting in the morning sun. Imagine finding your presents under the tree just as you're learning that the kid next door had everything looted by the Grinch. That's how I felt for a few good seconds, before I got my hands on the SLYSR.

It was sleek-yet-tough and premium-built, the only kind of scooter I could imagine carrying Tony Stark or Bruce Wayne, which got me wondering: "Where'd you get the money for these?"

"You know, it's the funniest thing," Sunny replied. "I won the Powerball lottery last night."

A head rush of excitement hit me so hard it almost felt like panic. "You won the *POWERBA—*"

Sunny covered my mouth.

"Technically it was Mrs. Ramirez who won it," she whispered, cautiously removing her hand. "I gave her the numbers; she gave me a cut. Sweet old lady."

It made perfect sense. If Sunny came from the future, it would be no problem for her to predict the winning Powerball numbers for any given day. In fact, she'd probably arrived with the digits scrawled into that Lesson Planner of hers. "Sunny, that's like 700 million dollars."

"Breathe, Jonah. I put in a few wrong numbers so I wouldn't win the full amount. It was only 700 grand."

I clutched my inhaler. "So you could've won the *entire* Powerball. But you didn't. On purpose."

"Do you want the scooter or not?"

"Hey, I'm not complaining." I knelt to admire the all-terrain eleven-inch wheels. Sunny tossed me a helmet. I snapped it on, mounted the scooter, and started it up, throttle in hand.

"Ready for some door-to-door recruitment?" Sunny patted me on the back.

"Sure . . ." I shuddered. The thought of another doorstep put a cold brick in my stomach. I'd been nervous when she made me knock on Gideon's door, and just look at what had been waiting behind Door #1: a runaway dog, a deadly pizza delivery, a death-defying time-jump, and a visit from two obsessive inventors from 2100. I'd rather pass on Door #2.

"Follow me," Sunny sang. She and her SLYSR took off down Ocean Ave like a bolt of stealth lightning.

We sailed along the sidewalks of Carbon Hill at twenty-five miles per hour, and the Model-Z ran smoother than a dream—closest I'd ever come to flying. I was riding on air, but it didn't make a difference. I still had the brick in my gut.

The Crossgates housing development was supposed to feel like a throwback to 1950s suburbia—sidewalks, porches, and white picket fences. And that's exactly how the first few blocks of it looked. The rest, however, was nothing but empty streets and abandoned jobsites. The place was a work in progress.

We stopped at the last house on Apple Pie Road. An American flag hung from the front porch, flapping gently against a backdrop of rock piles and open-pit foundations. A bundle of half-deflated foil balloons hovered around the bright red mailbox. One of them said *I love you Grandma*. Another said *Welcome home*.

"So . . ." I cleared my throat and straightened, pretending my nerves hadn't turned to spaghetti. "Who's up?"

Sunny checked her Lesson Planner, tilting it out of my view, then clapped it shut. "Her name is Rashi Kapoor."

I recognized Rashi's name, but she wouldn't know mine. I'd never even shared a class with her. The closer Sunny nudged me toward that cherry-red front door, the higher my questions piled up. Every time we took a step, I stopped Sunny with another one.

"Is it because Rashi was class president last year? Is it because of her future? Is that it? Is it something Rashi is going to be?"

Sunny stopped me at the foot of Rashi's porch. "You've really gotta stop worrying about the future, Jonah."

"About the *future*?" I raised an eyebrow, Mom-style. "You're kidding me."

Sunny raised an eyebrow back. "I said to stop worrying, not to stop caring. You need to work more and worry less. It's like my dad says: 'Let tomorrow worry about itself. Today'll keep you busy.' Come on." She pulled my hand toward the porch.

I leaned away and went limp, not caring that it made me look like a seventh-grade toddler. "I'm not moving until you tell me what you know." I folded my arms. "Why. Rashi."

Sunny closed her eyes. "I'll make you a deal. For the rest of this mission, I'll give you five more facts about the future. That's it. So, if you want to use Future Fact #1 right here, then knock yourself out."

Future Facts. It had a nice ring to it. And, as much as I hated a five-question limit, it was a lot better than having Sunny ignore every question I asked.

"Okay." The tension in my neck let up just a little. "You told me that we absolutely *have* to strike on October twenty-eighth. 'Zero Hour' is what you called it. But what does it all mean? What's so special about 'Zero Hour'?"

"Pass." Sunny moved up the steps. "You don't need to know that yet."

"You can't 'pass' on Future Facts!" I put my foot down—literally—on Rashi's front porch.

"My future, my rules." Sunny folded her arms. "Pass."

"Fine," I said, "then what is it about Rashi Kapoor? Why is she our campaign manager?"

Sunny flicked me the side-eye before answering. "Future Fact: Rashi Kapoor is a future US president's Chief of Staff. Basically, she'll run the White House." Sunny took a long breath, giving a weary, are-you-satisfied look. "Needless to say, she's good at managing things."

" . . . the White House."

"Yes, Jonah. The White House. That's number one." Sunny mashed the doorbell and stood back. "You've got four Future Facts left."

The door flung open to reveal an old woman in a pale blue cloth that draped over her shoulder and wrapped around her side.

Sunny waved. "Good morning."

The woman peered at us through large old-lady glasses that looked almost exactly like the ones my Great Aunt Linda wore. She folded her arms, waiting for us to talk first.

"Is Rashi home?" I blurted.

The woman's eyes narrowed. She shuffled back into the foyer, stepping around a small mountain of luggage and shouting in a language I couldn't place. I'm pretty sure I heard a "Rashi" in there somewhere.

Another woman, about Mom's age, passed through the foyer lugging a foot bath and a lamp. Her oversized T-shirt said *Let's Have a Moment of Science.*

"Mummy, you've gotta speak to her in English, she doesn't—" She froze in her tracks as a starstruck smile leapt across her face.

"We've been over this, Mom." Rashi Kapoor hobbled down the steps with her face obscured by not one, but two open books—an algebra textbook and *Learning Basic Hindi.* "I need to be immersed. Nani, *don't* speak English with me, okay?"

She lowered the books and froze just like her mom had. Except Rashi didn't smile. She watched us as warily as her grandmother had.

"Deepak!" Rashi's mom called across the house. "It's the YouTube kid!" She grinned at me like I was some kind of celebrity.

"Mom, his name is Jonah," said Rashi. I couldn't believe she knew my name.

A man emerged from the kitchen with a batter-coated apron. He threw out a floury hand.

"Jonah!" he said, shaking mine. "This is such an honor. I'm Rashi's dad—I mean, my *name* is Deepak, but I am Rashi's dad, too, and I just want to say, as a professor of Earth Science—"

"*DAD*," Rashi groaned. "I know you're excited to meet Jonah here and—" She gestured to the time-traveler beside me.

"And Sunny," I said.

"But I don't think they came here to sign autographs." Rashi stepped in between her dad and me. "What's up, guys?"

"We need you." Sunny spoke with a depth in her voice that took me back to Martic Pinnacle.

Rashi checked the time on her phone. Her eyes darted with calculations, like she was organizing dozens of fifteen-minute time-blocks in her head.

"Come on." She turned for the stairs. "We can talk in my office."

Rashi called it her "office," but it was really just a nice bedroom with a big desk and lots of bookshelves. Broadway playbills decorated the walls. Rashi was exactly the type of straight-A student to find her fandom in Broadway plays. As for me, the only play I'd ever heard of was *Hamilton*, and that's only because Rashi used one of its songs in her class presidential campaign.

Rashi offered us a couple of pink inflatable chairs and settled in behind the desk. Its top was perfectly bare except for two objects: a picture frame and a little hourglass that she placed in front of me and Sunny. The sand filled the upper chamber of the glass—all the way to a measuring line labeled *3 minutes*.

"Let's cut the chitchat," she said, tenting her fingers like a Disney villain. "I can guess why the two of you came to my doorstep. Given the content of your YouTube video, I assume you're building some kind of climate activism group at Creekside Middle. Now you need someone like me to help you get it off the ground. Am I wrong?"

Sunny and I both shook our heads.

"Now, I can only guess that you're approaching me in particular because I happen to be the two-time class president, national champion mathlete, and all-around smartest kid in school. Also, one heck of a party planner. Am I wrong?"

Again, we shook our heads. The hourglass was down to two and a half minutes now.

"I've seen your video, Jonah. Several times, in fact—thanks to the fanboys and fangirls downstairs. Kudos, by the way. I think the whole thing was very well stated. But I need to be honest with you: this year I'm taking extra classes at Carbon Community College, I'm a member of every school club, I'm leading *half* of those clubs, and I'm running for reelection in November."

Rashi closed her eyes and shuddered, as if she'd overwhelmed herself just by saying it all out loud.

"So," she resumed. "As much as I believe in what you're doing, I just literally, physically, humanly do not have the *time*." She pointed at the little hourglass in front of me. "How much is left?"

"Two minutes." My mouth had gone bone-dry.

Rashi nodded. "So, you've got me for the next 120 seconds. Anything else on your mind?"

Sunny rested her hand on my shoulder. "We hear you," she began. "But you might want to listen to my friend here before you make up your mind. Jonah, take it away."

I opened my mouth, but nothing came out for a good ten seconds. My lungs flared up with that tight, itchy feeling. The girl was clearly an intellectual heavyweight. If we had any chance of winning Rashi over, it would have to be with cold hard facts. I clutched my inhaler and reached back into my deepest, most advanced Wikipedia studies.

"So there's this group at the United Nations." I cleared my throat. "Dedicated to studying the climate."

"The Intergovernmental Panel on Climate Change?" Rashi tossed me a mini water bottle from her desk. "Yeah. I've heard of the IPCC."

"Right, the IPCC." I twisted off the cap and took a quick sip. I could've stayed here on this inflatable chair for the rest of the twenty-first century and never once remembered that name. "So that's a ton, *thousands*, of scientists putting their heads together to see what's going on. According to them, if people don't change what they're doing, we could see the Earth heat up by—"

"Five point seven degrees," Rashi said. I'd been planning to say *lots*.

"Exactly," I said between sips. "Now you might not think 5.7 sounds like a lot, but—"

"That's in Celsius." Rashi's eyes darted to the picture on her desk, then back to me. "In Fahrenheit, we're looking at 10.2 degrees—no, 10.26. If you've got a fever that high above normal, you might want to dial 9-1-1."

"Great!" The conversation got me weirdly excited. I'd have a hard time finding an adult who understood this stuff so well—let alone somebody my age.

Rashi snatched up the spent hourglass. "Time's up."

I rocked in my inflatable chair, all pumped up on adrenaline. I hadn't felt this way since Mom let me and Gideon try Monster energy drinks in fourth grade. The squeeze of my asthma had loosened up entirely. Three minutes with Rashi more than proved that she didn't just know how to get it all done, she understood why it all mattered. We'd found our manager.

"So"—I rose to my feet—"what do you say?"

Rashi stood up and extended a hand. "I say it's been a pleasure talking with you, Jonah Kaminski. I'll show you the door."

So long, adrenaline.

Half-heartedly, I shook Rashi's hand, watching her eyes trail to that picture frame one last time. Now on my feet, I could see the photo inside. It showed a sprawling fortress, built from ancient-looking red stone and decorated with pointed arches. In the picture, Rashi posed arm in arm with her grandmother on one side and a jolly-looking old man on the other. Rashi wore half a smirk, and the old man leaned against her in mid-laugh, like it was something she had said.

Rashi walked us outside. As she and Sunny made small talk, I stared at the abandoned construction site beside her home. That's how I felt at the moment. Trapped in a project that'd never get off the ground. I had thirty-one days to organize 600 students and, to quote Sunny, I would never be able to do it alone. Too bad I couldn't get a single person to help.

I slumped off the porch steps without even saying bye. Something poked me from behind. I looked back.

Sunny glared at me like I'd just taken a part-time job in the ice-cream truck. She turned to Rashi with a polite smile. "Can you give us a minute?"

"Thirty seconds. Tops." Rashi waited on the porch.

"*Jonah,*" Sunny whispered. "Just come out with it already."

I patted my pockets to show how little I had to give. "Come out with what?"

"I'm not a mind reader," Sunny whisper-shot back, "but I can tell you've got something on your mind. So come out with it."

Rashi headed for the door. Sunny prodded me again. What was I supposed to say? In a panic, I went with the first thing that came to mind:

"Who's the old man?"

Rashi froze. "Come again?"

"The old man," I said, as the asthma tickled its way back up my chest. "From the picture on your desk."

"What does it matter?"

"Because." I took a breath. "In the three minutes we spent in your office, I saw your eyes move to that photo at least three times."

Rashi folded her arms tight and took a seat on the top step. "That's Nana—my grandfather." She stared at the desolate construction site. "We visit Nani and Nana in India every summer. We used to, I mean. Before this year."

"The heat wave," Sunny whispered. Rashi nodded.

Mom had told me about the one in New Delhi. It was the hottest temperature ever recorded in that city—120 degrees Fahrenheit. When a road-melting heat wave transforms your city into an oven, you've got no choice but to take shelter and pray that you don't suffer a heat stroke—which is how thirty-six people lost their lives last summer. Now I wondered if one of those people was Rashi's grandfather, the smiling man in her picture. It hit me right in the heart. For all the thought I'd given the climate apocalypse over the last several months, I'd never once stopped to consider that some people might already be living it.

Rashi swallowed hard, still looking away. "After the last heat wave, my parents tried to make them move here, but they didn't want to leave home. Now it's only Nani moving in."

I glanced again at Rashi's mailbox. *Welcome Home*, the half-deflated party balloon said. But Nani's arrival couldn't be less of a party. They were all just doing their best to manage in a world without a man who laughed in family photos and made his granddaughter smile.

"It's not right," Sunny said to Rashi, while resting a hand on my shoulder. "But it's going to happen again. And again, and again, and again. Some of the biggest cities in that part of the world won't be livable at all—if we don't do something about it soon." She gestured to the little hourglass Rashi was still holding. "We're almost out of time."

"I know you're busy," I added, closing my eyes to manage the nerves. "You can't do it all. But I guess that's the good thing about having a Crew: you won't have to do this alone."

Rashi looked down for a long moment, cradling the hourglass in her hands. She dabbed her eyes and turned to face us. "When do we start?"

"Tomorrow," Sunny said. "Lunch period. Room 329."

"What if the teachers are still on strike tom—" I stopped myself in the nick of time. No way was I gonna let Sunny blow another one of my Future Facts. I had only four left.

"So . . ." Sunny held out a double thumbs-up, grinning expectantly. "Room 329?"

"Three twenty-nine at noon." Rashi tossed her the hourglass. "I'll make time."

STEP 2:

DRESS UP FOR SCIENCE CLASS

Wednesday, September 28

30 days until Zero Hour

Sunny was right. We did go back to school. The Carbon Hill School District Teachers Union renegotiated their contract and ended the strike immediately.

They'd won.

That meant Sunny was right about one more thing: a strike was a good way to make things happen. Strength in numbers. And if there was one way we Creekside students could outdo our teachers (besides burping the alphabet), it was in our numbers. Of course, I still had no idea why Sunny believed that one student strike—no matter how big—would do enough to rewrite the twenty-first century, but not even all four of my Future Facts could buy me that answer.

It was easier to show my face in school after the teachers' strike. Instead of replaying Jonah Kaminski's viral doomsday video, most students were discussing how otherworldly it felt to see our teachers on a picket line—like looking into some alternate dimension where your silliest sixth-grade teacher has always been a steely-eyed freedom fighter. My YouTube rant came up once or twice, but never for long. I got one pat on the back. One fist bump. I didn't notice any negative reactions, mostly because I was avoiding Lindsay Allister at all costs. But the moment I reached my locker, I knew that Lindsay and her thugs had not been avoiding me.

FAKER.

The word slashed across the face of my locker in fat red permanent marker.

I didn't care what Sunny said about her; I refused to believe that Lindsay Allister was "not half-bad."

After homeroom, I had science with Ms. Alecci. Room 329—the same room Sunny had pegged for our first Crew meeting. I had no clue why she thought my strictest teacher's classroom would make the perfect environment for plotting our student rebellion.

Come to think of it, I didn't know much of anything about today's meeting. Why Alecci's room? What would we discuss? And how in the world did Sunny plan on joining us? Would she crawl in through the window? Would she freeze time to stroll through the front entrance undetected? Not unless she wanted to catch heat from the ice-cream truck.

My classmates drifted into the room and found their seats. Still no Alecci. With no teacher in the room, chaos reigned. Science class went apocalyptic. We were minutes away from boarded windows and burning cars.

Finally, the door swung open, but it wasn't Ms. Alecci. The door revealed a man in a secondhand suit, looking a bit past due for a haircut. He had a head of salt-and-pepper gray hair, but a face as young as Mom's. The man pushed a bin up to Alecci's desk and, with one methodical sweep of his arm, dumped every paper, book, and desktop calendar into the trash.

The classroom erupted in protest. Even Terry DiMarco, the most disrespectful student in my class, rose to defend the sacred honor of Ms. Alecci's stuff. "What do you think you're doing, man?"

"Oh my word," Stasha gasped from the back of the room. "She's dead, isn't she?"

"No." The man surveyed our faces, blinking in confusion. "What kind of a monster do you think I am?" He carried Alecci's belongings into the hall and returned, shutting the door behind him.

"Skin cancer," Terry said. "In detention last year, I saw this huge mole on the back of her neck."

"Listen." The man looked around for some chalk. "Nobody's dead. Nobody's got cancer. Under the new teachers union contract, Ms. Alecci can finally collect her hard-earned pension. She put in for retirement—starting today. As we speak, the lady's halfway to Costa Rica. So let me introduce myself." He found a tiny chalk nub and slashed his name on the board: D-A-N. "My name is Mr. Dan, and I'm not asking for your respect. I'm not even asking you to listen to me. All I ask is that you SPEAK. UP."

Mr. Dan scribbled *SPEAK UP* on the board in handwriting almost as bad as mine.

"Two reasons for that." He sat on the edge of Ms. Alecci's—no, *his*—desk. "The first reason is that I am literally, legally deaf." Mr. Dan removed two dangly hearing aids from behind his ears, the kind with circular magnets in the back. "Cochlear implants. Without these processors, I can't hear jack. But even with them"—he hooked the processors back behind his ears—"I can't hear mumbling voices worth a dang. Which is kind of a shame, since your voices are so dang important.

"And that brings me to the second reason I need you to speak up." He took center stage in front of the class. "Kids are the smartest people on the face of the earth. I mean it. The smartest adult is an absolute blockhead compared to any kid. Not that you know more than adults do. I mean, I'm a pretty well-read person; I know *way* more stuff than you guys. But you guys are smart because of all the stuff you *don't* know. You don't take anything for granted. You don't accept the world like it is. And absolutely no one should. So please, for the love of the scientific method, SPEAK UP."

I could swear he was looking straight at me.

Suddenly, it all made sense. This was precisely the kind of teacher who would let a Crew of climate rebels hold their meetings in his classroom. That this particular teacher would start working in this particular classroom on this particular day—Sunny must have known it from the start.

Kat Pucillo piped in from the back of the room. "Mr. Dan, isn't this supposed to be science class?"

"Of course it is. You think science is for people who *don't* speak up?"

At that very moment, as if to answer Mr. Dan's rhetorical question, Sunny stepped into the room. I leapt to my feet. I'd never seen Sunny outside of a recruiting mission.

Principal Rivera stepped in behind her and sized up the room. The wild-eyed YouTuber in the front row must've caught his eye. "No cause for alarm, Jonah. Just a new student."

As soon as I heard a few voices snickering behind me, I dropped back into my seat. I shouldn't have been so shocked to see her. How else did I expect Sunny to lead our first Crew meeting if she wasn't attending Creekside Middle?

"Of course," I said to Mr. Rivera. "I don't know her or anything."

More tittering came from the back of the class.

"I wouldn't expect you to know her, Jonah." Principal Rivera looked confused. "She just flew in last weekend."

Sunny nodded brightly. With a bow clipped onto her braided updo and a long flowery dress, Sunny didn't look like herself—which made sense. She was going undercover as an ordinary student. Unfortunately, Sunny didn't have any idea what an ordinary student wore to school in the 2020s. The dress was fabulous, of course, very Sunny, but maybe a little extra for science class.

"I'd like to introduce your new classmate," Rivera went on. "She's temporarily joining us here at Creekside through an international exchange program called . . ."

"22nd-Century Kids," Sunny said.

"Funny name," Principal Rivera remarked to no one in particular. He led Sunny to the empty seat beside mine. "Your new classmate has traveled across the world to learn with us—all the way from *France*. Her name is Sunday." He squinted at the letter in his hand. "Sunday Lafrance."

Sunny greeted the class with a modest wave. "Bonjour." She didn't speak with the slightest hint of a French accent.

"We're still sorting out the paperwork, but it looks like she'll be attending Creekside for the next few weeks. So, I hope you'll all give

Sunday a good Creekside welcome." The classroom pattered with light applause as Principal Rivera left the room.

Mr. Dan took a seat on top of his desk. "Jonah, can you get Sunday up to speed?"

I turned to Sunny and tuned out the rest of the classroom, hoping to keep my nerves at bay. "Speak up," I summarized, "because grown-ups don't listen."

"Or don't hear so well." Mr. Dan showed Sunny his cochlear implants. "And kids are worth hearing. So, here's the only homework I'll ever assign: At some point this year, I want you to find one pointless thing that people take for granted. Ask a grown-up why and see how much they squirm."

I scribbled the assignment into my notebook: *Put grown-ups on the spot.* By the time class ended, Mr. Dan had already passed into legend as the greatest teacher of my middle school career.

The P.A. system beeped, and every student got up to leave Room 329. Everyone but Sunny and me.

"Mr. Dan." Sunny remained at her desk, raising her hand even though we were the only students left in the room. We'd have to work on her classroom protocol.

"Ms. Lafrance." He played along, pointing to her.

"Jonah here was too shy to ask," she began, tossing my dignity to the curb, "but he was wondering if you might let his new club meet in your room over lunch today."

Mr. Dan looked suspicious. "What's the club?"

I answered with the totally confident and not shy "It's about, um, the climate . . . and . . . um . . ."

"Putting grown-ups on the spot," Sunny interrupted. "That's what the club is for."

"That"—Mr. Dan furrowed his brow and stroked his chin—"has got to be the most punk rock thing I have ever heard in my life." He broke into a grin. "Mi casa, su casa."

STEP 3:

THINK BIG

By lunchtime, Mr. Dan's classroom had gone completely cinematic. It was dark, lit only by the digital blue glare of the classroom projector. Sunny took a wide stance at the head of the classroom, her Lesson Planner held open like a Bible at her chest. She surveyed her army of three: me, Rashi, and Gideon (still grounded, but not grounded from school). Mr. Dan sat in the corner, but he'd given us strict instructions to pretend he wasn't there.

Steam snaked up from the ramen bowls Sunny had ordered for our lunch, catching the projector light like cigar smoke in a room full of top intelligence officials.

"Lady and gentlemen"—Sunny glanced at the Lesson Planner—"this job will not be easy. Each of you deserves to understand the task we're facing." She tapped her watch and instantly overrode Mr. Dan's projector, just like she'd done with those TVs at the Superstore. A CGI globe flooded the screen now, painting Sunny in its blue gridlines. Then a single word animated over the globe in bright block letters: *BRIEFING*.

"Whoa!" Mr. Dan pointed at the projector. "What kinda watch does that?"

I coughed up a noodle in mid-slurp. "It's . . . um . . . French?"

Mr. Dan leaned back, folding his arms. "A French smartwatch . . ."

He looked genuinely intrigued. But when it came to Sunny and her time machine, the last thing we needed was a curious adult.

"It's an early prototype," Sunny chimed in. "I'm not supposed to talk about it."

"Cool," Mr. Dan chirped before innocently delving back into his ramen.

Sunny was good in a pinch—better than I was, anyway.

"Now"—Sunny folded her hands and faced Rashi, Gideon, and me—"back to the mission." She motioned to the globe behind her. "I'm going to assume that all of you understand the basics of climate science. At this point in human history, it's about as well understood as the laws of gravity."

"Sorry." Gideon raised his hand. "I don't know much of anything about climate science, one way or the other. I mean, besides what I heard in Jonah's video."

Sunny half smiled, like she was waiting for the punchline. "You're serious."

A twenty-second-century visitor like Sunny wouldn't understand that there was nothing unusual about Gideon. Here in the 2020s, there were plenty of kids—grown-ups, too—who still hadn't quite noticed the story of the century. For every historic wildfire, we had an army of Chewbagoats waiting to drown out the news.

"It's not his fault," I piped up. "I'll get him caught up after the meeting."

Then I swallowed hard. Even now, the thought of a one-on-one conversation with Gideon made me sweat. Where would we even begin? I couldn't just start tutoring the guy on climate science without addressing at least *one* of the many elephants in the room. But which elephant came first—the condolences-for-his-dad elephant, the years-long-silence elephant, or the elephant of the well-deserved grudge that Gideon must've been holding against me?

"Look," Gideon said. "I just want my dog back. And if you, Sunday Lafrance, are telling me that this is important, then sign me up. I mean, you're literally from the future—"

I bolted to my feet. "The Future Scientists . . . of America . . . Academic Leadership . . . Smart Kids Program." It was the best I could do. We hadn't told Rashi about Sunny's secret, and the less other people knew, the safer Sunny would be. Anything to keep word away from those ice-cream creepers who were trying to track her down.

"How about we cut to the chase?" Sunny said without losing the momentum in her voice. She tapped on her watch, and the screen filled with the photo of a hulking factory, topped with smokestacks and wrapped in a chain-link fence. I'd resented this place since well before I knew anything about carbon emissions because, for as long as I could remember, whenever Mom would leave me for work, this was the place that took her away.

"Tell me, Jonah," Sunny said. "What's this building for?"

"It's the Allister Energy Plant. They burn coal to make electricity."

"Sorta," Sunny replied. "That's what the building is for *today*. It wasn't always like this."

To my astonishment, the modern picture morphed into a reel of old film footage. The same building now looked different, younger. It had no fence. No razor wire. Fewer smokestacks. It was a proud brick factory, festooned with buntings of red, white, and blue. I never thought I'd feel this way about the Allister Energy Plant, but the place was beautiful.

"Carbon Hill," Sunny said. "1946."

"Doesn't look like much of a coal plant." I stroked my chin.

"It *wasn't* a coal plant," Sunny replied. "During World War II, the government turned this abandoned building into a propeller factory. They hauled in new equipment, trained new workers, and offered a good job to everyone in town."

"We get it," Rashi said, as if she were speaking for all of us. I, for one, did not "get it." But I figured this was one of Rashi's powers; she had a way of thinking a few dozen steps ahead of everyone else. "If Carbon Hill could make propeller blades during World War II, we could make windmill blades today."

"Or solar panels," Sunny said.

"Or geothermal energy coils," I added, now thankful for all those hours I'd spent anxiously googling green technology. Sunny's vision was beginning to click. To really save the world, we couldn't just board up the Allister Energy Plant; we had to turn it into something new.

"I see head nods," Sunny said. "So, you get the idea. But this has to be a whole lot bigger than Carbon Hill. This kind of transformation needs to happen all over the United States of America—just like it did during World War II. This is all or nothing. Do or die. It's gotta be big."

I finally saw what had motivated Sunny's Produce Aisle Address about how grown-ups were thinking too small about saving the world. It was probably the same reason that she'd said my video "could use some work." I'd burned a solid minute ranting about family cars, vacations, shopping lists—the hundred little ways that everyday people are chipping in to the crisis. But Sunny didn't want to talk about the little stuff. Sunny wanted to do something huge.

"But how's that ever gonna happen?" I said, always the one to rain on Sunny's crusade. "How exactly can one climate strike in one small town trigger a worldwide energy revolution?"

"I'm glad you asked." Sunny tapped her watch, and an old man with a cheesy smile appeared onscreen behind her. I knew that face. "United States Senator James Lyndon Budley. 'Senator Bud' for short." Sunny gave his giant cheek a little pat. "Meet your target."

The lights switched back on.

"Alright, kids." Mr. Dan had stopped making himself invisible. In fact, he now appeared in full-blown Responsible Adult mode at the front of room. "I'm cool with secret plans to save the world, but I draw the line at 'targets.' You guys are starting to sound like the Mafia."

"It's not violent." Rashi leapt to Sunny's defense. "Every movement has a target. The abolitionists had President Lincoln. They needed him to pass the Thirteenth Amendment. The civil rights movement had President Johnson. They needed him to pass the Civil Rights Act. All Sunny's saying is our movement has a target, too: Senator Bud. We need him to help us save the world."

"You know what?" Mr. Dan took off his hearing aids and held up a dog-eared paperback novel. "I think I'll mind my own business." He gave us a wink, switched off the lights, and went back to his desk.

Sunny was beaming. "This is why we need you, Rashi."

"Don't mention it."

Sunny's smile fell away as she returned to the topic at hand. "Jim

Budley loves this town. Grew up here, in fact. Unfortunately, he grew up to be one of the greatest hypocrites in human history." She closed her eyes and breathed for a moment, reining in her temper. "He mentions climate change in every single stump speech, but he's collected more donations from Allister Energy than any other person in the US government. And once this country is ready to make a big change, you can bet he'll stand in the way."

I wasn't about to waste a Future Fact, but I could hear the traces of one in her words. Sunny wasn't *betting* that Senator Bud would keep our country from stopping the apocalypse. She knew it for a fact. Someday, I guessed, in the not-too-distant future, the government would pursue a climate plan big enough to avert the apocalypse, and Bud's vote would single-handedly kill it.

"So now"—Sunny shut the Lesson Planner and trained her eyes on me—"a question—"

Please don't say my name.

"—for my dear friend, Jonah." I glanced around to make sure there wasn't another Jonah in the room. Nope, Sunny was looking at me. "How does anyone motivate a guy like Senator Bud?"

I blinked for a slow second as the Jonah Kaminski Nerve-Machine fired up like an internal combustion engine. My palms started sweating, which had a way of drying out my mouth. I swallowed, which seemed to knock my heartbeat into overdrive. The heartbeat woke up my asthma, which tightened my lungs—just enough to crank my nerves higher, making my hands sweat more. And so on. Why was I so terrified of three kids in a classroom? My body was making no sense, but no amount of shame could break this feedback loop. I'd have to think my way out of it.

I squinted at Sunny's projection of Jim Budley and his needy, oversized grin. How should I know what motivates a US Senator? His desperate-looking smile reminded me of the yard signs from his last reelection campaign. All of them bore a star-spangled thumbs-up with the words *I LIKE BUD*. Perhaps that was the key. I stared at my desk and forced out the answer:

"He wants to be liked," I said. "He *needs* to be, I mean, if he wants to get reelected next year. So, I guess, um, if you wanna win him over, you've gotta make it impossible for him to say no without looking like a jerk."

I glanced up from the sweaty palm prints on my desk and found Sunny staring aghast. But not at me.

"Why aren't you guys writing this down? Jonah Kaminski gets people—most of the time. And he's dead right about Senator Bud. So, here's what we're gonna do." Sunny made a pink October calendar light up on-screen behind her. "On Friday, October twenty-eighth, we need to launch a climate strike big enough to rock this entire town. We're not just gonna make the local news. I'm talking national. Global, even. We're gonna put more pressure on Senator Bud than he's ever felt before. We're gonna make him care more about protecting our future than he does about protecting Richard Allister."

October 28, I remembered. Zero Hour.

"And now"—Sunny brought up the lights and gave a light curtsy with her frilly yellow dress—"I would like to announce my retirement."

"What?!" shouted Gideon, surely remembering that Einstein's fate depended on our Crew—and on Sunny, most of all. "You can't leave!"

I took as much offense as Gideon did. "What do you mean 'retirement'?! We still have thirty days to go!"

Sunny placed a hand on each of our desks to quiet us down.

"I'm not going anywhere," she said. "I'm just trusting someone else to lead. If things ever start to get really impossible, I'm your guy. But from now on, all official business goes through the campaign manager."

Rashi took Sunny's place at the front of the room as Sunny settled down to bask in the steam of her takeout ramen. She was the only one who hadn't eaten.

"Well"—Rashi squared her shoulders—"you heard the woman. That's thirty days to get this entire school mobilized. It's not impossible. But we'd better get to work."

STEP 4:

CRAFT UP A STORM

Thursday, September 29

29 days until Zero Hour

For lunch the next day, Sunny ordered a whole stack of Maroni's pizza—the first dairy product I'd tasted since putting my "carbon footprint" on a diet. That was four months ago. But now, reclining in Mr. Dan's room for our second Crew meeting, I gazed lovingly at my steaming slice of extra cheese. For once, I didn't feel guilty for eating. What this Crew was building together would be so much bigger than a lifetime's worth of uneaten mozzarella.

"Amen." Sunny finished blessing her broccoli pizza and dug in. So did I. Sunny had dressed more casual today, already embracing her newfound retirement. Rashi, on the other hand, was too professional to respect the "lunch" in "lunch meeting." She paced the front of the classroom while the rest of us finished our slices.

"This isn't my first campaign," said Rashi Kapoor, two-time class president. "And I know how to win. We are going to mobilize this school in the same way I won class president last year. And that's with lots. And lots. Of posters."

Rashi raised a giant rubber bin and dumped its contents across a lab table. It looked like a craft store had exploded into a multicolored mess of poster board, construction paper, cut-out letters, and glue sticks.

"I hope you're gonna clean that up," Mr. Dan said from behind a giant stromboli, his napkin tucked in like a bib.

Rashi threw him a thumbs-up since he wouldn't hear her voice. Mr. Dan had removed his hearing aids at the start of our meeting. He'd said he wanted to bask in blissful silence, but I suspected it had something to do with a legal term I'd heard from Mom: *plausible deniability*.

"You'd be surprised what you can accomplish with a little arts and crafts." Rashi gestured with a hot glue gun. "Last year, I hung twenty-three extra-large poster boards around the school for my campaign. I think that's a good place to start."

"I like it." Gideon held up a bulk package of mini American flags. "Very patriotic."

Rashi took the flags. "This is all leftover from my presidential run. The stars and stripes were kind of on theme, you know?"

I shrugged. "We think our country can save the world. What's more Captain America than that?"

"Hear, hear." Sunny unscrewed a giant glue stick. "Let's get crafting like the state of our union depends on it."

So, craft we did. For the rest of that week and a bit of the next, Mr. Dan's science classroom spun into a cyclone of creative brilliance. Construction paper whipped into words of power. Glitter-glue zigzagged onto poster boards like lightning. Gold star stickers showered our creations like fire from the gods. Our magic? Invisible tape. Our weapon? Safety scissors. When we'd finished, the team had produced twenty-three posters, each looking a little something like this:

By the following Tuesday, we'd plastered them all over Creekside Middle—anywhere with a bulletin board. We hung posters near the entrance, in the cafeteria, beside the front office, and in just about every science classroom. We gathered for a quick huddle and a round of high fives before leaving school that afternoon.

"We did it," Rashi announced. "The U.S.A. has officially gone public."

"Now all we gotta do is sit back and watch the members roll in." Gideon wore the same confident half smile I'd seen on his eight-year-old self after we'd mixed our first batch of watery lemonade, absolutely certain of our future success in the beverage industry. I could only hope that these new posters would perform a little better than the lemonade stand had.

STEP 5:

MEET SHAKESPEARE

Friday, October 7

21 days until Zero Hour

"Where did we go wrong?" Rashi paced the front of the classroom, clutching a burrito the size of her head.

She looked all broken up, more flustered than I'd ever seen her, and she had good reason to be. After all those posters, we'd gained only one new recruit, and even that was on a technicality. Little Mike Callahan "joined" for exactly two hours this morning; he'd heard that we always got free takeout for our meetings. This much was true (it's nice having a Powerball winner on your Crew), but Little Mike quit the U.S.A. the minute he found out that we'd ordered burritos. Apparently, Little Mike was more of a pizza guy. One recruit gained; one recruit lost.

"You'll figure it out. This room is full of ideas," Sunny said with a wink.

Did she know what I was thinking? Or was she just being chill as heck? Retirement suited her—literally. Today she had come to school in a bright-pink tracksuit, a cross between the astronaut costume and whatever Ms. Alecci would've packed for her new life of leisure. How had Sunny gotten more relaxed while the rest of us were only getting more high-strung?

"I like your optimism, Sunny," Gideon replied as a chunk of guacamole plopped from his burrito onto his desk. "But the plan isn't holding up."

"It's leaking." Rashi kept pacing while she battled her own burrito at the front of the room.

"We hab shum bapkins uppear," Mr. Dan said through a mouthful of fajita veggies. He slid a stack of napkins to the corner of his desk.

The words on the board behind Mr. Dan's head were taunting me this afternoon: *SPEAK UP.*

No, I thought back, *why can't somebody else speak up?* The problem with the posters was obvious enough.

Rashi sighed as she mopped up burrito juice from the floor. "Posters just aren't going to cut it."

Sunny shrugged. "I wonder if *Jonah* has any thoughts."

I *did* have a hunch about our problem, but I wasn't in the mood to speak up. Life was so much easier when I didn't have to talk, and Rashi seemed to be working it out on her own.

"Well, for one thing," Rashi noted, "they're not much use when they keep getting trashed every day." A fair point.

As if we hadn't already burned enough time on arts and crafts the week before, we'd spent most of this week remaking the originals. They were getting vandalized or shredded faster than we could crank them out. Most were graffitied with the word *FAKE*, so I figured Lindsay Allister and her Bacon friend had played a role.

"The posters are too vulnerable," Rashi continued. "Too easy to sabotage."

"Yeah," Gideon joined in. "And most people still don't seem to understand what this group is really about."

He was probably referring to himself as much as anyone else. I was supposed to follow up with him on the science of things, but I dodged that conversation every chance I got. I still hadn't kicked my talking-to-Gideon allergy. Every time I thought of trying, I wound up choking on another doubt: Did Gideon really care about any of this? Wasn't he just in it for a dog? Was he only putting on a nice face while, deep down, he couldn't stand the sight of his deadbeat former friend? Whenever I tried to speak to him, one of these questions clogged up my throat.

"I'm not sure *what* the issue is," Rashi concluded. "But we can't move forward unless we figure it out. I'm not wasting any more days."

"Yeah." Sunny straightened and shot me a glare. "If only we had *someone in this room* who knows how to motivate people."

I looked away, and my eyes landed back on Mr. Dan's chalkboard. *SPEAK UP.*

Fine, I thought. But instead of raising my voice, I raised my hand—a very cool and normal thing to do during a conversation with three of your peers.

Rashi raised an eyebrow and called on me. "You in the front."

My mouth went suddenly dry. I took a sip from my bottle of tamarind soda. "Something I noticed right after we put the posters around." I wiped my sweaty palms with a burrito napkin. "Right after, actually. Jace Marasco stopped at one of them. He kinda tilted his head, then tilted his head the other way. Then sorta shrugged. Then walked off."

I waited for Rashi and the others to put it together. It seemed plain enough to me. But not even Gideon could see my point.

"Um . . ." he interjected as nicely as anyone could. "The end?"

"You guys don't see it?" I was frankly a little shocked. "Jace read the whole thing, tried again, then eventually gave up. After that I reread the poster, and something hit me: people need the bigger picture. It's like advertising a movie with all posters and no trailers. We're not giving them the story."

Rashi froze mid-bite. Over the last week, I'd learned that this kind of buffering meant she had officially entered Deep Thought Do-Not-Disturb Mode. It was best not to interrupt.

"Lit!" she said, snapping out of it. "That's what we need."

"What's *lit*?" I asked. Sunny and Gideon seconded my question.

"*Lit* means cool!" Mr. Dan announced from behind his newspaper with all the eagerness of a grown-up who just learned how to floss and wants every kid on Earth to know it.

"Wrong 'lit,'" Rashi groaned.

"This is why I never listen in." Mr. Dan popped off his hearing aids and went back to the *Times*.

"It's short for *literature*." Rashi closed her eyes to search the massive database she carried in that head of hers. "When my mom ran a donation drive for Liberty House, she printed thousands and thousands of fliers—lit. Basically, they explained the organization with plenty of detail—certainly more than you'd fit on a poster."

"Lit." Sunny smiled and propped her feet up on the desk. "I knew you'd figure something out."

"But I haven't told you the best part," Rashi said. "I know just the guy to write it."

It was a five-minute SLYSR ride from Creekside Middle to the Liberty House townhomes, but it took us more than twenty. That's because every time we heard the faintest tune of that ice-cream truck, Sunny would hit the brakes and suggest an alternate route. Rashi followed along, deeply puzzled by our irrational fear of frozen dairy products. She'd borrowed Gideon's scooter because he was lucky enough to still be grounded.

The homes in this neighborhood were built close together—each squished up against the other. They were colorful, newly built, and overflowing with life. In these vibrant hours just after school, they looked like a United Nations block party. I saw old women wearing layer upon layer of wildly patterned fabric. Young men blasting Spanish-language pop from their phone speakers and defying the laws of physics with a soccer ball. One big gaggle of toddlers clustered around the front porch of a house for story time.

"They're all refugees of one kind or another," Rashi said. "All of them lost a home somewhere far away. Now they're doing their best to make a new home here. Like Nani." Her eyes flitted from house to house before she pointed to one at the end of the block. "I rolled the carpet in that one."

Rashi's family had been volunteering at Liberty House for years, she explained, which was why she knew so much about the place.

"I'd always wondered who lived here," I said.

"Kings and queens," Rashi said in a hushed, majestic tone. "The first ones burnt by the flame they never lit. The world's unluckiest. They'll always deserve more than anyone can give. These ones—

these ones—inherit the earth."

"Very . . . poetic?" I replied, puzzling at Rashi's sudden Shakespearean turn.

"It *is* a poem," Rashi said. "A twelve-year-old boy wrote those words in Puerto Rico after a hurricane took his home. It won him a bit of award money, enough to move his whole family to a new home in Pennsylvania—but he'll be the last one to tell you that. Paco isn't one to brag."

"Did you just say 'Paco'?" Sunny threw out her arms, like she was catching her balance. She unzipped her backpack, whipped out the Lesson Planner, and started furiously paging through it.

"Yes, Paco," Rashi answered. "'Paco' Francisco Mercado Baez. He moved here last year."

"To Carbon Hill?!" Sunny's mouth hung as wide as it could go. She gave up on the scrapbook and packed it away, her face still frozen in shock.

"Do you already know him or something?" Rashi asked.

Sunny broke into a nervous laugh. "Of course I don't know *Paco*," she said bashfully, trying to pull herself together. "I'm just glad we found a qualified writer."

"Rashi, can you excuse me and Sunny for a minute?" I power walked Sunny to the other end of the block. Obviously, she knew something we didn't.

"Future Fact," I said.

"Are you sure? This'll be two out of five." Sunny covered her mouth with both hands. I guessed this was one Future Fact that she didn't want to give away, which made me all the more desperate to hear it.

"I don't care," I said. "You've gotta tell me why you're freaking out over this Paco guy. Is he your long-lost grandpa or something?"

"You watch too many movies. Reality is a lot more interesting." Sunny folded her hands ceremoniously. "Future Fact #2: 'Paco' Francisco Mercado Baez is best known to the future as Paco. Just that. He's one of the great twenty-first-century writers. They call him the Shakespeare of Climate Change. But hardly anyone in the future can tell you much else about the man."

"Why's that?"

Her fangirl smile fell away. "Because he never tried to publish a single thing. Kept all the writings to himself. It wasn't until after he'd passed away that his work started getting around. He never lived to see the power of his own voice."

Sunny had been right to hesitate.

"That's a heavy one," I muttered.

"Don't forget, the whole future's on the table. Maybe things will be different after Paco joins the Crew." Sunny looked up to the sky and smiled. "You know the lady who helped me plan this mission? Even *she* didn't see Paco coming. It's nowhere in the notes. Just goes to show that there's always a higher plan. And I've got a feeling it's a blizzing good one."

"I hope so." I took a hit from my inhaler. If we wanted a climate strike big enough to change Senator Bud's future vote, we were going to need something a lot more powerful than glitter glue and poster board. Maybe the Shakespeare of Climate Change was exactly the "blizzing" help we needed.

"Three Future Facts left." Sunny gave me a pat and headed back to Rashi.

We approached the gaggle of toddlers, all gathered for story time. They assembled near one of the porches, where an older boy perched on the stoop. He wore an oversized T-shirt and moved his arms in grand sweeping gestures as he delivered the end of some electrifying tale:

"The old city was greatly outnumbered. So the people took up candles instead of swords, and they filled their streets with singing."

He repeated himself in Spanish. As he did, a woman in a headscarf beside him translated into yet another language.

Then Paco went on: "It was their one last night of peace. They had no idea that just a few hills away, the invading forces could see their candlelight dotting the streets. It looked like a vast and mighty army. Suddenly, it was the invaders who felt outnumbered. So they fled the island and never . . . came . . . back. The end."

Once "the end" had been translated across a few languages, the toddlers whipped into a passionate protest. Three-year-olds aren't big on endings. They shot to their feet, each naming some other story and demanding that Paco select it for his next act. He waved at them to sit back down, wearing a warmer and more mature expression than I'd seen on any person my age. It made me think of how those commercials for invisible braces will talk about "the perfect smile." One of Paco's top teeth was a little bit chipped, but when he observed his crowd of adoring fans, 'Paco' Francisco Mercado Baez had the perfect smile.

"Paco!" Rashi called.

The moment he heard his own name, the boy shrank. His smile closed up.

"Rashi." He gave a small, polite wave. "Hi."

As Rashi and Sunny sat by him on the stairs, the toddlers scattered across the shared front lawns. The woman from the stoop bounded off to keep her two little ones from toddling into the street. I sat in the grass.

Rashi first asked about each member of Paco's family (somehow, she knew them all by name). Then she launched into the standard pitch about how the world's gonna get a heck of a lot worse if we don't do something now, and if you wanna help, join the Crew.

I sat on pins and needles the entire time. I, for one, hadn't had much luck with recruiting. But surely Rashi Kapoor, future White House Chief of Staff, had the stuff to get Paco on board.

"I'll make this easy for you." Paco eyed the cluster of mini fans already circling back for more stories. "You've got the wrong guy."

My heart sank.

"But we need a writer," I objected, my disappointment overcoming my nerves. "And you've won awards for that, haven't you?"

"Barely," Paco said, struggling with a few three-year-olds who now tried to mount onto his shoulders from the higher porch steps. He wiggled free and chased a couple of them into the lawn, calling back, "The award was mostly luck."

"I'd hardly call it luck, Paco. I've read your stuff," Rashi said while Paco Frankenstein-walked over the tiny front lawn with toddlers clinging to each of his legs like koalas. One of them tugged on a hole in Paco's jeans, tearing the pant leg all the way from knee to ankle. The toddler scurried away, apologizing in Spanish.

Paco hadn't been puffed up before, but now he looked utterly deflated.

"Look," he muttered, his eyes glued to the tear in his jeans. "I don't have a computer. I don't have a printer. My handwriting is . . . embarrassing. And I'm not nearly as good a writer as you think I am. I can't give you what you need." He slumped down onto the grass, right across from me.

It seemed like a good time to say something smart, but Rashi had used up all the best points. All I could do was pick at the grass.

"*We're losing him,*" Sunny mouthed at me.

"I'm fresh out of ideas," I muttered.

"I don't need your ideas. I need your eyes," she whispered. "What have you noticed? What makes him tick? Just come out with it already."

Sunny poked my chest like I was a vending machine, and, sure enough, a solution tumbled right out me.

"What's his name?" I said, pointing at one of Paco's tiny fans.

"Antonio," Paco replied.

Sunny swaggered with an I-told-you-so smirk and plopped onto the grass beside Paco. She plucked a tiny flower and dropped it into his hand.

I cleared my throat. "And . . . how did Antonio get here?"

Paco spun the flower between his fingers and winced, like it physically hurt him to think of it. "Antonio's family owned a coffee farm in Honduras for three generations. But by his generation, the weather had changed so much that they couldn't grow coffee there anymore. They lost everything."

Sunny found another baby flower and dropped it into Paco's hand. "What about her?" She pointed at a toddler with her hair done up in tiny locks.

"Georgieta?" Paco closed his eyes and took a long breath. "Well, she's too little to understand it, but her father, her brothers, and her sisters are all gone—along with her home in Sierra Leone. They got an abnormal amount of rain last year, and one day, a whole muddy mountainside just slid right onto their town."

"And what about you?" Sunny asked, handing him yet another flower.

"What *about* me?" Paco folded his legs and leaned back. "This isn't about me. It's about Jose. My best friend back in San Juan. His house was destroyed, too. Same with Gabriela and Paola and Diego and Miguel. All of us lost our homes. I'm just the lucky kid who won a free replacement. That's why I'm here. Luck."

"Fine," Sunny replied. "You're lucky, and they weren't. So do this for them . . . unless you're too busy to help."

Paco laughed. "All my neighborhood friends go to bed before eight o'clock. Who said anything about busy?"

Guiltily, Rashi inspected a little crack on the stair beside her. Even after joining the Crew, she was still the Queen of Busy.

Paco went on: "I'm not saying I don't want to help. I'm saying *you* don't want my help. Trust me. I'm not as talented as you think I am."

"Dude." I kept my eyes down and pushed through the tightening of my chest. "Look at who you're talking to. My only talent is YouTube freak-outs."

"*Not true,*" Sunny fiercely interjected.

"Just trying to make a point." I closed my eyes. "What I'm saying is . . . if I can help, then anyone can."

I peeked over at Paco.

He shook his head and stared at the little flowers that Sunny had placed in his hand.

Then he nodded. "I'm in." He tucked the tiny blossoms into his torn-up jeans pocket. "I can't promise a good job. But I can give you my time."

"It's all we ask," Rashi said.

I let the relief sink in. And the pride. With my help, Sunny had nabbed one of the greatest writers of the twenty-first century.

Paco returned to his stoop and lifted a loose brick. He reached into the nook underneath and retrieved a pocket-sized notebook. He invited us to the white plastic chairs neatly arranged on his family's front porch.

"No use in waiting." Paco grabbed the pencil he'd kept tucked over his ear. "What's the piece?"

"A flyer," Rashi said. "One sheet."

Paco waved his hand. "What are we trying to *say*?"

For some reason, Rashi and Sunny both turned to me. Since when had I become a spokesperson for the U.S.A.?

"I don't know." I fidgeted with my hands. "I mean, we wanna stop the apocalypse. And we want people to get started before it's too late."

"Of course," Paco said.

"It'll take a big, historic change—especially over the next ten years," I said, remembering everything Sunny had shown us about the assembly lines America pumped up during World War II. "We need to change our buildings, change our vehicles, change our power systems. Everything."

I folded my arms. Paco nodded, but said nothing. I got the feeling he'd heard all this before. What else was there to say?

"It's like during World War II," I blurted. "America needed a huge amount of new machines. So the whole country got to work. All together and all at once. They brought factories back to life—whole towns like this one. We need to do that here again."

"But not just here," Paco said. "America can't save the world alone." He was beginning to sound like Sunny.

"Then I guess it's kind of like a *World* War, isn't it?"

"A peaceful one," Paco said. "And this time we're the ones who start it."

I whistled and tilted back in my plastic chair. "It's almost like we're trying to start World War III."

Paco's eyes and nostrils flared. "That's it." He attacked the little notebook with his tiny pencil nub. "That's the headline."

He finished writing, and flipped the pad around for us to read:

LET'S START WORLD WAR III

I tapped the page. "Well, I'd say that's impossible to ignore. Now what else do we—"

Paco held his finger up for silence. He'd already started writing the lit.

"I'm good," he said, trancelike. "I got this."

STEP 6:

Zoom In

Saturday, October 8

20 days until Zero Hour

The crew of heroes marched as one. Each wore the same armored Quantum Suit, a uniform perfected for the rigors of time-travel. Their fearless leader offered a few words before they jumped into the fight of their lives. No do-overs. They had one last chance to save the world. Whatever it takes. But suddenly the heroes and their captain, every surviving Avenger, froze in time.

"Oh. My. Word." Sunny had shot to her feet, pointing at the TV with Gideon's remote.

"Do you hear it?" Gideon turned white, glancing out the windows for any sign of the ice-cream truck. "Is it them?"

"What. In. The. World," Sunny said.

I held my breath, lungs bracing for impact. But I couldn't hear even the faintest strains of the national anthem down here in Gideon's basement bedroom.

Sunny clicked the TV zoom button several times until the face of Black Widow filled the screen. "You're telling me that *this* is Black Widow?"

Gideon and I each allowed ourselves to breathe out.

"Well, yeah." I leaned back into my seat on the couch. "Scarlett Johansson."

"You mean Scarlet *Witch*?" Sunny hit the Zoom button one more time.

"No, that's Black Widow." Gideon reclined on the couch on Sunny's other side.

Sunny threw up her hands and looked at us like we were trying to pull a prank. "Then why isn't she Black?"

"Are you thinking of Black Panther?" I offered. "Or Shuri?"

"I know my Avengers," Sunny answered with a heavy dose of side-eye. "I'm talking about Natasha Romanova. Founding Avenger. Black Widow."

"Sorry, Sunny." I gestured to the TV screen. "This is the only Natasha we've got in the 2020s."

Sunny shook her head. "The 2052 Avengers are the best. They've got a *Black* Black Widow. Wolverine's in it, too."

"Sounds amazing," Gideon said. "I'll have to preorder some tickets."

Gideon's bedroom hadn't always been in the basement. It used to be upstairs, but that changed after his mom remarried. When his stepbrothers moved in, he'd graciously offered his room and volunteered for the worst one in the house—literally the bottom of the barrel. Gideon had told us all about it as he welcomed us in today, but he also let us in on his little secret: this bedroom was a dream-come-true.

I could believe it. We always used to look for excuses to play in this basement, back when this was his dad's music room.

Most of the rustic folk music posters remained, even the one I still remembered best. It was a photo print of an old man's hands cradling a banjo, with a sentence scrawled around the banjo's circular face: *This Machine Surrounds Hate and Forces It to Surrender.*

"Who's hungry?" The door at the top of the stairs swung open, and a jubilant woman paraded into our basement hangout. She wore a billowing tunic and colorful patterned leggings. Gideon's mom came bearing a tray of malted chocolate milk and homemade kettle corn.

I felt a little guilty, watching the snacks arrive. We were the only ones in the Crew who had taken Saturday off. Rashi was still remaking posters, and Paco was writing up a storm. We, on the other hand, were watching *Avengers: Endgame*—Sunny's orders. Whenever I questioned this piece of the plan, Sunny held to the same cloudy answer: I still hadn't finished my first mission. *Round up your Crew—a team of your closest friends.*

But I couldn't do it. Anytime I tried to talk to Gideon, the words stopped up somewhere between my straining lungs and my dried-out mouth. So, planted here in Gideon's own bedroom, I was spending the afternoon trying to blend in with the couch cushions.

Gideon's mom had other ideas. She never took her smiling eyes off me, even as she propped up the TV tray and presented our junk food feast.

"Thanks, Mrs. Baylor. I mean, Mrs. Smith." I kept forgetting that Gideon Baylor's mom no longer shared Gideon's last name. But for the moment, with Gideon's stepdad working and his stepbrothers who knows where, she seemed so much like the Mrs. Baylor I remembered, lavishing us kids with her grand achievements in the art of snack craft.

I picked up the popcorn bowl.

"You used to *love* my kettle corn, Joni Boy." Her eyes twinkled.

"Mom," Gideon groaned. "It's just Jonah, okay?"

"Well, pardon me." Mrs. Smith winked at me like the two of us were in on the joke. "MISTER Jonah, that is. Mister *famous*." She waved her phone in the air.

I stuffed some homemade kettle corn into my face and nodded vigorously. "Still the best," I said through a mouthful.

"How's your mom doing?" Mrs. Smith asked with a warm smile, sounding every bit the former nurse. But the warmth wasn't enough to cut through the cold guilt I carried whenever I thought about Mom.

I shrugged. "She's fine."

But Mom was not fine. She was sad. Just that morning, she'd been so eager to learn that I was spending time with Gideon again. "Gimme the whole story," she'd chirped while settling into her cushy morning chair with an enormous mug of coffee. But I couldn't tell her about our mission without risking her job and flipping her life upside down. So I didn't tell her anything at all. I shrugged and let the hurtful silence hang between us—just like I was doing now with Mrs. Smith.

"Liquid chocolate?!" Sunny had taken a sip from her foamy glass of Ovaltine, and now she straightened, eyes wide. "I forgot people used to do this!"

The front door opened upstairs. Bootsteps entered the living room above our heads. My breathing tensed up. I imagined two Soda Jerks, dressed in white, creeping through the house, ready to drag every one of us back to their smog-ridden future.

"Finished up at the Fairview Village property." A man's voice came down from the kitchen, directed at no one in particular. It was the same expressionless monotone you'd hear from a kid reciting the Pledge for the 697th time. Apparently, Gideon's stepdad had gotten home early.

Gideon sighed an enormous breath. At first, it sounded like relief, but the look on his face told me something more complicated than that. I knew it had something to do with Mr. Smith's robotic voice. Gideon's stepdad seemed like the kind of workaholic business owner who was always too busy to be friendly—basically, the opposite of Gideon.

Mrs. Smith borrowed the remote from Sunny and turned the volume down to seven percent.

Gideon sank into the couch. "We can't even hear it, Mom."

Mrs. Smith gave a sympathetic look. "Dad has a migraine. He just texted."

Gideon said nothing as she fluttered back up the stairs. His cheeks went red.

"For the record," he grumbled, "I have never once called Mr. Smith my 'dad.'"

He stared at the banjo poster. The hollowness in his voice made me think of everything he'd lost. Sure, Gideon had lost a father. But, in so many ways, he'd lost a bit of his mom, too. Her attention was divided as she looked out for a whole new family of migraines, perfectly polished pickup trucks, and stepkids who always forgot their house keys. Maybe Gideon felt like she wasn't there for him as much anymore—not like Mom was there for me.

Sunny elbowed me gently. She gave me a say-something glare,

but all I could think to say was *sorry*. Sorry for being jealous of all the sympathy. Sorry for taking the other sidewalk. Sorry for leaving him when he was most alone. But not a single one of those words found its way to my mouth.

Gideon sniffed and pretended to watch the movie. Sunny elbowed me again. Her eyes flickered with a glint that I couldn't quite place. Was she angry? Was she sad?

"I'm gonna show you something." Sunny cracked open her Lesson Planner and plucked a photo from its back folder. She slapped it onto the ottoman. Gideon and I leaned forward in unison. It was a picture of dirt, with a bit of freshly planted grass peeking through. Behind the dirt stood three stone tablets:

GEORGE TURNER	**VERA TURNER**	**MONDAY TURNER**
2063–2099	**2065–2099**	**2092–2099**

These were the graves of a family.

Sunny removed her pink glasses and sat across from us on the ottoman, just beside her photo. She folded her arms tight and looked away, the beginnings of tears in her eyes.

"Sunny," I said. "Is this—"

She nodded. "We've all lost people."

I patted her on the knee, utterly helpless when it came to condolences. Gideon passed her a tissue box.

"I told you guys all about *what* I was here to do." She dabbed at her nose. "But I never told you *why*."

Of course. Why else would a kid travel all the way back in time on a mission that could go wrong in so many ways?

"You've got nothing to lose," I said.

Sunny chuckled through the tears. "No, zoozle-brain. It's not like I wanna die or anything. I just wanna see them again. It's silly, I know, and unscientific, I'm sure, but every day I check this photo to see if those stones have disappeared like your newspaper headline. Because if I can change the future just enough, then maybe I can fade the stones away. And if I can fade the stones away, then maybe I can bring my family back, too."

I *was* a zoozle-brain. From the moment Sunny had saved my life, I'd been thinking of her as something supernatural, beyond human. I hadn't stopped to wonder what was in it for her. But now I understood.

"I hope you can bring them back," Gideon said. "But I wish you'd never lost them at all."

"That's the whole idea." Sunny brandished the time machine around her wrist.

"I'm sorry you lost your family," I said.

"Well, that's what *I've* been holding back." Sunny took each of us by the hand and looked me in the eye. "Your turn."

"Gideon . . ." I looked away, and my eyes wandered back to Sunny's photo. "I'm not the best at saying things at the appropriate time. And I know this is coming a couple years too late. But . . . I'm sorry, man." I lowered my head. "I'm sorry about your dad." Those words were all I could manage. I could only hope they'd be enough.

"No, man." He rose and paced in front of the TV. "I'm sorry about *your* dad. I'm sorry I didn't talk to you for all these years. It's just that I felt so bad, you know. Everyone did all this stuff to help me and Mom, but nobody seemed to act like anything was happening to you. Like you were invisible or something. And I didn't do any better than they did." Shaking his head, he dropped back onto his spot on the couch.

I couldn't understand it. Why was Gideon apologizing? Had we really been avoiding each other all this time just because each of us felt bad for his own made-up reason?

"I'll forgive you." I turned to face him. "But will you forgive me?"

"No hard feelings." Gideon closed his eyes and nodded briskly.

"Shake on it," Sunny said.

And then something happened that not even Sunny could have predicted. Instead of shaking hands, we did a fist bump. Then a bop-bop, slap-slap, shake-shake, before sliding into a final thumb-clasp. Gideon cracked a smile. I couldn't help but do the same. We'd made up that handshake all the way back in third grade.

For these last two years, I'd been telling myself that I had no friends. That Gideon and I had nothing in common anymore. But the two of us still had *everything* in common. All that time, we'd been saving up that secret handshake, and I hadn't even known it.

Sunny burst out laughing.

"You guys are such blorks," she said, wiping her eyes. With a self-satisfied grin, she turned to me and mouthed, "*Mission accomplished.*"

I grabbed the popcorn as Sunny reclaimed her spot between Gideon and me.

She gawked at the TV screen as a musclebound, mohawk-wearing man went cave-diving with Jeff Bezos. "Wait. So that's how Thor used to look?"

"No. That's Smash Kelly," I squeaked as pent-up laughter flooded my belly like a party balloon. "Somebody sat on the remote."

That's when the balloon popped. All three of us laughed ourselves to tears until Gideon's mom shushed us from the top of the steps.

I dug out the remote and switched back to the movie. Steve Rogers and Tony Stark exchanged a silent nod as the Avengers readied for launch. Their team was reassembled at last, and the future wouldn't know what hit it.

STEP 7:

SAVE THE EGG ROLLS

Monday, October 10

18 days until Zero Hour

We were late to start our lunch meeting, since everyone was still sopping wet.

Last period, the entire school had cleared out for a routine fire drill. Unfortunately, there was nothing routine about the surprise downpour that hammered us as we headed back in.

Still damp, I stared out Mr. Dan's window, watching the rain form little streams along the sidewalks of Creekside Road. Beyond them, an ice-cream truck crept by, glowing with amber bulbs and cranking out that creepy rendition of the national anthem.

"How many times is that?" Sunny joined me at the window, drying off the back of her neck with a paper towel.

"Third time today."

For all the days their truck had been patrolling Carbon Hill, the Soda Jerks hadn't zeroed in on Sunny. They'd paid no attention to Creekside Middle. Today, that changed.

I'd first spotted them during the fire drill. I'd been waiting on the sidewalk in my gym shorts when their glitchy truck suddenly appeared a few blocks away. But it wasn't just the truck this time. The

Soda Jerks had company. A winged reptile the size of a giraffe clung to their windshield wipers and pecked at the rooftop. Apparently, they'd taken a wrong turn into prehistoric Carbon Hill and picked up a hitchhiker along the way. I watched them scramble madly inside their malfunctioning time machine until the entire truck—pterodactyl and all—vanished from the block.

A second later, the ice-cream truck had reappeared in mid-motion, speeding down Creekside Road and screeching to a halt in front of the evacuated school. The Soda Jerks burst out and sprinted into our building. A while after that, the two of them came racing out from behind the school, bolted back to their truck, and peeled out.

I couldn't make sense of it. Why today? Why had Creekside Middle suddenly attracted them after all this time?

Behind me, Gideon broke into a peal of laughter, nearly choking on his egg roll. He'd been playing the Chewbagoat video on loop since he'd settled in for lunch.

"Amazing." He dabbed a tear from the corner of his eye. "It just went up last night and they're already at three million views."

"Can you please keep it down?" I had nothing against Chewbacca or goats or funny videos, but it was hard not to resent the video that would have upstaged my dying message to the world.

Paco appeared in the doorway.

"Our poet!" Sunny declared. "Mr. 'Paco' Francisco Mercado Baez!"

Gideon broke into a light golf clap while his phone looped the Chewbagoat roar.

I didn't join the applause, but I was thrilled beyond words to see Paco hit the scene. This guy would bring us more than a notepad.

He was packing words of power, something that could propel our message into the stratosphere. If we had any hope of rounding up half the school in time for Zero Hour, we would need exactly that kind of energy.

"I'm here to apologize," he said, eyeing his pant leg. The jeans that tore on Friday were now lovingly stitched back up from ankle to knee. "I can't join you guys today."

"What are you talking about?" Rashi said. "You're here, aren't you?"

Sunny made a sad face and held out a paper plate. "I got you egg rolls and everything."

Paco looked at the lunch order and caved. "I can't let good egg rolls go to waste." To be fair, they did smell incredible. Paco pulled the notepad out of his back pocket and slumped into a desk. "Did you get these from the new Thai pla—hey!"

No sooner had Paco sat than Sunny had swiped the notebook from his desk.

Paco relaxed, playing it cool. "Flip away," he said. "That's why I came to apologize. I didn't write anything."

"You what?" I burst out of my seat. My egg rolls and my hopes tumbled helplessly to the floor.

Rashi stormed over and grabbed Paco's plate. "I made fifteen replacement posters over the weekend—gave up *Wicked* tickets and everything—and you couldn't find the time to write one single word?"

Paco shook his head. "Not any *good* ones."

"So you *did* write something," Gideon said through a mouthful.

"The plot thickens." I brushed the floor dust from my fallen egg rolls. Five-second rule.

Paco dug into his side pocket and pulled out a few twisted scraps of paper. "It was all trash," he said. "Like I told you before, I'm not your guy."

Rashi snatched up the papers and gave back his plate. "I'll be the judge of that."

She untwisted the pages and read the first little sheet. She cocked her head, flipped the sheet, and froze into Deep Thought Do-Not-Disturb Mode.

Suddenly, she sprang into action. She opened her personal laptop and began typing, her rapid keystrokes joining the pitter-patter of raindrops on the window.

"What are you doing?" I asked.

"Managing the campaign." Rashi punched fingers at the keyboard for a good minute or two. When I peeked over to read the words, she swatted me away. "Just eat."

After she finished, Rashi fired off a sheet from Mr. Dan's printer and dropped it onto my desk. "Read."

My chest constricted at the thought of performing for the Crew. I glanced at Gideon, who was already waiting with a reassuring thumbs-up. I cleared my throat, straightened, and read:

LET'S START WWIII

Grown-Ups Gave Us a Monster.
Now We'll Give Them a War.

The monster was born out of smokestacks.
It bottle-fed on tailpipes. It cut its teeth on

methane-spewing trash. Already the monster is making trouble, starting fires, swelling rivers. Even now, so young, the monster has scorched our California forests and flooded our Iowa farms. But when we grow up, the monster will grow up, too.

It will swallow our beaches, roast our woodlands, melt the whole North Pole. It will burn us, starve us, steal the ones we love. Maybe then, we'll fight the monster. Even go to war. But the monster will be much too big.

We are the last generation with any chance to stop it. Not then, but now. We can do it. We can beat it. We can go to war. It will be a war without bullets, guns, or bombs. One great war for the last generation. A war for the greening of the world.

We call it World War G.

It all starts here. We are the United Students of America, and if you're ready to start a war, join us.

"World War G," I whispered. "This is everything we've been trying to say."

"Take it from a guy who didn't know climate anything a couple weeks ago," Gideon chimed in. "I would've signed up after reading that."

Paco laced both hands over his head. "That was all me?" I couldn't tell if he was horrified or delighted.

"Look, Paco." Sunny grabbed the sheet and slapped it down in front of him. "You've got a superpower. How about you drop the secret identity?"

"Everyone needs to read this," I said.

Rashi waved to Mr. Dan, who dropped his book and popped a hearing aid back on.

"Mr. Dan," Rashi said, "how many more of these can I print?"

"Looks like"—he checked the printer on the floor beside his desk—"three more. Paper's almost out."

"Three?!" Rashi groaned.

My emotional high took a nosedive. "We need, like, 300."

"Try 1,000," Rashi said.

"The teachers' lounge!" Gideon tapped a little ditty on his desk. "They've got a professional-grade copier. Top of the line." His expression dimmed. "But kids can't use it without permission. Plus, it's weird in the lounge. In September, Ms. Alecci sent me there to copy some worksheets, and the whole place smelled like leftovers."

"Mr. Da-an?" Rashi sang. We all put on our best set of puppy-dog eyes.

The man smirked and shook his head. "As much as I admire your powers of manipulation, I'll have to pass. Every teacher has their own access code for that printer. But I don't have one yet. Plus, I'd probably get dinged for blowing that much paper." He mouthed the word *sorry* as he took off his hearing aid and returned to his book.

Paco sighed. "So it's impossible."

"Did somebody say impossible?" Sunny cracked her knuckles and straightened, assuming a posture that reminded me of the pink astronaut. She was coming out of retirement—at least for the moment. She turned to Gideon.

"How fast is it?" she asked. "The copier."

Gideon raised an eyebrow. "'Bout sixty pages a minute. Oh, that baby ought to be fast enough for ya."

"Perfect," Sunny said.

I was still trying to figure out why Gideon talked about a copy machine like it was the Millennium Falcon when Sunny pulled both of us aside. "Would you two join me in the storage closet?"

STEP 8:

Engage Operation Ditto

12:18 p.m.

Leaving Paco, Rashi, and Mr. Dan in dumbfounded silence, the three of us stepped into the tiny closet at the back of the room. Sunny shut the door behind us. We were surrounded by dusty beakers and microscopes.

"What are we doing?" I asked. "Besides the world's most awkward game of hide-and-seek." I'd gotten used to taking strange orders from my futuristic friend, but this was getting ridiculous.

Sunny held the printout up to our faces. "This is a godsend. We can't wait until Friday for people to see it."

"Friday?" I puzzled. "Tomorrow's Tuesday. We can get some copies by then."

Sunny took me by the shoulders and shot me a knowing look. "It won't be Tuesday. Or Wednesday. Or Thursday. It happens today, or we wait for Friday."

"Okay, okay," I whispered, not ready to blow another Future Fact. "But how's a storage closet gonna make it happen?"

"Try to keep up," Sunny said. "We need to use that copy machine, which means we need access to that faculty lounge for fifteen minutes at least."

"But it's lunchtime," Gideon said. "That room'll be crawling with faculty right about now."

"Exactly," Sunny said. "*Right about now* we can't use it. But forty-five minutes ago . . ."

"The fire drill," I said. "Of course." All we needed was to jump forty-five minutes back in time, and the entire school would be cleared out—including the faculty lounge. That would buy us more than enough time to crank out a thousand copies of Paco's super-powered lit.

Gideon grinned. "Chewie, hit the hyperdrive."

Sunny poked at her watch and grabbed me and Gideon by the arms. The closet bubbled around us. The bubble popped.

11:33 a.m.

We stepped into a bright and empty classroom. The sun was still shining. We'd gone back before the rain, early in the fire drill. The entire building was ours.

The three of us approached Mr. Dan's classroom window and watched hundreds of students horse around on the school's front lawn. We had nearly half an hour until the rain started, when everyone would rush back into the school.

I spotted past-Me on the sidewalk and shivered. If you've ever felt weird about seeing yourself in a video, just multiply that weirdness by a hundred and you'll get a pretty good sense for how it feels to watch your own past in real time. You'll never feel less like yourself.

"Do I always look so grumpy?" I asked.

Gideon shrugged. "It's just your resting-face, man. Everyone has a resting-face."

An ice-cream truck screeched to a halt outside. Past-Me snapped to attention as the vehicle spat out the two Soda Jerks.

"Oh right," I choked. My heart rate kicked into double time. I took a quick puff from the silver inhaler.

Gideon clamped his hands over his head and stumbled back a few steps. He started panting, as if he were the asthmatic one. "They're attracted to the time-jumps. How could we forget that?"

"Speak for yourself," Sunny said.

Outside, past-Me and past-Sunny watched the Soda Jerks race toward the school. Back then, I had wondered what they were after, but not anymore.

"I had a hunch that our future selves would have *something* to do with this. And now I know why." With holy reverence, Sunny patted our one copy of Paco's lit. "It's worth the risk, getting this out today. Let's be quick."

We followed Sunny out of Mr. Dan's room and into 328 across the hall. We switched off the lights and peeked through a crack in the door. The Soda Jerks rushed into view. They looked ridiculous—still dressed up like professional ice-cream scoopers from the 1950s. Only now, they were winded and wild-eyed, even more desperate than before.

"It's a kid." The short, mustached man spoke like he desperately needed to clear his throat. "Has to be."

"Likely," the tall woman shot back. "Given the location." She wore a set of headphones connected to a couple of flashlight-looking instruments—some kind of time-jump detectors, I could only assume.

"Remember," Sunny whispered. "The inventors never even saw

my disguise."

"Got it," Gideon whispered back, his panic hardening to resolve. "We can't let them see you with the timepiece."

The woman's instruments led them into Mr. Dan's classroom, where we'd emerged from a supply closet only seconds before. They shut the door behind them, and we crept back into the empty hall.

"The lounge." Gideon broke into a jog. "This way."

We'd passed the water fountains at the corner when we heard the Soda Jerks leave the classroom. We froze. From around the corner, we couldn't see them coming, but we could hear them. Their old-timey footwear must've been designed for tap dancing, because those heels clacked as loud as a haunted grandfather clock with every menacing step.

Tick. Tock. Tick. Tock.

"*They're gonna see me*," Sunny mouthed.

"Library," Gideon whispered, opening a set of doors behind us. "The lights are off."

We tiptoe-bolted down a darkened aisle and pushed through a door that exited near the cafeteria. But this was one of those emergency-only exits, the kind that sets off a screeching alarm. The electric scream resounded through every quiet corner in Creekside Middle. No use tiptoeing now.

"Follow me!" Gideon shouted, dashing across the cafeteria, cutting a right at the art display and bursting through a half-opened door. Sunny and I tumbled in after him.

Everything in this room was brown—walls, carpet, couch. A mess of brown chairs surrounded a big brown table. The table was littered with Tupperware and half-eaten lunches.

"Smell that?" Gideon leaned triumphantly against a massive copy machine. "Leftovers."

We were safe for now. But I didn't feel safe—not with those Soda Jerks so close.

"It's a beauty." Sunny grazed a hand over the hood of the copy machine.

"The VistaMax 200 Series," Gideon announced. "My grandma's retirement home has one. I get to mess around with it when my mom cleans there on Saturdays."

"Cool name." Sunny pointed gun-fingers at Gideon. "VistaMax 200!"

"Vista . . . MAX." Gideon shot gun-fingers back.

"Shhhh." I didn't understand how they could remain so chill in a moment like this. At any second, those frantic, desperate inventors could burst through that brown door and drag us away to their precious polluted future.

"You know how to start this thing?" Sunny looked back at Gideon. She'd already poked a few buttons without much response.

Then it hit me.

"Bad news," I announced, hoping the two of them had braced themselves for a crushing disappointment. "We don't have a code." The three of us had just traveled through time and risked being captured only to return empty-handed—if we even returned at all.

"Oh, right . . ." Gideon's voice trailed off. "The access code. I mean, Ms. Alecci did give me hers when I came here before the strike . . . and I did write the code on my arm . . ."

In a flash of theatrical flare, Gideon tugged back his shirtsleeve.

". . . in PERMANENT MARKER."

The numbers were faint but unmistakable along Gideon's forearm. I figured he would've learned his lesson about Sharpies after those black mustaches we got in so much trouble for in third grade, but thankfully not.

Sunny applauded. "You do shower, right?"

"Often." Gideon laughed. "But who actually *scrubs* their arms, anyway?"

I politely raised a hand, but Gideon had already blown right past me. He punched in the five digits, and all three of us waited for a few agonizing seconds. Would Alecci's access code still work a whole two weeks after her retirement? The VistaMax 200 sounded a friendly chime and rolled into motion:

ACCESS GRANTED.

"Showtime." Gideon hit the *start* button and stepped back as sheet after sheet leapt out of the mighty machine.

Minutes passed, and pages piled up.

"That's all of them." I gathered up the heavy stack of fliers, crisp and hot from the printer.

Sunny checked her watch and grabbed the door handle.

I stopped it with my foot. "Can't we just jump back from here?"

"I wish," Sunny said. "But that would put us in this room at twelve eighteen."

"Lunch break." Gideon shuddered. Spontaneously appearing in a room full of teachers would not be a great way of keeping Sunny's cover.

She cracked the door, and we listened. The alarm had settled. The rain went on tapping outside, but we heard no *tick-tock* of the Soda Jerks' shoes. She opened the door the rest of the way, and we crept out on tiptoes, me last of all. With Paco's lit piled in my arms, I couldn't stop the door from slamming behind me.

BAM! The sound of it echoed through every cavernous hallway in the building.

Tick-tock-tick-tock-tick-tock. The Soda Jerks were running now, so we ran, too.

On instinct, I took us through the cafeteria and into the kitchen. Better to hide out somewhere random than get captured en route to Mr. Dan's room—the location of our last jump was the first place they'd expect us to go. The kitchen was eerily quiet. No *tick-tocks* here.

"So this is where the magic happens," Gideon whispered in wonder.

Most students had never laid eyes on the school kitchen. But there we stood. I found it more impressive than I'd imagined. Almost every surface was a reflective stainless steel.

"Looks like the lab," Sunny said.

"No. Way." Gideon picked up a barrel-sized can of fruit cocktail. "The menu always says '*Fresh* Fruit Medley.'"

I huffed. "Lies!"

Sunny threw a hand in front of my face. "Listen."

Tick-tock-tick-tock-tick-tock.

We dove behind a counter and backed up against the shelves. I checked the time on a clock nearby: one minute until lunch period.

The footsteps got closer. It was only one of them, from what I could tell.

Tick. Tock.

The steps entered the kitchen, creeping in from our right. Sunny crawled to the left. Gideon and I had a little more trouble—me with my stack of paper and Gideon with the giant can of fruit he'd forgotten to put down. My hands were sweating so bad that I had to be careful they didn't soak through Paco's words.

Tick.

We crawled behind another counter just in time.

Tock.

The dead silence of Creekside Middle suddenly dissolved under the rain. Beyond the kitchen, the relative quiet of our school building gave way to a clamor of young voices and wet, squeaking feet. The Soda Jerks' shoes *tick-tocked* rapidly out through an exit to the lot out back. All clear.

I dropped the lit and sprawled flat, panting on the cold laminate floor.

"Close call." Sunny stood up and kindly kicked my foot. "Come on."

We slipped into the hallway and joined the crowd of soaking students, keeping our heads low to avoid being spotted by our past selves who walked only a few shoulders ahead. As everyone rushed to their lockers and the bathrooms to dry off, our present selves slipped back into Mr. Dan's room, back into his closet, back to 12:18.

12:18 p.m.

"Find any secret copy machines?" Rashi snarked as we popped back out the closet door, mere seconds after we'd first gone in.

"As a matter of fact"—Gideon scooped the one thousand pages from my arms—"we found a VistaMax 200. Top. Of. The. Line." He dropped the pile onto Rashi's desk.

"That's impossible." Paco rushed toward the closet door.

"Dude." I stepped in his way. "You'll only be more confused."

"No, seriously." Rashi flipped through the pile of still-warm pages. "How did you do it?" She shot a look at Paco, probably wondering if he'd assisted in whatever bizarre magic trick this had to be. Paco looked even more dumbfounded than her. It meant a lot to see the Shakespeare of Climate Change at a loss for words.

"Sunny's got a knack for the impossible," Gideon said. "Let's just leave it at that."

Barely concealing a grin, Sunny plopped onto her seat and tore into another egg roll. They were still warm.

"This is some powerful stuff." Mr. Dan, who had just read over one of the fliers at his desk, hooked a hearing aid back onto his ear. "You know, at your age, my idea of rebellion was drawing butts on the bathroom wall, not starting a global revolution."

I shrugged. "It's not like we have any choice."

"And we're running out of time." Sunny wagged her egg roll.

"So what are we waiting for?" Rashi said. "Let's drop some lit."

I nodded slowly, wearing what must've looked like an evil grin. I felt like a troublemaker—the good kind. Surely, I thought, if we deployed Paco's powerful words far and wide, we'd finally see a volcanic reaction from the Creekside student body—a reaction big enough to earn us 600 new recruits and a climate strike so powerful that Senator Bud would have no choice but to fall in line.

STEP 9:

DIG DEEP

Thursday, October 13

15 days until Zero Hour

Sunny was right. Again.

We couldn't have spread Paco's lit on Tuesday or Wednesday. At 4:00 a.m. Tuesday morning, an electrical malfunction knocked out the school's power. Mom blamed Richard Allister, who had paid for a lot of the school's construction years ago—and used the cheapest electricians in the tristate area. Class was canceled until the school got our lights back on, which didn't happen until Thursday—and Thursday was our seventh-grade class trip. If we hadn't managed to drop that lit on Monday afternoon, we would've been waiting until Friday, just like Sunny said.

But Sunny wasn't right about everything. We'd all expected to show up Thursday to a bumper crop of new recruits. After all, we'd gone for broke on Monday, sowing enough of those fliers to reach every last student in Creekside Middle. Thursday morning came, and we reaped the fruits of our labor: fist bumps. Lots of fist bumps. More fist bumps than I'd ever gotten in my life. But it didn't go any further than that.

Even though students were loving Paco's flier, we couldn't seem to turn that energy into new recruits. After 1,000 fliers, we'd managed to add exactly zero new members to the U.S.A.

"Don't say I didn't warn you," Paco droned, leaning his head against the school bus window. We hit a pothole, and he bumped his forehead. "'I'm not your guy'—that's what I told you." He leaned back in his seat, rubbing his head. "And now look at us. The lit's not working."

"Don't you *dare* resign," Rashi shot back. She slouched there beside him with a sack lunch resting sadly on her lap. The four of us—Paco, Rashi, Gideon, and I—hunched together at the back of the bus, on our way to the annual Carbon Hill Historic Coal Mine field trip. The only Crew member absent was Sunny, who stayed back for permission-slip reasons (her parents hadn't been born yet).

Cautiously, Gideon chimed in from the other way-back seat. "*I* think the lit's working. This morning, kids kept chanting *U.S.A.* whenever they passed me in the halls, and I'm, like, eighty percent sure they weren't making fun of me." He paused before correcting the record. "A few were."

It wasn't all fist bumps for me, either. That morning, I found a few copies stuffed into my locker with the word "FAKER" scrawled across the face of them. Handiwork of Lindsay Allister, I thought, or at least one of her popular friends.

I peeked over the seat to check on Mom, who'd volunteered to chaperone the trip. I'd ditched her at the front of the bus when we first got on, just to keep her clear of the U.S.A. It killed me to shut her out, but what choice did I have? If Mom knew about our mission, I knew she'd support it any way she could. And if Mom supported our mission, then she could get herself in trouble with Allister

Energy. And if Mom got in trouble with Allister Energy, she could lose her job, her law school grant—everything she'd worked so hard to achieve.

She seemed to be enjoying her impromptu parent-teacher conference with Mr. Dan up there, but even that made me nervous. What if Mr. Dan wound up accidentally ratting us out? Even though he'd kept us on mute most days, the guy knew way more about Sunny and the U.S.A. than any grown-up had a right to.

So, as Rashi and Paco bickered away from Creekside to the coal mine, I rode beside Gideon and crossed my fingers that Mr. Dan wasn't sharing any classified information.

After we'd filed off the bus, I ditched the Crew and looked for Mom.

I spotted her waiting beside the bronze statue of a coal miner. A placard nearly as big as the statue itself made sure everyone knew who to thank for installing it: *Generously Donated by Allister Energy*. The closer I got to Mom, the worse I felt that too-familiar pinch of guilt in my chest. I avoided eye contact, remembering the pain I'd left on her face at the front of the bus. It was a pain I'd seen too many times lately—after every story I'd hidden and every conversation I'd cut short. For the last three weeks, I'd been ghosting my own mother, and on some level, she knew it. But when I reached Mom at the statue, for once she wasn't wearing that knowledge on her face.

Mom gave me a peck on the head. "You didn't tell me about your new science teacher!"

"Yeah." I shifted back. "He's pretty cool."

"He's hilarious," Mom said. "Did you know he worked five years as a full-time anti-war activist?"

I nodded, even though this was the first I'd heard of Mr. Dan's past life. I was just glad Mom wasn't spouting facts about the U.S.A.

"Yeah, I thanked him for his service." Mom smirked, glancing at where her foot would've been if the government hadn't sent her to Iraq. She was joking, but not really.

A steam whistle blasted, which signaled the start of our tour through the Carbon Hill Historic Coal Mine. We joined the throng of students and faculty, though I kept Mom far from Rashi and Paco. I avoided eye contact with Gideon, too, which felt painfully similar to my pre-Sunny lifestyle. Painful or not, I had to keep Mom out of this.

Our class gathered around a bony bald man with suspenders and a bow tie. He cleared his throat.

"I'm Gervis Archibald, spokesman for the Carbon Hill Historical Society, generously sponsored by Allister Energy, and I would like you all to know how honored we are to welcome this *particular* class onto our grounds today." He never once broke eye contact with Lindsay Allister, whose dad's donations probably paid his salary. Lindsay rolled her eyes.

"Join me on a journey through time," he said, his voice trembling theatrically. "The year? 1921. The place? A coal miner's humble abode."

To the surprise of absolutely no one, Gervis did *not* lead us on a "journey through time." Instead, he led our group through a gift shop and into a tiny house with a few wooden dividers that were supposed to pass for walls. Only half the students fit inside.

"This fully restored structure shows how the typical coal-mining family was housed in the early 1900s. Some coal miners would happily nest a family of up to *nine people* in a modest structure such as this." The man smiled vacantly.

Mom raised her hand. "Nine?"

Gervis cupped his ear. "I beg your pardon?"

"A family of nine," Mom repeated. "A family of *nine* would live *happily* in a place this small?"

Gervis swallowed hard. "These quarters were supplied by the Allister Coal Company, and these workers were *proud* to reserve a portion of their wages to pay off the company's home loans."

"Loans?!" Mom was getting way out of line, and most of my classmates were eating it up. The student body crackled with incredulous laughter, and Mom kept at it. "So first you tell us that Johnny Coal Bucket was happy to cram his family of nine into this postage stamp of a house, and now you're saying that Johnny was *proud* to be neck-deep in debt for it, too?"

Apparently loving Mom's smackdown on Carbon Hill history, Mr. Dan sang a little taunt from the corner of his mouth: "That's why they started a un-ion . . ."

Rashi interrupted immediately, asking about this union that Mr. Dan had just added to Gervis's historical record.

"It's no secret," the sweaty tour guide answered. "The United Mine Workers were active in early twentieth-century Carbon Hill. And, yes, they did manage to improve housing here—in collaboration, of course, with Richard Allister the First. Your great-great-great-great-grandfather." He bent low, beaming at Lindsay like she was a baby in a stroller. But the smile dropped straight off his face when his eyes landed back on Mom.

The whole ordeal was exactly why Mom could never know about

the Crew. If she learned what we were fighting for, she would roll up her sleeves and join the brawl in a hot second. Next thing you know, Mom would somehow wind up cornering every powerful person in Carbon Hill with the pummeling lecture of a lifetime. It would be epic, no doubt, but it wouldn't be worth her job.

As our cable car descended 300 feet underground, Gervis explained how biological matter transformed into anthracite coal over millions of years. But all that Rashi, Paco, and Gideon seemed to care about was the United Mine Workers.

"How did the workers do it?" Paco asked.

"How did they bore this hole into the earth?" Gervis replied.

"No," Paco said. "How did they get better houses?"

Even in the dim, subterranean lighting, it was easy to see Gervis rolling his eyes. "Well, they staged a rather large strike. One of the strategic advantages of organized labor, I suppose: strength in numbers."

"But how did they get their numbers in the first place?" Gideon asked. "Like, how exactly did they recruit so many people?"

"I don't know." The man spoke with a tightness in his chest, like he was holding back a scream.

I knew why they wouldn't stop asking. Hearing about that union had offered a glimmer of much-needed hope. Carbon Hill had united, defied Allister, and fought to make things better. We'd done it before, so why couldn't we do it again?

We unloaded from the cable car and shuffled single file through the darkness with nothing but a few electric lights posted around the tunnel walls. Gervis led us to a wax figure display of a mule and a boy in a hard hat.

"Believe it or not," he said, "children your age would work these mines as well."

Gideon raised his hand, but the man pretended not to see him.

"The mules," Gervis went on, "were blinded by the darkness."

Gideon kept his hand up, stretching onto his tiptoes like a first grader pleading for a bathroom pass. The man couldn't ignore him any longer. "Is this a question about the mule-boys?"

"Yes," Gideon said. "Were the mule-boys in the union?"

Gervis flashed so red that I was surprised his bow tie didn't pop off like a champagne cork.

"Young man," he whispered. "I am a spokesman for the Carbon Hill Historical Society, not a labor movement historian."

"But you are a historian." Rashi shoved her way to the front of the group. "So gimme some history. How did the first unions form? How did they expand their ranks? Did they post advertisements? Did they print literature?"

Yes, yes, yes, I thought. Rashi was asking for everything I wanted to hear.

"Isn't it *obvious*?!" The historian threw up his hands and accidentally knocked off the mule-boy's helmet. "These people spent half their lives working in a hole, just to stay in a hovel of a house that the company never quite let them pay off. A union recruiter could get them on board without uttering a single word. *Everyone* had reason enough to join."

"That's it!" Gideon shouted like he'd just struck gold in a coal mine.

After Gervis apologized profusely to the bored Lindsay Allister, he carted our group back up to the light of day. I slipped off to the Crew before the buses loaded up.

"Try to explain it again," Rashi said to Gideon. Paco seemed just as mystified as Rashi.

"It's like the guy told us," Gideon said. "We don't have to *say* anything. People will just, like, *join*."

"So your big idea," Rashi said very slowly, "is to do nothing?"

Gideon groaned. "That's not what I'm saying at all."

But nobody seemed to be seeing his point. No one, except for me.

"Think of it this way." I spoke up without meeting anyone's eyes, my thoughts returning to all the times Sunny had pushed me to intervene with new recruits. "The only success we've ever had with adding members was Rashi and Paco. And how did we recruit you?"

"Door-to-door," Rashi answered.

"Right," I said. "One-on-one recruitment. And even then, we almost failed. We hit you with every reason in the world, and both of you refused to join. Nothing worked until we stopped trying to reason with you . . . and let you find a reason of your own."

"My grandfather," said Rashi.

"My neighbors," said Paco.

For me, it was my asthma. For Sunny, it was the family she'd lost. For Gideon, it was a fluffy dog named Einstein.

"Each of you had a reason," I continued. "It never came down to any of the reasons we tried to feed you."

"Genius!" Rashi said. "Instead of giving them facts, we should be getting their stories."

"Collecting them," Paco said.

"And if they give us their stories"—Gideon swelled with pride—"they'll give us their time."

STEP 10:

WIELD AN ANCIENT WEAPON

Friday, October 14

14 days until Zero Hour

"Canvassing . . ." Rashi paced the top of the bleachers like a general addressing her troops. The troops were me, Gideon, Paco, and a super chilled-out Sunny. She lounged on a long stretch of bleacher with a light, blankety sweater and a pair of pink sunglasses.

"Canvassing is an ancient art," General Rashi went on, "dating back as far as the Roman Empire. And it's really quite simple: when you need a bunch of recruits, you go talk to a bunch of people. One. By. One. For political campaigns, it happens on doorsteps, but for us, it'll happen right here on the schoolyard."

"So we're canvassing recess," Retirement-Sunny remarked from her perch. "I love you guys."

Rashi presented a stack of retro composition books like the ones I'd used for my zombie survival guides.

"This is your turf," Rashi said. "It's a set of names in alphabetical order. Every student in our grade. What we'll *do* with that turf . . . well, that's where Jonah's little stroke of genius comes in."

"Gideon's idea, mostly," I noted, keeping my eyes on the bleachers. "But yeah. The trick is to let *them* do the talking. Not you. Think of it this way: all you need to do is collect one story from each student."

The whole Crew listened intently, which made this all the more uncomfortable. Here I was, instructing them on how to canvass the schoolyard when I had absolutely no intention of doing it myself.

I had it all worked out: Rashi still had a lot to plan for the day of our strike, and if you'd ever seen my extensive collection of zombie survival guides, you'd know that I was pretty good at documenting a strategy. While everyone else hit the schoolyard, I could stay back and serve as Rashi's notetaker, her scribe—an essential job that would most unfortunately keep me from canvassing.

"Collecting stories," Rashi continued. "Ask them how the climate crisis has already affected them or their family. Find out why this fight matters to them. Once you've gotten that far, it's just like Gideon said: if they give us their story, they'll give us their time. You can invite them for a canvass training in Room 329 on Monday. Then, every day, we'll start the whole process again—as many times as we need between now and October twenty-eighth. Recruit, train, repeat."

My mouth went dry, just thinking of how much talking Gideon, Sunny, and Paco would have to do. "That's a whole lotta canvassing."

"It's a whole lotta world to save," Sunny replied.

"So, each of us gets a slice of the alphabet," Rashi said. "I'll do A through E."

Rashi was canvassing, too? She doled out the rest of the alphabet in notebooks of purple, pink, and blue. Then she got to the yellow one.

"V through Z goes to Jonah." She tossed the notebook to me.

Yes. To me.

I opened my mouth, swallowed, opened my mouth again. I stood frozen, holding that yellow notebook like it was a warrant for my own arrest.

Rashi hopped off the bleachers. "Sound like a plan?"

It was all head nods and "Let's go!"s from everyone on the Crew—except for me, of course.

My stomach felt like a small man had climbed inside and started practicing the Dougie. I couldn't handle this. Even around the Crew, I still had a pretty serious case of talk-phobia. To me, it wasn't a question of whether I'd skip today's canvassing session; it was only a question of how.

An arm flung around my shoulder. Gideon wore a hang-in-there smile, but all he said was, "Wanna buddy up?"

Did. I. Ever.

Lucky for me, Gideon's version of buddying up consisted of me tagging along as he canvassed through his own book of turf. What can I say? He knew me well. The man in my stomach switched from the Dougie to the worm. Manageable. Gideon started with the first name in his book, Dariq Wallace. Dariq was one of the tallest, most popular guys in class, but Gideon didn't seem intimidated.

"Hey, man." Gideon threw down an easygoing handshake, then asked if Dariq had a climate story. It turned out Dariq did. Just two years ago, his family had to cancel their vacation to South Carolina because of a runaway hurricane. When they returned last year, their favorite little shrimp shack was gone—blown right off the face of the earth.

Just like that, Gideon had landed a new recruit.

I couldn't believe it. Gideon was not the most passionate person on the Crew—or the most knowledgeable. He'd only gotten involved for a chance to save his dog. But now I saw something in Gideon that even Sunny couldn't match: he knew how to make people feel comfortable. I'd always known this about Gideon's personality, but I'd never realized just how powerful that personality could be.

"See?" Gideon crossed off Dariq's name in his purple turf book. "If I can do it, you can do it. I mean, you're Jonah flippin' Kaminski, world-renowned YouTube activist. You've got this."

I nodded slowly, hands sweating through my yellow book of names. His words meant a lot, but I couldn't make the encouragement sink in—no matter how badly I wished it would. Gideon's superpower was making people feel comfortable; my only power was dodging discomfort with superspeed agility. I'd been doing it for years.

So before Gideon found his second recruit, I came up with the perfect way to handle my own turf for the day.

"I gotta go to the bathroom," I announced.

STEP 11:

TAKE A STAND ON THE TOILET SEAT

I paced the empty bathroom and waited for recess to end. That was Jonah Kaminski's Grand Strategy for Saving the World. With the entire seventh grade outside, our hallway felt like the set of some post-apocalyptic zombie movie. Dead silent. But dead silence was better than a forced conversation. If I had to choose between bathroom-bound boredom and my greatest mortal fear, I'd take the toilets every time.

But the silence soon gave way to the last sound I'd ever want to hear while alone in an empty building.

Tick. Tock. Tick. Tock.

I peeked out of the bathroom entrance. No Soda Jerks in sight. Only a couple of custodians: one tall, lanky woman and one short, stocky man.

A chill gripped the back of my neck. These were, in fact, the Soda Jerks, but poorly disguised as a Creekside cleaning crew. Of *course*. They knew that their thief would be somewhere around the middle school, so why not stay put and stake the place out? Certainly must be better than time-traveling their way into another pterodactyl attack with that glitched-out ice-cream truck of theirs. As usual, their getup was more of a costume than a proper disguise. They looked like custodians from a kids' picture book, with gray jumpsuits and tool belts loaded with spray bottles and plungers. Each had a white name tag sewn on, but the name tag only said *Janitor.*

Their voices approached down the hallway, stopping outside the boys' bathroom. I rushed into a stall.

"It's empty in here," the man croaked. His voice got closer, accompanied by the squeaky wheels of a mop bucket. They crept right into the bathroom. I stood on top of the toilet seat and crouched low.

"Did you see the playground?" he stammered.

"Recruitment," the woman said.

"Any record of this happening here before?"

"How should I know?" the woman grumbled. "It's not like we have a record of every conversation on every schoolyard in the entire history of Pennsylvania. We'll just have to watch and see. If a big change happens, we'll know the thief is involved."

"We're close now." The man let out a sharp breath.

My stomach churned. Thanks to Sunny's last time-jump, these creeps had finally gotten their first real lead, and our mission had gotten ten times harder. We'd have to organize our October 28 action—the climate strike that could sway Senator Bud and remix the century—with agents of Sunny's old future lurking around every corner.

One of their walkie-talkies sounded off, and I heard the voice of Principal Rivera crackle through.

"Vomit situation in the cafeteria," he radioed. "Could someone bring a mop? Two mops. And a couple gallons of disinfectant. Thank you."

The two Soda Jerk Janitors groaned in unison before exiting with their squeaky bucket.

Vomit was better than they deserved. But poetic justice was not enough. We had to win. We had to take the future back from people like them. I pictured Gideon out there on the schoolyard, expanding the U.S.A. with every passing minute. That kid was fearless. A warrior. Changing the world. Meanwhile, I cowered over a toilet pretending to suffer major digestive issues.

Gideon said it himself: if he could face the schoolyard, then so could I. I flushed the empty toilet, washed my hands, and marched back out into the light of day.

Rashi stood near the soccer net, chatting with the poise of a seasoned professional. Paco canvassed by the Gaga ball pit, happy to let his latest recruit do the talking. Sunny took her time with another potential Crew-mate, changing his life forever, I assumed. Gideon, meanwhile, was probably talking to his tenth recruit by now.

My turn. I cracked open my composition book and flipped to the first name listed on my turf: Sarah Vogelsburg, a new student at Creekside Middle.

I found her sitting on the grass, alone with a giant sketchbook and the most extensive marker set I'd ever seen. Sarah noticed me approaching, and my guts did a somersault. Was it awkward? Of course. But this time I wouldn't let awkward hold me back.

"Hi, Sarah." I joined her on the lawn. "I'm working with the United Students of America, and we're trying to talk to every student in the seventh grade about the climate crisis. How has your family been impacted by extreme weather?"

Sarah straightened. "*My* family?"

Without hesitation, she told me about her former California home—a stylish, throwback kinda house, like something from a 1970s sitcom. She explained that wildfires in California had gotten a lot worse since the house was built. Bigger, stronger . . . deadlier. Just five weeks ago, her neighborhood had burned to the ground. Now her family stayed with grandparents in Carbon Hill, and Sarah didn't have a friend within 2,500 miles.

The more I heard of Sarah's story, the less awkward I felt. I knew what it meant to have no friends. So I told Sarah about how I'd met the founders of the U.S.A. and how the Crew was basically one big group of friends. They could be her friends, too.

Sarah dropped her marker. "Are you serious?" She seemed ready to cry.

Rashi hadn't trained me for this, so I just smiled and nodded my head.

After that, Sarah Vogelsburg signed up. That's right: I, Jonah Kaminski, added one whole member to the United Students of America. And I was only getting started. I talked to lots of students that day, students I'd never really known, whose names I could recite but whose voices I'd hardly ever heard.

McKayla told me about her cousin's flooded condo. Reggie talked about the spring pollen, and how it had gotten so bad that his sister had to skip their Easter egg hunt last year. Bell told me about the stuffed koala she'd had since she was a baby, the one she couldn't even look at anymore without remembering the thousands of koalas that were lost in the Australian bushfires.

Was I actually *good* at this? Not entirely. I still felt spectacularly awkward every time. But I did find it easy to spot that little thread that tied a person's life to the fate of our planet. After I found the thread, all I had to do was give it a tug.

It got me thinking about something Sunny had told me on the night we first met. It wasn't my video that brought her to Martic Pinnacle, but something the video had shown her about me. Finally, I could see it for myself: Jonah Kaminski knew how to make things personal. That's how I saw the climate apocalypse in my asthma, in Gideon's dog, in Rashi's grandfather, in Paco's little neighbors. I thought back to the years I'd spent overthinking every conversation, inspecting every facial expression, and replaying every awkward interaction. For the very first time I started to wonder: maybe this was more than a defect. Maybe I had a gift—a superpower all my own.

I passed by Gideon near the soccer net. We shared a grin and, without a word, popped out our secret handshake—the one that had hung invisibly between us all those years we'd spent not talking. The stories were a lot like that, I thought, each one a secret handshake, an invisible bond that connected each person to everyone else on Earth.

It took only a conversation. One name at the top of a list. That's all it would ever have to be—a matter of performing one simple task. Then doing it again. And once more after that.

Recruit, train, repeat. It would work, and there was no way a couple of Soda Jerk Janitors from a wasted future could stop it.

PLAN C:

ACTION

STEP 1:

WATCH YOUR TEACHER SNAP

Tuesday, October 25

3 days until Zero Hour

They say time flies when you're having fun. But if you ever want time to fly so fast that it practically breaks the sound barrier, try saving the world in a single week. It felt like no time at all.

The view outside Mr. Dan's window had changed. Most of the leaves had blown off in the storm that started raging last weekend. Even today the rain kept up, setting an October record for Carbon Hill. But inside the walls of Mr. Dan's room, a different kind of storm was brewing—and that storm was the U.S.A.

The previous week had stretched us, but it had grown us, too. For one thing, we were finally more than five. After a week of recruit-train-repeat, we'd managed to expand into chapters across each grade level at Creekside Middle. By our last count, the United Students of America now had 307 Creekside students in our ranks.

Make that 320, I thought, glancing back at Gideon. He was coaching thirteen new recruits at the back of the room. With three days left before Zero Hour, Mr. Dan's classroom had transformed into a full-blown Avengers Compound. We packed every corner with training, planning, and strategizing of one kind or another.

Rashi, Sunny, and I had combined our desks near the window.

"How's it goin' over there, Paco?" Rashi called to the opposite corner of the room, where Paco was pulling his hair in front of her laptop. As our writer, it was his job to draft our official letter to Senator Bud.

"I'm going to let you down," he groaned.

Rashi tried to conceal a laugh. "Just make sure your writing 'lets us down' by the end of today. We've gotta send that letter by tomorrow morning. No later."

By now, it was a running joke among the Crew: the only person who didn't have total confidence in Paco's power was Paco himself.

Rashi turned back to me and Sunny. The three of us huddled around a hand-drawn map of the streets surrounding Creekside Middle. Rashi circled the school's front lawn. "In phase one, we'll need a strong show of force. Something for the news cameras. Let's run the picket line right here along the front entrance."

"Too close," Sunny replied—the first thing I'd heard from her all day. "We can't do that."

Rashi wasn't having it. "Reason being?"

"Safety." Sunny clenched a fist and rested it gently on her desk. "Just keep them away from the building."

"You mean, like, the fire code or something?" I clarified.

Sunny pretended to agree. "Sure. Fire code."

She hadn't been herself all week, not since the storm set in. She wore less color and didn't smile nearly as much. My guess? It had to be something about October 28. She'd always called it Zero Hour, after all, not Hero Hour or Super Time or Freedom Friday. She must've seen something on the horizon, the same something that made her insist on scheduling our strike for that *particular* day in history. I would just have to wait and see. Sunny's rules were clear enough: No Future Facts about Zero Hour.

"Would you guys PLEASE quiet down?" Mr. Dan shouted with a cell phone squished against one of his hearing aids.

The room fell silent. He'd never yelled at us like that before.

"I just want you to be careful," he murmured into the phone. "Of course I'm watching the news. But you never know. Okay. Bye." He hung up and turned to us. "Sorry about that." He pointed to his hearing aids. "The processors, you know. Extra noise makes it hard." He closed his eyes and rubbed his temples.

"Who was that?" Sunny asked.

"My ex-girlfriend. She lives outside of Redding, California. Before that, I was talking to my grandma in Myrtle Beach. It's all getting a little scary for me, you know?"

"What's a little scary?" asked Gideon, who obviously hadn't been following the news.

"The Twin Horsemen." Rashi reached into her backpack and pulled out today's paper. "Keep it. I bought a whole stack of these this morning. I figured that's what you do when you're living through history," she muttered.

I felt sick when I saw the front page. It showed a woman about Mom's age crumpled to the ground in anguish as she watched an apartment complex burn. The sky looked like a furnace. The photo felt obscene, like something I wasn't supposed to be seeing.

The headline read:

A WEEK OF INFAMY

Twin Disasters Strike Two Coasts;

Thousands Missing, Many Feared Dead

"Hurricane Rex is the biggest storm ever to hit the East Coast this far north," Rashi explained. "It's why we've been seeing so much rain, even out here in Carbon Hill. And on the West Coast, Northern California is battling the biggest wildfire on record. It's two apocalyptic disasters striking the United States at once. People are calling them the Twin Horsemen. Both could die down, but—"

"They won't." Sunny snatched Mr. Dan's phone and foisted it back at him. "Your grandma and your ex. Make them leave. Say whatever you have to. Just get them out of there."

Mr. Dan stared at her for a moment. Tilted his head. Then nodded and took the phone. "Better safe than sorry, right?"

"Right," Sunny said, slumping back into her seat.

I wasn't about to waste a Future Fact because I'd already worked one out for myself. There had to be some connection between the Twin Horsemen and the date that Sunny had chosen for our strike. I'd never felt such a stomach-turning mix of fear and excitement.

Whatever happened over the next three days, it was going to be big.

STEP 2:

GET PUNKED

Wednesday, October 26

2 days until Zero Hour

"...With liberty and freedom for all."

Over the school loudspeaker, Principal Rivera thanked Tony Torricelli for leading us in the Pledge. He was nice enough to pretend that Tony hadn't butchered half the words.

I slouched low, waiting for Ms. Colarusso's homeroom to end. None of the Crew shared this period, which made it the one part of each day that felt the most like Before, like those lonely old days when I'd actively fought to be friendless. Homeroom was perhaps the most depressing form of time-travel ever invented.

The classroom door crept open as Rivera's voice read off the announcements. A short man with a long, drooping mustache poked his head into the room.

"Any spot-cleaning?" he asked. The Soda Jerk Janitor spoke brightly, as if trying to hide the gravely grind of his polluted voice.

"No," Ms. Colarusso said flatly. These check-ins were a little much. Since Sunny was smart enough to hide the timepiece in her backpack, the Soda Jerk Janitors hadn't had much luck in the last week of searching. In their desperation, they'd started checking each classroom daily with an extra-thorough "spot-cleaning" service. But most teachers didn't welcome the interruption. Before closing the door, the man spaced out for a second, like his entire life was flashing before his dark-rimmed eyes. He saluted Ms. Colarusso and sleepily moved along.

The announcements continued. Basketball tryouts next week. Leave your phones in your locker, please. And finally, a "very special announcement."

"How many of you Creekside students would like to 'go green'?" Principal Rivera asked.

Hard pass, I thought. The Crew didn't care much for those empty eco-slogans. Sunny had given us a word for it: *greenwashing*. "Going green" was the kind of weaksauce catchphrase companies liked to put big on their tote bags and social posts, even though they didn't mean it. The whole thing was about encouraging people to make itty-bitty personal changes for an itty-bitty impact, even while the world fell apart in a great big way. Greenwashing was a deadly distraction.

"Well," Principal Rivera continued, "all you environmentalists out there will be happy to hear that Creekside Middle School is hosting its very first Green Kids Forum tomorrow afternoon!"

The classroom gave a thin smattering of applause. Mostly it was Ms. Colarusso, who tried to model the appropriate level of excitement by clapping with her face like a WOW emoji. I, on the other hand, could not have been less excited. Something was off. How exactly did a "Green Kids Forum" suddenly appear on the schedule for the day before Zero Hour?

"But that's not all," Principal Rivera said over the loudspeaker.

"To host this forum, we are bringing in someone very special." He paused for a moment of suspense. "Smash Kelly from HeTV's *Punk-Work with Smash Kelly*!"

That got the room's attention. In fact, it lit the room on fire.

"Is he serious?"

"The *real* Smash Kelly?"

"He used to be my favorite wrestler!"

Applause morphed into a rumble of fists on desks, a tremor that grew into an earthquake that echoed across the school.

I sat there, still as a stone of the non-quaking variety. Was this good or bad? It didn't feel like the *best* idea, but how could a "Green Kids Forum" do more harm than good?

"This is bad," Sunny said during lunch in Mr. Dan's room. She hadn't touched her cheese fries. "Never saw it coming."

"It's corny," I said, "and probably useless. But it can't be the end of the world."

"You're not listening." Sunny grabbed my shirtsleeve. "I *never saw it coming*."

Now I understood. In all the Future Facts of her Lesson Planner, Sunny had never seen any reference to a celebrity visit at Creekside Middle. This was something new, somehow triggered by all the work that our Crew had done.

"But still," I said, "maybe we're just having an influence."

Sunny raised an eyebrow. "You haven't seen the posters yet, have you?"

Just then, Rashi burst into our little Avengers Compound and slapped a glossy sheet onto my desk. "What in the corporate world is this?!"

The poster featured a heavily filtered photo of Smash Kelly cradling a cartoon globe with one hand and flashing a rock sign with the other. His tongue was sticking out. The top of the poster said *GREEN IS THE NEW BLACK*. The bottom said *Sponsored by Allister Energy*.

"Now that's some premium, unleaded nightmare fuel," Gideon said.

I rubbed my eyes and looked again. It seemed ridiculous that a coal company would want anything to do with a "Green Kids Forum." But that was the problem with "going green." Allister Energy had no issue with folks in Carbon Hill tweaking a few lifestyle choices, so long as we never changed anything big enough to take away their power.

"They're trying to distract us on the day before Zero Hour." Sunny crumpled the poster into a ball. "They couldn't know *everything* we've planned, but they sure as zooph know we're up to something."

"Gideon." Rashi snapped into her best General Leia impression. "Get in touch with our chapter leaders. Fifth through eighth. We've gotta keep our strike plans under wraps."

Lucky for us, most recruits didn't have all the details just yet. They understood our goals, our dreams—that we were building a movement—but so far, nobody but the Crew knew we were planning a strike. And they certainly didn't know we were planning a disruption big enough to knock some sense into Senator Bud.

"But the strike is Friday," Paco said. "If our plan stays top secret, how's anyone gonna know what to do?"

"The assembly," Sunny answered. Her expression turned brighter than I'd seen it since the storm rolled in. "We'll have the whole U.S.A. in one room."

"A room sponsored by Allister Energy," Gideon said. "How could we possibly announce anything there?"

"I think you forgot." Sunny tossed the crumpled poster. It sailed across our headquarters and sunk clean into the trash. "The impossible is my specialty."

Sunny unlocked our SLYSRs from the rain-spattered bike rack after school.

"What are you going to do?" I pressed.

Sunny smirked under the dripping hood of her yellow raincoat. "You asking for a Future Fact?" She pulled back the hood and clipped on her helmet.

"Hey!" I raised a finger in defiance. "I'm asking for a plan. Not a prediction. There's a difference."

"Somebody's ner-vous!" a familiar voice rang behind me. It was one of Lindsay Allister's cronies—Bacon, or whatever they called him.

He ran over with a sporty-looking golf umbrella, a few of his fellow eighth-grade friends clustering around him with big, pricey umbrellas of their own. Their gang had only one seventh-grade member, and that was Lindsay. She wore a distant look, as usual.

Bacon's phone swept in from around my shoulder and snapped a wide selfie of me blinking in the rain and him pretending to choke.

"Delete that," I demanded.

"Can't." Bacon winced sarcastically. "It's in the cloud."

"Quit embarrassing yourself," Lindsay muttered—to me, I assumed. But her scowl was mostly trained on Bacon.

"Sorry, guys," the eighth grader fake apologized. "It's on the internet. That's permanent."

"*Nothing* is permanent," Sunny shot back. She reached into the backpack pocket where she'd hidden her watch, and Bacon's phone screen went completely blue. He tapped furiously at it, tried to shut it down. Nothing worked. He shoved it into his jeans with a babyish grunt, then pointed his umbrella at me like a rifle.

"Whatever you're planning for Friday, it's not gonna work," he raged as the rain flattened his hair. "Everybody knows your club is up to something. Us. The principal. Even Mommy's boss." He poked me with the tip of his umbrella. If Bacon mentioned Mom again, I would send him home with more than a broken phone.

Out of nowhere, Lindsay gave him a shove. "Do you ever stop talking?"

"Alls I'm saying is maybe we've got some plans of our own," Bacon said. "Right, Lindsay?"

"Just put a lid on it." Lindsay stormed away. Apparently, it wasn't just the U.S.A. who'd hatched a secret plan; the Allisters must've had their own designs already in play.

"You've got the *money*," I shouted so that Lindsay could hear me. "We've got the Crew." I snapped on my helmet for a little punctuation. It sure beat "phone head," as far as clapbacks go.

With twinkling fingers, Sunny waved bye-bye in Bacon's face, and we both zipped off on our electric scooters.

"See you at the assembly," the boy shouted. "You're gonna love it!"

STEP 3:

MAKE IT STOP

Thursday, October 27

1 day until Zero Hour

The auditorium simmered with anticipation—oddly quiet for a room that had just packed in the entire student body for our final period of the day. Every kid sat stock-still with a backpack between their feet. Sunny and I took up the centermost seats of the centermost aisle. Neither one of us spoke a word.

The room fell dark. Then silent.

The entire school day had felt like a ticking time-bomb, but now the ticking would come to an end. I pictured the glowing digits on the side of a detonator: Three. Two. One.

The speakers piped up. Prerecorded drumsticks clicked off the tempo—one, two, three, four—and then a single guitar chord crunched out, followed by a rapid-fire punk rock beat. The crowd went wild as the theme from HeTV's *PunkWork with Smash Kelly* kicked into high gear.

Then came the man himself. He blasted onto the stage, both hands lifted in a horn-fisted rock sign. The students roared, some chanting *PUNK! PUNK! PUNK! PUNK!* Smash Kelly totally looked the part. He had the build of a jock, but the style of an outcast. His Thor arms were sleeved in tattoos that overflowed up on his neck. His nose was pierced with a thick gold ring. Topping off the look, his hair was spiked into a six-inch mohawk.

Someone offstage tossed him a skateboard, and Smash and the skateboard became one. He soared from the left to the right, jumped a quarter-pipe ramp, and ground across a metal beam to stick a perfect landing at center stage. He lifted his arms once more, and the crowd gave a standing ovation. Then he popped the board into his hands and smashed it over his knee (must be how he got the name). The crowd stood in applause as a massive banner unfurled at the back of the stage:

GREEN IS THE NEW BLACK

Sponsored by Allister Energy

At the right-hand corner of the stage, nearly concealed by the old red curtain, I spotted a tall man in a swanky-looking suit. The red hair gave him away. This had to be Lindsay's dad, Richard Allister himself. Of course he would be here. Bringing a celebrity like Smash to Creekside must've cost a fortune.

"*PunkWork* is all about the world's most successful rebels." Smash strode along the front of the stage. "Businessmen who build half-pipes in their headquarters. Entrepreneurs with gauged ears. Millionaires who still like a good mosh pit. Punks. People who smash the status quo and make a lotta money doing it. And you know what? You can be punks, too . . . when it comes to going green. You can shake things up. You can smash the status quo . . . and *save* a lotta money doin' it."

Here's how to be a "Green Punk" and "save the planet" according to Smash Kelly:

1. Turn off the lights when you leave a room.

2. Use less AC on hot summer days.

3. Buy the *PunkWork* reusable shopping tote collection.

4. Turn your empty shampoo bottle into a pencil case with this one weird trick.

I felt queasy. It all took me back to a story I had been telling our new recruits this week, the story of my lonely, miserable, "green" summer. I'd switched off our AC units, turning our house into a tropical rain forest. I'd given up meat, cheese, and Cheetos. I'd even asked Mom to cancel our vacation to Great Aunt Linda's in Miami Beach, since that one round-trip flight would melt exactly ten square feet of the polar ice caps. I'd spent the whole summer torturing myself, and yet, for all my efforts, the world still hurtled toward apocalypse. "Going green" would never be enough.

Looking at Sunny, I saw I wasn't the only one cringing at Smash Kelly's Band-Aid solutions. She did everything in her power to restrain herself, closing her eyes, breathing slowly, clutching the armrests for dear life.

Smash took a knee at the edge of the stage. "Real talk, guys." He assumed a kinder, gentler tone. "If you wanna make a real difference, you're gonna have to work together."

I was shocked to see Sunny nodding in agreement.

"You'll have to team up."

"Exactly," Sunny whispered.

"To organize."

"*Yes.*"

"That's why I'm totally jacked to introduce a new way for you punks to go green at Creekside." Smash stood up and raised a fist.

"Ladies and gentlemen, give it up for the all-star Creekside Middle School G-Force!"

Smash's entrance music cranked back to full blast as a thin layer of fog spread across the stage. Green laser lights slashed wildly around the auditorium as a team leapt out through the curtains: Green shirts. Green jerseys. Matching green sweatbands. Every piece branded with a globe and a block-letter G.

This was the Allister-sponsored G-Force.

Each teammate carried a shiny green trash can. They arranged their bins in a line and, one by one, tossed in a crumpled sheet of green paper. Bacon, the most bombastic of the bunch, did a little jump shot through his legs.

Smash dealt them all high fives and addressed the auditorium. "Now, how about we see what this new team is all about? Let's talk to the *captain* of Creekside's G-Force, your very own Lindsay Allister."

Lindsay Allister? Fossil-fuel-rich Lindsay Allister? The same girl whose thugs called me a "faker" and vandalized my locker—just because I spoke up about the climate apocalypse?

She stepped through the curtain at center stage, sporting the same ridiculous uniform as the rest of her gang. The ranks of the G-Force clapped like clowns, Bacon most of all, but Lindsay didn't seem too excited. In fact, her face showed no expression at all. Smash held out for a fist bump, and Lindsay answered with a half-hearted fist tap. Her eyes drifted across the audience.

"So, Lindsay," Smash said as the music faded, "what would you say is the purpose of the G-Force here at Creekside?"

"It's pretty simple, Smash." Lindsay delivered the words with cold precision, literally reading them from a sheet of paper. "The G-Force is here to save the planet."

"Wow!" Smash clapped his meaty hands in hopes of starting a round of applause. It didn't catch on, which made me prouder of our U.S.A. recruits than words could possibly express. My Summer-of-Band-Aid-Solutions story must've really stuck.

Smash soldiered on: "And how exactly does the G-Force plan on saving the planet?"

Lindsay paused a little too long. Again, her eyes traced the auditorium. They landed smack in the center of my middle row. Was she looking at me?

The red-haired man coughed loudly offstage.

Lindsay snapped back to attention. She read the next response, her voice wobbling just a little. "We are going to get rid of all plastic straws in the cafeteria."

Smash nodded. "Anything else?"

Lindsay's father coughed again, louder this time. Lindsay lifted the page and took a breath, then locked up completely.

Footsteps clopped rapidly across the stage, and Smash glanced over with a start.

"Well, what a treat." His voice cracked. "Let's all welcome the president of Allister Energy, Mr. Richard Allister."

The spotlight wobbled to stage left, and the man behind the coal plant marched into view. He squeezed out a smile and tore the microphone from his daughter's hand.

"So, Miss Allister," Richard piped into the mic, his voice thinner and more gravelly than I'd expected. "How exactly does the G-Force plan on saving the world?"

He pointed the microphone at her face.

"Well, there's the straws. Um. The plastic straws," Lindsay stammered.

I shifted in my seat. This whole moment felt wrong, out of place, like all of Creekside Middle was spying on some private family argument.

"What. Else." The man didn't ask so much as demand.

Lindsay read straight off the page. "We will patrol the hallways to make sure no student leaves on the lights in an empty bathroom."

Richard snatched her notes and jammed them into his expensive jacket pocket. "And. What. Else."

Lindsay said nothing. Her eyes returned to the audience, and this time I had no doubt that she was looking at me.

"What about the *recycling* bins, Miss Allister?" Richard prodded.

No response. Lindsay's eyes were watery now. Desperate. She looked at her dad. Then at the floor. Then, once again, Lindsay looked at me, her expression sinking into deep, sorrowful regret.

She leaned into the microphone.

"I could've done so much more." Lindsay spoke like we were the only two people in the room. "Not just open a *door* for you."

She burst into tears.

I'd never expected to find myself feeling sorry for Lindsay Allister. Why pity the richest kid in town? But I had never witnessed a scene more pitiful than this. Or more puzzling. What door was she talking about? Had she really been speaking to me? She hadn't so much as glanced in my direction since she called my name from the Murder House on the morning of the teachers' strike.

If she was losing her mind, I couldn't blame her. Because for all the pain on that poor girl's face, her own dad wouldn't cut her one inch of slack. In fact, the sadder Lindsay appeared, the madder Richard got. And the whole scene was playing out in front of our entire school. Someone had to make it stop.

"Hate to interrupt!" a girl blurted beside me. Sunny, of course. She stood up in her bright yellow raincoat, projecting her voice so firmly that I could've sworn she was holding a mic. "I have a question for Smash."

The TV star chuckled and flashed a grin. "Looks like G-Force just got a new member."

A few people laughed. Mostly teachers.

Sunny smiled with a furnace of rage in her eyes.

"Maybe!" she sang, straining to keep a chipper tone. She cleared her throat. "Anyone watching the news knows that, not far away, our country is battling the biggest natural disasters ever to strike us all at once. Hundreds of people could die, and a lot more could lose their homes. So why do you think shinier recycling bins will keep that from happening?"

Smash blinked, processing the question. He looked at Richard for permission to answer. Richard gave a tiny nod.

"Well, every little bit helps, right?" Smash answered.

"But that's the problem, isn't it?" Sunny shot back. "The little bits *distract* us from the big stuff. 'Little' is not enough. The world has known about climate change for decades now, and the world has done *nothing* but little stuff. A new kind of expensive car. A new kind of light bulb. Another pinch of change here and there. Don't you think all these little things might be keeping us from the big things that need to happen?"

It felt like watching a boxer corner her opponent on the ropes.

Sunny was on a roll, channeling that same righteous indignation I'd once witnessed in a produce section full of soon-to-be-extinct fruits. Smash blinked harder and smiled wider. A big, painful I-didn't-sign-up-for-this smile.

He brought the microphone to his mouth, but Sunny cut him off. "And Richard, how can we trust you to help us save the planet while every day you get richer by cooking it?"

Richard's fake smile faded as he took the microphone back. He opened his mouth like a fish but said nothing. His eye twitched.

"So the guy's rich! What's your point?!" Bacon shouted from behind him. "At least the G-Force is doing something real—unlike your fake team with fake asthma and fake disasters."

A few of his buddies on the G-Force started chanting onstage: "FAKER! FAKER! FAKER!"

Richard Allister broke into a bashful grin.

"That's enough, boys." He silenced them with a wave of his hand, then pointed his smug grin right back at Sunny. "Call me what you like, kid. But Deacon here is right about one thing: I am the real deal."

"I guess you're right. Everybody knows Richard Allister is the realest guy in town." Sunny returned to her seat before bouncing right back up. "I mean, what's more *real* than someone trying to become a reality TV star?"

The man's smile melted faster than a polar ice cap. He glanced at Smash, who cowered behind his palms in a show of innocence.

"I have no idea what you're talking about," Richard whispered into the mic.

"Sure, you don't," Sunny said. "*Rickster.*"

Richard's face went as white as a bleached coral reef.

The students broke into little streams of whispered chatter. Apart from Richard and maybe Smash, not one of us had a clue what Sunny was talking about. But something told me we were all about to find out.

Let's back things up for a moment, shall we? To really appreciate what happened next, you should know what Sunny later explained to me:

Richard Allister had a dream. It wasn't more money—the man was already rich enough. What he wanted more than anything else in the world was to be rich *and* famous. To achieve his dream, Richard Allister saw only one sure path: becoming a star on reality TV. Specifically, a star on HeTV's *PunkWork with Smash Kelly.*

It seemed like a sure thing. After all, the whole show centered on people who were both 1) lovers of extreme sports and 2) rich. Richard Allister had #2 on lock, so all he had to do was fake #1.

It was all too perfect. As a popular kid in the 1980s, he'd managed to buy the respect of all his classmates—except for the skaters and the punks. But he'd show them. For the audition video, Richard got a sleeve of temporary tattoos up his arm. He bought a clip-on nose ring. He paid a stunt double to skate the half-pipe while wearing one of his suits. He even made up a nickname and claimed that people had been using it for years: Rickster.

A few months later, in total secrecy, the entire *PunkWork* production team showed up in Carbon Hill to shoot Richard Allister's episode.

The shoot did not go well.

At all.

In fact, the footage was so thoroughly embarrassing that the network refused to air it. They deleted the files, every megabyte, like they were stamping out a nasty piece of malware. Still, they missed one file: Rickster.mov. The audition video had already been automatically backed up to the HeTV cloud server. There it remained until 2032, when all their data leaked out to the public. By 2100, Richard's audition had become a Chewbagoat-level internet classic, the kind of absurd masterpiece that most people could quote from beginning to end.

One of those people was the young Sunday Turner.

And so, when it came time to travel back to the 2020s, Sunny added Richard's audition to her wristwatch database. She couldn't imagine why she'd need it. Perhaps just for a laugh. Or perhaps, she thought, in some odd twist of history, she just might find herself needing evidence of Richard Allister being Carbon Hill's most spectacular fake.

Now Sunny stared daggers up at Richard Allister.

A few teachers started gathering around the edges of our row, but Sunny stood smack in the middle and far from their reach. No stopping her now. She grinned, looking good and ready to teach this coal baron a precious lesson: when you've spent your entire life plundering the world of generations to come, never pick a fight with the future.

"Come on, Rickster." Sunny slapped the timepiece onto her wrist like she was Miles Morales with a loaded webslinger. So much for secrecy. "Are you *sure* you don't know what I'm talking about?"

Richard swallowed hard.

"Fine, then." Sunny tapped her gunmetal wristwatch. "I'll refresh your memory."

"They call me Rickster." The recording rippled through the auditorium, popping out from several hundred little speakers. Then several hundred students reached into their backpacks to see why their phones had suddenly started talking. In one fell swoop, the entire population of Creekside Middle School beheld Richard's video on an ocean of little screens. They couldn't even shut them off.

Sunny wore the same satisfied look you'd find on any kid who'd ever broken a pointless rule in the name of justice. We shared the briefest of fist bumps.

"Please silence your cell phones!" Richard Allister bleated from the stage.

But the video played on as the entire school choked with laughter—and that was even before the man in the video started pretending to rock out. "Rickster" donned a heavy-metal guitar and ripped through a blistering solo. Only problem? His fingers didn't match the sound. Another phony moment.

"Disable the Wi-Fi. Now!" Richard Allister's voice distorted through the speakers. Principal Rivera did his best to comply, but the man was powerless. Sunny was running the show.

With another tap on her timepiece, Sunny made the video stop. She lifted a finger, and the auditorium fell silent.

"Students of Creekside Middle: If you wanna be a fake hero, go ahead and join Rickster's G-Force. But if you wanna save the world for real, the United Students of America have already gotten started. Tomorrow morning, we strike. Eight o'clock. Right in the shadow of Creekside Middle. Join us!"

Mayhem set in. No one at Creekside had ever made a show of rebellion as glorious as Sunny's. People cheered. Mr. Dan, a few rows away, turned to flash Sunny a quick thumbs-up. Apparently, she'd aced his assignment to "put grown-ups on the spot."

Sunny smiled back as the entire student body rolled into a roaring chant: "U-S-A! U-S-A! U-S-A!"

I just about blew my voice out.

STEP 4:

FLEE THE SCENE

Richard Allister had lost the crowd. Smash Kelly walked off the stage. So did Lindsay. That left only Richard, Bacon, and half a dozen other goons chanting "G-FORCE!" as hard as their throats could handle.

I barely heard them over the crowd.

Sunny tugged me into a low crouch, huddled below the chaos. "Check the back," she said.

The Soda Jerk Janitors had posted themselves beside the rear exits.

Sunny pulled me lower. "They saw the whole thing. Me, the video, the timepiece, all of it."

"I gotta get you out of here," I said.

For the first time, the so-called inventors had Sunny in their sights. After everything she'd done for me, I couldn't let Sunny get dragged back into that barren future of theirs.

"We have more exits near the front," I told her. "I'll keep the Janitors distracted."

We switched jackets, and I pulled up Sunny's yellow hood to cover my head. She did the same with mine.

Then I leaned up to a guy beside me. "The buses are here! School's out!" I shouted.

The rumor spread like a California wildfire. I could hear "bus" mentions popping all over the auditorium.

The crowd began to move. In a not-so-orderly fashion, rows of students spilled into the aisles. They stuffed every open space, effectively clogging any path from the Janitors to me and Sunny.

Before we separated, Sunny caught me by the arm. "Meet me at the bike rack."

"Bike rack," I repeated, and elbowed my way into the still-chanting masses.

When I made it to the back exit, a meaty hand grabbed me by the raincoat. I recognized the smoker's voice immediately. "How stupid did you think we are?"

The Soda Jerk Janitor flipped me around and shoved me against the wall at the back of the auditorium. But the moment he set eyes on my face, his sneer dropped away. He'd expected Sunny, thanks to the yellow raincoat.

The woman stepped in behind him. "Front exits," she croaked. "I'll cut her off."

"Don't wait up for me," the man replied. "I wanna see how much he knows."

My body went cold as my chest burned up, desperate for the silver inhaler.

The tall Soda Jerk raced out the doors as the short man returned his attention to me. His grip tightened. So did my lungs. With all the chaos that Sunny and I had just set off, this guy could drag me kicking and screaming back to their truck without anyone batting an eye. One zap from that gas-pump thing, and I'd be locked in a smoggy cage with Einstein before you could say *asthma attack*.

"I've seen you with her," he growled. "If you don't tell me everything in five seconds, I'm gonna—"

The man's eyes widened as his entire body thrashed backward to the floor. That sinister face was replaced with a friendlier one.

"You're lucky I'm a pacifist!" Mr. Dan shouted as the man scrambled away. The teacher turned to me. "Are you okay?"

I puffed at my inhaler and gave a thumbs-up.

"And Sunny?" Mr. Dan looked worried.

The bike rack, I thought. Sunny was waiting. I had to move, and fast. So I ditched Mr. Dan and ran for the exit.

I splashed down the rainy sidewalk and found Sunny all clear for takeoff—helmet snapped on, scooter powered up.

"Yellow really is your color," Sunny said, looking the raincoat up and down. "Now come on. I can't stay here." She threw me my helmet. I grabbed my SLYSR.

I could already hear that creepy rendition of the national anthem whirring to life just a couple blocks away. The ice-cream truck. Sunny took off on her scooter and slashed across Creekside Road. I followed through the cold October rain as we raced for the Reservoir Park Wilderness Preserve.

STEP 5:

SAY GOODBYE

"You're leaving?!" My voice echoed through the softly dripping woods.

Sunny shushed me and finished rolling up her tent.

"But the strike is tomorrow!" I couldn't believe it. Sunny skipping the strike was about as unthinkable as Santa skipping Christmas. "This is everything we've worked for."

"Everything *you've* worked for," Sunny said. "I've been in retirement since September twenty-eighth, remember? I've got faith in the Crew." She zipped the bulging backpack and flung it over her shoulder. "If you want tomorrow to be anything more than a never-ending scooter chase, I can't be there."

As usual, Sunny had a point.

"And besides," she went on, "I think I've earned a little sightseeing before I head back to 2100."

"You know"—I held up the inhaler she'd used to save my life—"I never did say thank you."

Sunny took the inhaler and examined the sleek silver device in the fading light of the forest. The clouds had broken just enough to bring in some of the golden sunset. She laughed. "I had to travel back to the past to find any hope for the future. You gave me that hope. So don't lose yours. And don't stop caring too much. And please,

Jonah Kaminski, please don't stop making friends."

"I won't," I said, fighting back tears. It was a losing battle.

Sunny pulled me into a hug. Then she pushed me back, gripped my shoulders, and stared with that same flat resolve I'd seen when she first popped off the pink astronaut helmet.

"Future Fact #3," she said. "Use it."

I appreciated her generosity, but I wasn't about to use up my Future Facts just for the heck of it. I'd gotten so used to saving them up. "I'll pass. Maybe we'll meet again."

"Number. Three." Sunny pointed right between my eyes. "I need you to use it now."

I wasn't about to argue. "What do you need me to ask?"

She held up the photo she'd shown me and Gideon a couple weeks earlier: three names, three graves. Her eyes sparkled with tears. "Ask me how it happened."

I took a puff from my inhaler. I had only ever asked for the nice-to-know Future Facts up until now. Not once had I considered asking about something like this. My heart raced. "How did your family die?"

Sunny turned away.

"I'm sure you noticed me acting a little different this week," she began. "That's because it's the anniversary. October 27, 2099. That's when I lost them." She turned back to face me. "It happened right here. Except in 2099, these woods are older, dirtier, full of litter and a whole city's worth of tents. Rich folks call it a slum. Poor folks"—Sunny patted a hand over her heart—"call it home."

Sniffling, she settled onto the trunk of a fallen tree.

"It was the perfect day, as far as days go in the end-times. So we all played hide-and-seek like my sister Monday always begged us to do. Even Daddy. I hid in the branches of a great big tree. Before long, my parents and Monday were all looking for me, but they weren't even close." Sunny swallowed. "After I'd been perched up there for a while, I felt this rumble. Then I heard a roaring sound, like a massive ocean wave. And then I saw the water."

She closed her eyes and took in a sputtering breath, like she was stepping into the chilly tide right then.

"So muddy and angry and strong. Every tent got swept away. Even some trees gave out. Mine didn't. I closed my eyes and clung to it for a long, long time. When the water went down, I climbed down to look for my family." Sunny held up her rugged pink backpack. "Mom's rucksack was all I found."

"Was it a tidal wave?" I whispered, sitting down beside her on the tree trunk.

"Too far inland," Sunny said. "It was an old dam. None of them were made with this century's weather in mind. So they'll give out. They'll break. Sometimes even on a perfectly sunny day."

"It's not right." My heart ached for Sunny. I imagined her wandering these hills, soaked to the bone, orphaned at a moment's notice. "It must've been so scary."

Sunny wiped her eyes. "It was. And the same thing is about to happen here, Jonah. That's why I'm telling you."

My chest tightened. "What do you mean, 'here'?"

"I mean *now*," Sunny said. "The rain might've stopped, but it's already too late. Not far from here, the Happy Valley Dam is blocking off more water than it ever has before. They built it a hundred years ago, after the last one gave out. But they never expected this much rain. Just after midnight tonight, the dam will breach, and these woods will look like a river until the state finds a way to plug it up. By then, the waters will have already flooded the Little Delaware Creek."

I took another puff from my inhaler. Already I could picture myself braving the waist-high waters to rescue stranded pets and small children. "Tell me what I have to do."

"Classic Jonah." Sunny tapped me on the chest, right over my heart. "Always trying to save the world alone. As a matter of fact, there's nothing you have to do. No one's gonna be hurt, this time. But promise me you'll stay away from Creekside Middle until tomorrow morning."

"Why?"

"At three a.m., the flood waters will peak, and the school—well, they don't call it Creekside for nothing. All the classrooms will flood."

"Our school?" My stomach twisted into a knot. "I can't even imagine it."

"It's worse than that," Sunny said. "All that water soaking the foundation will flatten an old coal mine that runs under the building. Half of the cafeteria will cave in, and damage from the collapse will trigger an electrical fire that spreads into the gymnasium and the art rooms. By strike time, the waters will recede, and the fire will burn out, but the school? History."

This must've been why Sunny plotted our picket line so far away from the building. The knot inside of me gave out, my stomach plummeting into a mine shaft. Silly as it sounds, the first thing I pictured was a drawing I'd done in art a few weeks back. I'd drawn a wolf, perched on a pristine, snowy knoll. We'd had to choose one form of shading for that sketch, and I'd picked pointillism—turning thousands of little pencil dots into scratchy ice shadows. It had taken me hours to finish. Now all I could picture was my perfect snowy hill curling into flames on the art room wall.

"Can I stop it?"

She shook her head. "Not this time. But if our strike succeeds, you can keep a hundred other dams from breaking." She held up the photo of her family's grave site. "Even this one."

Gazing at the picture under our tree-covered twilight, I could feel my spirits climbing up from the mine shaft of despair. One thing I knew for sure: If my sheer willpower could have changed the future, all three of those graves would've vanished right then and there. "I promise you, Sunny."

"And I trust you, Jonah," she said. "Tonight the climate will strike Carbon Hill, and tomorrow the students of Carbon Hill will strike back. Tomorrow is when history takes a turn for the better."

All at once, every one of Sunny's riddles came into perfect focus, and I finally understood.

"Zero Hour," I whispered.

Sunny slid the photo into my shirt pocket. "Zero Hour."

STEP 6:

MAKE A HUGE MISTAKE

Night came quickly. I walked home after helping Sunny pack up, still wearing her yellow raincoat. We'd forgotten to trade back. Forgetting was easy with so much to process. In one day, Sunny and I had launched a revolution, uncovered the meaning of Zero Hour, and shared our final farewells. The mission felt nearly complete, and yet so much work still had to be done. Senator Bud had not been swayed. The graves had not faded. The future had not yet been saved.

I reached my front door. Locked. I knocked, and the door thrashed open.

Mom looked even more upset than she'd been the first time I'd disappeared. She was still wearing her security uniform, her eyes were smudged with teary makeup, and she was glaring at me like I'd just violated every workplace safety law on the books.

I was late. Very late.

She thrust her phone up to my nose so I could see the number she'd just dialed. 9-1-1.

"I was just about to hit the *call* button," she said. "You are so lucky I didn't."

"Mom, I'm sorry. I just—"

She fanned her hands in front of my face and stormed deeper

into the house. I followed her a few steps in and finally registered the true horror of what I had done.

Streamers dangled in the living room. A cake waited sadly on the kitchen table.

I had made Mom fear for my life. For the second time in five weeks. But this time, I had done it on my birthday.

"You know"—Mom angrily cut the cake—"I thought it would be funny to pretend like I'd forgotten, then surprise you after school. But apparently, even birthdays don't matter anymore."

This time I'd really done it. To Mom, nothing could be more insulting than forgetting my own birthday. *My favorite holiday*—that's what she always called it. Heck, it was even the PIN on her phone. 1-0-2-7. Forgetting it meant forgetting about the things she held most dear.

Mom abandoned the cake. "Tell me, Jonah, what happened in school today?"

"Um . . . nothing really."

"Is that right?" She clasped her hands and straightened her back, striking a deadly pose somewhere between Mom the former soldier and Mom the future lawyer. "Nothing at all worth reporting?"

I shrugged.

"So you *didn't* have a celebrity come visit your school today, and you *weren't* there when somebody hijacked every student's phone to broadcast an embarrassing video of the most powerful guy in town?"

"Well, yeah," I said. "That happened."

I wanted to tell her everything, not just the headlines of the day, but about what all those headlines really meant. For me. For Sunny.

For the future of humankind. After all, Mom was still my favorite person to talk to, especially about the things that matter most. But I couldn't. Not if it'd cost her a job, a scholarship, a dream. Instead, I gave my heartbroken Mom one final shrug and kept my mouth shut—just like I'd been doing for the last five weeks.

Mom let out a long, labored breath. "I can't believe I'm doing this on your birthday, but I'm all out of ideas." She handed me a little plate. "Upstairs. You're grounded for the night."

I took my sad slice of birthday cake and headed for my room.

"Don't forget your gift," Mom muttered. She presented a little book with a big bow on it: *Why We Can't Wait*, by Dr. Martin Luther King Jr.

"I figured if you're still interested in changing the world, you'd better start learning from the best." She paused. "There's a fifty from Aunt Linda in there, too."

"Thanks, Mom." I leaned in for a hug.

Mom gave me a back pat and shooed me away. "Bed. Go."

This didn't feel like the night before a revolution. What kind of revolutionary gets sent to his room for time-outs?

I ate my cake in bed, then untied the ribbon around *Why We Can't Wait*. Mom had written a little note on the inside cover:

The title made me think of you. Happy Birthday!

Love,

Your patient Mom

xoxo

I flipped through the pages and landed on the glossy ones near the middle of the book. They were tiled with old black-and-white photos. One picture caught my eye. It showed a few dozen students under arrest in Birmingham, Alabama, for walking out of school to march against racial segregation. Those students had stared down evils far scarier than anything I'd seen in Carbon Hill. No contest. How could I ever be one iota as brave as those kids were?

Closing the book, I pulled Sunny's grave-site photo from my shirt pocket and read their names out loud: "Monday. Vera. George." If I was going to be brave, even one-iota-brave, I couldn't do it for something as small as myself. And when I really considered it, I couldn't fathom doing it for something as dizzyingly big as "the planet."

So, tomorrow, I would be brave for these three names: Monday. Vera. George. I wasn't fighting to save the planet; I was fighting for them.

Holding Sunny's photo to my chest, I shut my eyes tight and prayed I wouldn't let her down.

STEP 7:

WALK THE BATTLEFIELD

Friday, October 28

Zero Hour

The daylight woke me. I tore off the covers and leapt out of bed. Go figure: I'd tossed and turned all night and never once thought to set my alarm. It was 7:47 a.m., thirteen minutes until the action began and forty-seven minutes after the Crew was supposed to show up. I was late for my own revolution.

I threw on some dirty clothes, taking great care to limit myself to red, white, or blue. U.S.A. colors. But I did make one exception: the yellow raincoat. If Sunny couldn't be there today, then I would stand in her place. I tucked her family photo into the front pocket.

Creeping down the stairs, I was careful to avoid the kitchen, where Mom would be waiting. She would know about the school by now. She'd be ready to break the news. She'd want to talk about last night. She'd want me to stay home and keep safe.

Not today.

One last betrayal, I promised myself. Today I fixed the future. Tomorrow I'd clean up the mess.

I power-walked to school in the damp autumn air, and the closer I got to Creekside Middle, the more I noticed it—that thick, rolling blanket of sound. Was it the roar of the swollen creek or the voice of a crowd? I lost all doubt near the end of Ocean Ave. That's when I heard the chanting, the stomping, the claps.

I pushed through the droves of people that surrounded the intersection to Creekside Road—mostly parents, tagging along like field trip chaperones—and stepped into a picture that looked like something out of a history book.

Hundreds of students had flooded the blocked-off section of Creekside Road, where the waters had already receded. Everyone was chanting, waving WWG picket signs and wearing red, white, and blue. They looked like a great big American flag, flapping before the ruins of some terrible battle. Creekside Middle was the ruins.

It made me sick just to look at the wreckage. Beyond a short wall of sandbags, my school was surrounded by fire trucks and belching out smoke. The collapsed cafeteria hung off to the left. All the classroom windows were fogged up and dripping from the inside.

My fellow students looked even more broken up than the building. At one time or another, every one of us must've joked about our school being wiped off the face of the earth. But now that the joke came true, now that the place that had sheltered us 180 days a year was suddenly wrecked and defiled, it flooded us with a hateful feeling that we couldn't help but wear on our faces.

This was personal.

Climate change had finally hit home. The biggest East Coast storm on record had sent its rains as far as Carbon Hill, Pennsylvania, and taken out a school in Senator Bud's hometown. Channel 8 had already arrived. The senator would have no choice but to listen to us, to the voice of the future in the heart of Carbon Hill.

It took me a minute to find the Crew. Gideon, Rashi, and Paco were gathered in front of the Murder House. Gideon hovered a few steps away, looking nothing like his usual jolly self. He kept glancing back at the school, then quickly looking away, practically shielding his eyes.

I reached out for our secret handshake, but he met it with a loose high five. "Everything okay?"

Gideon nodded before glancing back at the school.

"For a dude with a megaphone, you sure seem awfully quiet," I said, fishing for a response.

All he did was blink at the megaphone in his hand, like he hadn't known it was there. Something more than Einstein was on Gideon's mind today.

"Looks like home—after the storm, I mean." Paco stared at the washed-out school. "I guess we were right to call it a war. That's exactly how it feels."

"It's not a war that any of us started." I set my eyes far down the street toward the Allister Energy Plant. "But you better believe we're gonna finish it." I took the megaphone from Gideon's hand.

"Not yet," Rashi said. "We're saving our YouTube celebrity for last." She eyed my yellow raincoat. "Where's Sunny?"

I hadn't even considered how I'd explain her absence to the rest of the Crew. "Well. Um. Sunny couldn't be here."

"You cannot be serious." Gideon started pacing. I gave him a firm look and pointed at my wrist—right where a gunmetal timepiece would go. "Oh." He got quiet again. "Them."

"I'll tell you all what Sunny told me." I zipped up Sunny's raincoat as I spoke. "She has faith in us. In all of us." I handed Rashi the megaphone. "So let's have some faith in each other."

Aside from a pile of sandbags, we didn't have much of a stage. So, we had everyone crouch low as Rashi stepped up to our homemade podium. She powered on the megaphone and kicked off the rally, Rashi-style—with ridiculously well-prepared remarks.

"Students, rebels, members of the media, and fellow members of the U.S.A., welcome to our battlefield."

The audience broke into a deafening cheer.

She gestured toward the wet, smoldering school. "It does look like a battle today. But it doesn't look like a battle we are winning." She held up a copy of Tuesday's front page. "Two coasts attacked by the climate. Our own school destroyed. And yet it's not the responsible adults who are stepping up to fight. It's us."

Some students started chanting: "U-S-A! U-S-A! U-S-A!"

"Today's strike is a message to Senator Bud," Rashi said. As a visual aid, I held up a giant poster with Senator Bud's face on it while Rashi explained just how powerful the man was, but just how little he had done. "We're here to tell him that his words are not enough. We demand action. And we've put those demands in writing."

I offered up a long sheet of paper that looked like the Declaration of Independence.

"This letter was written by our own Mr. 'Paco' Francisco Mercado Baez," Rashi announced. "I think it's only fair that he present it to you now. Paco?"

Paco approached the lectern, took the megaphone, and breathed in slowly through his nose. He surveyed the crowd for a moment, then turned back to Rashi.

"You read it," he whispered, backing away from the podium.

Rashi rolled with it. She must've known this was no time to argue. Clearing her throat and hoisting up the page theatrically, she began to read.

WHAT IS WORLD WAR G?

Dear Senator James L. Budley,

For an entire generation, the time you've served as our US Senator, the United States has done nothing but small, slow things to fight a big, fast problem. You saw the asteroid hurtling for Planet Earth, and you picked up a squirt gun. We think we understand why. When the worst of this apocalypse strikes the earth, many of today's senators won't be on this earth anymore.

But we will. We have no choice but to live with what you've left us. Our demand, we think, is a modest one: Show us a response to the apocalypse that's as big as the apocalypse itself. Get the whole world to fight—while we still have a chance of winning.

The climate apocalypse will take more from our generation than we lost in World War II. So our fight should be greater, too. That's why we're calling for a new World War. A war without bullets, guns, or bombs. A war that makes us healthier, happier, and—for most people—richer. One great war for the last generation. A war for the greening of the world. We call it World War G.

We demand that World War G replace oil, gas, and coal. We demand that World War G plant new trees in the billions. We demand that World War G revive our communities with good jobs and a livable future. And here's one part we won't let you ignore: We demand that World War G move quickly. We're talking years, not decades.

We don't want your words, Senator Bud. We want your votes. Not long ago, you voted to give tax money to polluters like Allister Energy. We the future were watching. Not long from now, our government will have to decide whether it's time to build an America—and a Carbon Hill—that doesn't need Allister anymore. When that day comes, vote YES for World War G. We the future will be watching then, too.

Ours might be the Last Generation to survive on Planet Earth, and we won't go down without a fight. Yes, we are rude. Yes, we are annoying. No, we will not knock it off. We are the United Students of America, and we are not asking for World War G. We're demanding it.

As Rashi recited the final line, a mountainous kid shot to his feet. It was Dariq Wallace, Gideon's first recruit, probably the only popular kid I *hadn't* seen with the G-Force. He pumped his fist and shouted, "World War G!"

It set the whole crowd off. The entire U.S.A. erupted into cheers and stomps and applause—a fury loud enough for Senator Bud to hear. Or so we hoped.

STEP 8:

UNLEASH YOUR STORY

As the crowd went wild, the local news pressed in to get a statement from our Crew. We made a statement, alright. One by one, members of the U.S.A. got in front of the cameras to tell their stories. These were the same stories we'd spent these last weeks collecting, our secret weapon, the invisible bond that had pulled us all together and made us into an army. Now we displayed the full force of this power for all of Carbon Hill—and Senator Bud—to see.

First came Rashi, who told the story of her nani and nana, the grandparents who had lost their home to the New Delhi heat wave. Somehow, she kept it together, even when she told us how that heat wave stole her grandfather, too.

Sarah Vogelsburg told her story of the home she'd lost, and how so many more were being lost in that firebomb still sweeping the West Coast. Some of our stories were short and painful, like Sarah's. Some were short and sweet, like Dariq Wallace and the shrimp shack. Even Little Mike, the picky eater who'd quit the U.S.A. for burrito-related reasons, had a story to tell.

"Let's face it," Mike concluded. "If I grow up in a world where only the strong survive, I'm gonna grow up dead."

I started to notice more cameras and lights popping up at the fringes of the crowd, with the big, colorful logos of national networks. This was going way beyond Channel 8. But of course it was. Yesterday, America had watched as the climate attacked our nation like never before. We kids were the first Americans to stand against it. That's why we weren't just going live to Carbon Hill—we were going live to the world.

"Paco," I said, "you're up."

"This is it," Rashi said. "Tell them your story."

Paco backed away and shook his head.

"If I can do it"—Rashi shoved the megaphone into his hands—"so can you."

Paco let the megaphone slump.

Rashi fumed. "We brought you onto the team for your voice. You're 'Paco' Francisco Mercado Baez. The poet. Our chief storyteller. And you seriously can't share a few words?"

I caught some folks in the crowd starting to spot the argument sparking around the podium.

But Paco wouldn't budge. "I'll ruin it."

"You're ruining it right *now*!" Rashi exclaimed, loud enough for all the crowd to hear.

She and Paco stared each other down, each daring the other to blink. Everyone was watching. For a long moment, it felt like our entire mission—and Sunny's—teetered on the brink of disaster.

"I have something to say!" Gideon scooped up the megaphone and approached the makeshift podium, reaching down to grab a crooked-looking duffel bag.

"I'll be honest," he began, "I didn't join the U.S.A. because I cared about this climate fight. It never meant too much to me. I just wanted my dog back." Of course, I was the only person in the crowd who knew about Einstein, but that didn't seem to matter. The conviction in Gideon's voice more than made up for it.

"Then this happened." He glanced darkly back at the ruined school. "And now I get it. This apocalypse will change each and every one of our lives. Either we change the world now, or the world changes everything. Anyways, it reminds me of a song my dad used to play."

He reached into the sleeping bag, pulled out his purple toy guitar—the one most people our age wouldn't be caught dead holding—and slung it over his shoulder. Even though his candy-colored instrument looked like a 4+ toy from the clearance aisle, Gideon had never looked so dignified.

He started to play. He was gentle at first, not strumming but plucking individual notes. His fingers went swiftly, leaping across the plastic strings like piano keys. It didn't sound like a cheap toy—not the way Gideon played it. The notes popped through the megaphone like the sound of some electric banjo, oddly beautiful.

The melody settled the churning crowd. Gideon began strumming in a loose shuffle-y beat, like the cadence of an old Celtic ballad. The chords were sad and stirring.

I knew the song as soon as he sang the opening lyrics. Mom loved this one: "The Times, They Are A-Changin'" by Bob Dylan, a battle hymn from the 1960s, around the time those students were arrested for marching in Birmingham, Alabama. But the words could've been written today. Gideon sang about accepting the truth, about admitting that the waters have risen around you, about grown-ups who should help us save the world, and about senators like James "Bud" Budley, who had to accept that change would reach them whether they liked it or not.

By the final verse, Rashi and Paco had patched things up and were swaying side by side. When Gideon finished, the whole U.S.A. stood dumbstruck. Silent. And then the whole host of students erupted in applause.

I leapt over to Gideon and jostled him by the shoulders. "Dude, how did you learn to do that?!"

"Same way you get to Carnegie Hall," Gideon answered, wiping his eyes. "Practice." Something told me he was quoting his dad.

At that precise moment, I could swear I felt a stirring in the air, like something in time and space had just shifted forever. Gideon wasn't just carrying along with some destiny that Sunny could've predicted from the start. He was plucking himself a new destiny. Changing his own story.

I checked Sunny's photo, just in case. Still there. It appeared destiny still needed some work.

STEP 9:

ENGAGE PHASE 2

The crowd was hyped, and the world was watching.

"Phase two," Rashi told Paco. Paco passed it on to Gideon, who sprang right into action. He hustled through the crowd, doling out instructions and rounding up our throng of fired-up students.

We called phase 2 the Endgame. The final boss battle. Even though today's action had gone better than I could possibly have imagined, the Endgame still scared the oxygen right out of me. (I felt for my inhaler: still there.)

This final stage would begin with our march to the Allister Energy Plant. Yes, *that* Allister Energy Plant, the place where Mom worked. After that, the others would clear a space for me to deliver my speech—the Big One, my first public message to the world since posting that viral video. This time I'd be speaking directly to Senator Bud, and this time the world would be watching. Live. All that attention would have to change the senator's mind. And it all came down to me.

I wasn't as nervous as you'd think, and I had Gideon to thank for that. He'd told me the same thing about 700 times as I rehearsed my lines over the previous week: "Just pretend it's YouTube." And it helped. A speech, after all, is way easier than a conversation. It's a straight line from point A to point B, just like talking into YouTube on

Mom's old phone, may it rest in peace.

Rashi blew a whistle, and we started on our slow, steady march along Creekside Road. Thanks to a few fallen trees that Sunny had almost certainly anticipated, the entire street was closed to vehicle traffic. The U.S.A. had safe passage all the way to the gates of Allister Energy.

As we left school grounds, I noticed the sky for the first time that day. The clouds had bubbled up dark and thick. More rain? Perhaps. But the weather had nothing on us. As hundreds of students marched as one, any reasonable person could see where the real power was brewing. We were the swelling thunderhead. We were the storm, a force of nature that no senator could possibly ignore.

I glanced back over my shoulder and couldn't see the end of our ranks. We looked like an endless tide of handmade signs and American flags. Lots of students waved copies of that "*A WEEK OF INFAMY*" newspaper like twenty-first-century newsies.

But even as this triumphant scene unfolded around me, I couldn't ignore the weirdness around town today. First, I noticed the telephone poles. Then the bus stops. Then the windshields. Every available surface was plastered with copies of the same yellow flier. *MISSING CHILD*, it said, with a big picture of Sunny underneath. *Call with details*. It had to be the Soda Jerks. But where were they? Not once today had I spotted them anywhere in the crowd.

I pushed them out of my mind. Their time was almost up. Soon I would put the last nail in that coffin of a future they'd worked so hard to preserve.

The smokestacks loomed closer now. This called for a nice deep puff on my inhaler. There would be no hiding this from Mom after I reached the gates of Allister Energy. Odds were a security guard like her would be staring me straight in the eye while I delivered my epic speech. After all, it's not every day that nearly a thousand protesters flooded the station's front lot. I could only hope that Mom would keep her head—and her job.

Rashi blew her whistle before our front ranks got too close to the plant. The crowd slowed for a moment as my original Crew gathered for a quick huddle.

"After we pass that fallen tree, we reach the gate," said Rashi, her eyes fixed on mine. "You ready for this?"

I combed my hair with my fingers and checked my fly. "Ready enough," I said. "Let's move in."

Backed by a cavalry of kids and a troop of protective parents, I marched at the head of the crowd. Behind me, the U.S.A. resumed their latest chant:

"BUD! PLEASE! WORLD WAR G!"

I led our battalion around the sideways canopy of a toppled birch. That's when I got my first good look at the Allister Energy Plant.

"Holy guacamole," Gideon said.

The front gates were shut tight, barricaded by a bright green stage. A giant banner flapped above it all: *GO GREEN!*

The whole display was decorated with green flags and green streamers, with green tables loaded up with green reusable water bottles. They even had a green medical tent like you'd see at some giant, green-themed music festival. It looked like the G-Force had thrown up all over the place. A grim realization came over me at once: the U.S.A. was not taking Allister Energy by surprise. They'd been expecting us. But how? We'd kept our strike plans under tight wraps. Only the original Crew knew we'd be marching on Allister, and none of us would have let that slip.

As our crowd pressed up to the stage, most of the students went on chanting. They weren't disheartened; in fact, some of them looked at this cheesy green display as some kind of victory, judging by the hoots and hollers behind me. Squished at the foot of the stage, I wasn't feeling so optimistic.

"Hey-o!" a godlike voice boomed from the speakers above. "Don't all join the G-Force at once!"

Rashi and Paco groaned in unison. It was Smash Kelly again.

His unstyled mohawk flopped to the side, and his smile looked ten times phonier than it had at the school assembly. "So inspiring, you guys. Seriously. The folks at Allister Energy couldn't be more excited by the awesome work you kids are doing to save the planet today. So give yourselves a round of applause!"

A few of the others clapped until they noticed that the Crew and I had folded our arms.

"Allister Energy built this stage for you. They wanna hear from the inspiring 'green' kids of Carbon Hill. So, I'd like to call on one of your fearless leaders. Mr. Jonah Kaminski!" My name popped through the speakers like an electric shock. "Step right up!"

Rashi gave me the okay.

"We'll be right here." Gideon threw down our secret handshake.

A few stagehands swarmed in. They rushed me to the back of the stage and clipped a small microphone onto my shirt.

I glanced at the sky. The clouds had grown so thick and dark that the tented space backstage felt almost like the night. Nothing had gone according to plan, but planning wasn't my job. I would deliver the speech. I would bring the thunder. I would grab the attention of those news cameras and, somewhere, Senator Bud himself.

The stagehands left. For a moment I was alone, waiting for Smash to finish his story and introduce me already ("—so I'd just chomped into the spiciest fish taco of my life, dude. I'm talkin' *fuego*—"). I took out my silver inhaler. I was going to need it.

Two hands landed on my shoulders. I spun and dropped the inhaler. It was them.

Both inventors stood together, now disguised as hotshot event organizers, each wearing a walkie-talkie and carrying a clipboard. The man bore a scabby slash across his cheek (maybe another run-in with the claws of some prehistoric beast?). They must have taken a few more glitchy spins in that ice-cream time machine of theirs.

I'd been wondering how Allister Energy was so prepared for the U.S.A., but now I had a good guess. The Soda Jerks could've watched today's events unfold and then taken another death-defying trip through time. A few days back would've done it. That way, they could tip off Richard Allister with all the time he needed to assemble this big green distraction.

"You sure put yourselves through a lot," I muttered, eyes on the ground, "just to keep me from stepping onto that stage."

They were positively beaming now. The man's chuckle sounded like a cough.

"We're not trying to keep you off the stage," the woman rasped, a happy glint in her buggy eyes. "Go on ahead. There's nothing you can do to stop *this*."

She revealed a crisp envelope, flaunting it like a billion-dollar bill. How exactly could a single piece of US postage bring these weirdos such deep satisfaction?

"Mr. Jonah!" Smash Kelly called out over the system. "My man!"

"Best of luck, sir," the man croaked while nudging me toward the steps. He smiled. "The future is watching."

I hit the stage, and the U.S.A. gave me a warm Creekside welcome. All of them cheered—everyone except the original Crew, who could read my face well enough to worry. Smash threw his Thor arm around my shoulder and whiplashed me into a side hug. Gideon frowned and mouthed something like *"Are you okay?"* I closed my eyes and nodded.

"A man of few words. I respect that!" Smash slapped me on the back. Apparently, he'd asked me a question while I spaced out in front of the crowd. All week I'd been prepping for a speech, not an onstage conversation.

The old chain reaction picked up from there. Heart rate: high. Palms: wet. Mouth: dry. Lungs: tight. I tried to wish it away, to force the asthma out, rehearsing the opening line: *It was right here, at this very building—*

"Now, before you address the troops"—Smash gave me a schmaltzy wink—"I've got some news you're gonna love."

The Soda Jerk Janitor Clipboard Lady tiptoed out and handed him an envelope, the one she'd brandished backstage. Smash slid out the paper. He dangled it in front of me like he was the host of some game show where the grand prize is folded sheets of paper.

"I happen to be in possession"—Smash paused—"of a letter"—he paused again—"from none other than US Senator Jim Budley!"

Rashi tried to strike up another chant of "BUD! PLEASE! WORLD WAR G!" but it dropped off as soon as she stopped using the megaphone. She looked offended, but I couldn't blame the crowd. All of us were waiting to hear from Bud.

Smash Kelly unfolded the letter, turned to face me, and read:

To Jonah Kaminski,
the United Students of America,
and G-Force,

I was so moved by the events you've held this week. From the climate strike to the Green Kids Forum, our little town of Carbon Hill has captured the hearts of a nation. In light of this week's national tragedy, it's beautiful to see how Americans can come together and heal. We can all agree there is always more we can do to take care of the environment. But here's where I'll respectfully disagree: this is not a war.

Wars have losers. And I've been around long enough to see that, when we come together as Americans, we can WIN—up, down, left, right, and all across the board. So, while I might not be about this "World War G," I am down with the WWG. To me, it stands for "Win-Win Green." Because in America, there are no losers, especially when Americans go green.

So here's what I'd propose: Let's rap. All of us. I'd like to gather the United Students of America, the G-Force, and Allister Energy to hold a "Win-Win Green" rally next Monday, October 31. I have accepted Allister Energy's generous invitation to host our event at their historic Carbon Hill energy plant.

There's no reason we can't protect the planet while also protecting Carbon Hill's biggest job creator at the very same time.

Let's Win-Win Green!

Respectfully,

James Budley
United States Senator

I couldn't speak. Rain hit the crowd with a few pits and pats, but it was nothing compared to the hurricane slamming my chest. I breathed slowly, in through my nose and out through my mouth like they'd taught me in the hospital.

After all the time we'd invested, I couldn't imagine a payoff worse than Senator Bud's letter. A "Win-Win" rally on Allister home turf? This was Richard's dream come true. The longer they kept us compromising, the longer he kept burning his coal.

Right on cue, the sky dumped its rain on the heads of the U.S.A. I pulled Sunny's photo from the pocket of her yellow raincoat. The graves were still there. I'd failed the mission.

"Now, we don't want any of you catching cold today, so grab yourself a G-Force raincoat from the staff." Smash nodded toward the side of the crowd, where a gaggle of Allister employees had lined up with bins of bright green ponchos.

I watched in horror as all our recruits morphed from red, white, and blue to an ocean of G-Force green.

Gideon chucked his poncho back at Smash Kelly. Smash caught it and pulled it over his own shoulders. "Sorry about the rain, boss," he said to me. "I was really jacked to hear your speech."

About a dozen school buses pulled in from the unblocked end of Creekside Road.

"Now, let's get you kids to shelter," Smash announced. "Everybody find your bus number and load up. They'll bring you home safe. And don't mind the security team! They're just here to make sure you all find your seats without getting hurt."

The word "security" snapped me out of my daze. I scanned the crowd, searching for Mom's face. For once, I actually *hoped* she would catch me in the act of activism. I'd never needed her strength more than I did right then, tongue-tied at center stage, unworthy of the yellow raincoat on my back. But Mom was not there.

The Crew got swept away in a riptide of green-uniformed students. Paco scuffled with a bald security guard. Rashi tried to start another chant. Gideon wrapped his guitar in a poncho to protect it from the rain. All the while, the rest of the U.S.A. were turning themselves in without a fight. Each school bus was a yellow sponge, soaking up all the students we'd worked so hard to recruit.

"Come back!" I shouted, but they'd already cut the mic. "Come ba—"

My chest locked up. I felt for my silver inhaler and remembered how I'd fumbled it backstage. Crumpling to my knees, I clawed at my throat.

Smash Kelly dropped beside me, his hands darting uselessly overhead. My vision twinkled. My tongue prickled.

The last thing I saw was a fleet of buses driving off with the future of the world in tow.

STEP 10:

WAKE UP

Where was Gideon? Rashi? Paco? Whatever happened to the Crew? I had been dreaming about those questions for I don't know how long—hours, maybe—when my eyes cracked open and adjusted to the failing light.

There wasn't much to see. Green vinyl all around. A thin, foil blanket and a thin, creaky cot, with me stretched out in between. The rain still fell, drumming on the roof of the medical tent where I'd been snoozing.

The on-duty paramedics must have rushed me here. I held the silver inhaler now, and I halfway remembered them returning it, right before I curled up for my epic nappy-nap. Apparently, my body had decided this was the perfect time to catch up on all the sleep I'd lost last night. How embarrassing.

But why was I the only one here? Why hadn't the Crew stuck with me?

"They're gone, sir." A woman's gravelly voice came through the tent wall. I couldn't hear the other side of her conversation. A phone call. "Only one remains on your property now."

I recognized the woman's voice as one of the inventors'. And I could guess which millionaire coal baron was speaking on the other end.

The woman gave a big, plastic laugh. "Well, let's hope so."

Silently, I slipped off the cot and collected my backpack. No way would the Soda Jerks send me home in peace. They knew that I knew about Sunny. If I didn't get out of that tent, I'd soon wind up sharing a smoggy kennel with Einstein himself.

I panicked, searching for a quiet point of exit. A strip of light shone at the corner of the tent room, where two sheets of green vinyl were Velcroed together. I gently peeled the walls apart, climbed out into the rain, and ran like it was the end of the world.

Judging by the tint of the sky, it was getting late. But I wouldn't go home just yet. After everyone in the Crew had practically left me for dead, I needed to see the one person who hadn't let me down today. The girl who *I'd* let down instead.

I walked forty-five minutes across town to check the Wayback Diner. No Sunny. I visited the Superstore produce aisle. No Sunny. Home Run Sporting Goods? No Sunny. Finally, I backtracked all the way to Creekside Road, past the smoldering school, over the swollen creek and into the waterlogged woods of the Reservoir Park Wilderness Preserve. No Sunny there, either—only the drooping, weepy trees of a forest that would one day claim the lives of Vera, George, and Monday Turner. The grave-site photo in my pocket proved well enough that I had not saved her family. Sunny was long gone from here, but still far from home.

I must've looked like a stray dog, soaked with rain but too scared to take shelter—even though my home waited right in front of me. The porch light was on, along with the living room lamps. A silhouette drifted past the blinds. Mom.

Would she ever look at me the same after she'd seen all the things I'd been hiding? Or would she treat me like the lying, sneaking, birthday-skipping son that I'd become?

Down the street, that perfectly polished work truck sat crooked against the curb, an unthinkably sloppy parking job for a guy as straitlaced as Gideon's stepdad. Mr. Smith must've come home in a hurry. I wondered why and wandered closer, until I found the reason splintered in a soggy heap beside their trash can.

It was Gideon's toy guitar, shattered worse than one of Smash Kelly's skateboards.

The sight knocked the wind right out of me. I'd always known Gideon's boring stepdad didn't understand him, and probably didn't respect him, either. But I never could've imagined that he hated Gideon enough to smash his guitar. And for what? All Gideon did was sing from his heart and bring a little joy to anyone who cared to listen. The thought of someone punishing him for that . . . I couldn't take it.

Shaking, I stormed up to the truck bed, peering into its obsessively organized tool buckets. My eyes went straight to the sledgehammer. The next thing I knew, the hammer was in my hands. I grabbed a can of spray paint, too.

Sunny had left. The Crew had run off. The U.S.A. was dead. It all came down to me, just like that first evening on Martic Pinnacle. But this time I wouldn't arm myself with videos or words or ideas. This time I would do something real.

STEP 11:

BREAK SOMETHING

How to Save the World Without Any Help from Anyone but Yourself:

STEP 1: Borrow a sledgehammer.

STEP 2: Go to Sil's Market for supplies.

STEP 3: Purchase one bandana, two egg cartons, four toilet paper rolls, and three packs of smoke balls on clearance from the Fourth of July.

STEP 4: Ride your electric scooter to the Allister Energy corporate office.

STEP 5: Conceal your identity with the bandana.

STEP 6: Coat the trees and shrubs with streams of toilet paper.

STEP 7: Shatter 24 eggs against the office building's shiny façade.

STEP 8: Spray-paint "FUTURE-KILLERS" as big as possible on the front sidewalk.

STEP 9: Use the hammer to shatter the main door.

STEP 10: Use smoke balls to trigger the sprinkler system, soaking every paper, desk, and computer in the joint.

I'd gotten as far as Step 4 when the SLYSR's battery died. I tossed it to the roadside, took a puff on my inhaler, and hiked it the rest of the way. Step 5 (the bandana) was easy. I tied it on as I walked. Nothing would slow me down tonight—except for the hammer, which was getting a little heavy. I marched as fast as I could. The world had run out of time, after all, and I was the only one who cared enough to save it.

The offices looked empty, unlit. I scanned the lot for cars, for any sign of a witness. All clear. Back to the plan. Step 6 was to toilet-paper the trees, but that didn't work so well in the rain. All the quilted Charmin stuck together in a single soaking roll.

I thought Step 7 would be a satisfying one: throwing two-dozen eggs against the squeaky-clean Allister headquarters. But the eggs had burst all over the inside of my backpack. Turns out sledgehammers and eggshells don't get along. Step 8 (graffiti time) was a non-starter. Like a true tactical genius, I'd grabbed a can of clear enamel Rust-Oleum, which was basically the color of air. So much for tagging Allister Energy as the "FUTURE-KILLERS" they were.

With every foiled step, my anger swelled. I hardened my resolve. The details didn't matter. I still had a hammer, and those front doors were much too pretty. Their reflective glass made me think of the windows at Creekside Middle, which now stood soaked and sooty and utterly destroyed.

I took up the hammer. My heart was hammering already. I tightened my grip and felt its sheer destructive weight. In one day, I had watched my school burn, my movement fail, and my friends disappear. This strike wouldn't be for Mom or Gideon or even the photo in my pocket. This one would be for me.

Just as I lifted the hammer back, the glass door began to flicker with a strobe of red and blue. A small siren chirped in warning, and a blinding floodlight overtook me. I was busted, caught on private property with spray paint, smoke balls, and a demolition tool. I let the hammer thud to the ground.

Turning slowly, I raised my hands. No sudden movements. The car door opened. Shoes clicked onto the lot. Keys jangled.

"I'm sorry," I called out, shakily.

"No," came the voice—the *last* voice in all the world that I expected to hear.

I peered into the lights and spotted a silhouette racing toward me. It met me head-on, nearly tackling me in its arms. It was an online university sweatshirt. It was Coconut Curls hair mist and aloe makeup wipes.

It was Mom.

"Don't you dare be sorry," she said.

STEP 12:

Endure a Cheeto Interrogation

Mom wouldn't let me talk until we'd moved out of the Allister security vehicle and into our own car. But even then, I couldn't find the words.

"Unbelievable," she groaned, pulling out of the unlit employee lot. "Look, Jonah. If you're gonna buy twenty bucks' worth of vandalism supplies, don't buy it all at the same shop." She glared at me with an eyebrow raised. "Sil called."

I covered my face and shook my head. It was an odd moment, realizing all at once how much of a fool I'd been and how little it mattered to Mom.

She reached into the back seat, dropped a party-sized bag of Cheetos onto my lap, and, using her best Good Cop impression, said, "Talk."

So I talked. I told her about the Crew. About door-to-door recruiting and making friends with Gideon all over again. I told her about Rashi and Paco and the 600 students of the U.S.A., and how things had ended as quickly as they'd begun. Mom said nothing. All she did was drive and nod. She remained stone silent when we pulled back up to the house, even as we headed for the front door. Not a word.

When I finished, Mom sat on the stoop and invited me to join her. "Thanks for being honest with me, Jonah." She took my hand. "There's just one part I still don't understand."

"What's that?"

"When exactly did you meet Sunny?"

I snapped my hand away in shock. Sunny was the one part I'd left out. "What? I mean—who?"

"Sunny." Mom shrugged. "Or is it Sunday? I'm not sure. Anyways, that girl from the future."

Hearing Mom utter the name "Sunny" was already enough to leave me speechless. But "girl from the future" knocked me straight into a stream of perfect gibberish: "From the—how the—but Sunny is—"

My mouth kept running on autocomplete until Mom patted my knee. "Dude, I'm your mom. I know things. Although, I haven't known about this one for long."

"Why didn't you say something?" All that time in the car and Mom never once let on that she already knew half of what I'd been telling her.

Mom took my hand back. "Force of habit? You're not the only one with a big-secrets problem."

I laughed. "I doubt you've got secrets bigger than a time-traveling climate activist."

Mom tapped her prosthetic foot. "I never told you why I lost it."

"Iraq," I said, through a mouthful of Cheetos.

"That's *where* I lost it." Mom confiscated the Cheeto bag. "I'm talking about *why*. I never told you the story."

I stopped and thought for a second. Mom was right. Thirteen

years of life, and I'd never once asked how my own mother had lost her foot.

"Then tell me." I braced myself for something big. "What happened in Iraq?"

It was hot. One hundred and ten degrees. Mom had spent her entire tour of duty working as a driver in Mosul, and most of those days had been boring. But not this one. An American executive was coming to town, checking on his company's "investments" in the area. He'd been warned about this visit. Too risky, they'd told him. But this executive was the kind of businessman who would've felt right at home on *PunkWork with Smash Kelly*. He liked risky.

Never mind that risky meant tighter security, which meant closed roads, which meant a more dangerous route for Mom. She never saw it coming. The roadside explosive was powerful enough to flip her vehicle upside down. Miraculously, no one lost their life, but Mom did lose her foot in surgery the next day.

"And here's the part you'll never believe," Mom said. "That executive? Richard Allister. He'd flown in to check on a power plant that Allister Energy had been paid to install."

"You're joking." I doubled over, mouth agape. "Does the company know about this? Do they know their president was responsible for what happened?"

Mom rolled her eyes. "Why else do you think they've been so nice to me?"

Every time I'd shut Mom out over the last month, every question I'd blown off, every lie I'd told, suddenly rose to the surface of my mind.

"All this time," I confessed, "I've been afraid to get you involved with the strike—*specifically* because of Allister Energy. I didn't want them to fire you."

"Fire me? They need me, dude. Besides, it's illegal to fire any employee based on their political work—climate stuff included."

I slapped my forehead, picturing the powerhouse version of Mom I'd seen on the coal mine tour. I could've had that in my corner all this time.

She gave me a sideways hug. "What I'm trying to say, Jonah, is I've given a lot to that company. Too much. And you can bet your behind I'm not letting them take this away from you."

She climbed to her feet and faced the door.

"Take what from me?" I joined her on the doorstep. "Mom, what are you talking about?"

"Your future"—Mom unlocked the bolt and pointed inside—"and your Crew."

STEP 13:

THROW A SURPRISE PARTY

In the movies, whenever a person witnesses something truly unbelievable, like talking-dog unbelievable, they blink extra hard to make sure that the thing is actually real and not just a talking-dog-shaped speck in their eye.

When I stepped into my house on the night of October 28, I blinked extra hard.

Because there I found the Crew, eating birthday cake and watching *Night of the Living Dead* on my TV. In my living room. On my couch. Surrounded by the leftover streamers from my ruined birthday. It wasn't a dream.

It was Rashi and Paco . . . and a girl with a superpowered watch.

Sunny swept in with one enormous hug. Had she always been this tall? I hugged her back. Few people could better understand how I'd be feeling after a day like this.

"So you're still here," I said.

"Never went far. Just a school talent show in Philly. Couldn't pass up seeing a young Pastel performing live in concert," she gloated.

"Who's Pastel?"

Sunny tightened her mouth. Future Fact required. "You don't need to know that yet. But your kids are gonna love him."

I turned to Mom. "So how long have you known about all this?"

Mom checked the time on her phone. "Two hours?"

"And you just believed it?" Two hours was an awfully short amount of time to make sense of the Sunny situation. It had taken me two *days* at least.

"Course I did!" Mom gave me a playful shove. "If all your friends are telling me that one of them is from the future, I'll believe it. The hardest part was believing you made four new friends in less than a month."

"I believe that's what you twenty-first-century folk would call a 'sick burn,'" Sunny observed.

I rolled with it, turning to Rashi. "So you've known about Sunny, too?"

"Since the whole copier thing," Rashi answered while jotting notes in a purple composition book. "You guys basically time-traveled right in front of us, remember?"

I laughed and recalled Operation Ditto from a few weeks back. It felt like a lifetime ago. Just looking at Sunny, I could've sworn she'd grown a couple of inches since then.

"I thought we were pretty discreet about it." Sunny chuckled. "You're up, Paco. Tell him what blew my cover."

"Gideon." Paco cracked a smile. "He accidentally told me during the coal mine tour. Then he tried to un-tell me, but there was no getting that toothpaste back in the tube."

"Classic Gideon." I'd never felt fonder of someone for totally dropping the ball. "Where is he, anyway?"

"Oh, this is a good one." Paco grabbed a popcorn bowl from the coffee table and kicked back on the couch.

"When the rain picked up," Rashi explained, "the security team started ushering us toward the buses. We tried to reach you, but the guards kept us back."

"Then Gideon saw you collapse," Paco said, munching on popcorn. "Talk about superpowers. If you wanna see Gideon hulk out, try messing with Jonah."

I felt myself starting to blush.

"So, while the rest of us were getting carried off to the buses, Gideon was squaring off with security," Rashi said. "Long story short, he kinda wound up punching a guard in the eye."

"Accidentally," Mom added.

I glanced back at her face to check for any sign of damage.

She shook her head. "Can you see Giddy Boy punching this no-filter work of art? They assigned me to headquarters today instead of at the plant. Missed all the action, unfortunately."

"It was pretty satisfying." Paco grinned.

"So, wait a minute," I said, pressing on my temples to jumpstart my brain. "Are you guys telling me that Gideon's in jail?" Out of all the rebels in the U.S.A., I'd never pegged Gideon as the stone-cold outlaw.

"His stepdad bailed him out," Rashi said. "Now he's just grounded for life."

I gave Mom a hard look.

Mom laughed. "Gideon's fine," she said, apparently back to her usual mind-reading ways. She held up her phone as evidence. "Danielle's been texting. Last I heard, Gideon is halfway through a Marvel marathon."

"But Mr. Smith smashed his guitar," I said.

Rashi and Paco shook their heads. "No," they said in perfect sync.

"That was the security guard he clocked in the head," said Paco.

Mom nodded. "Mr. Smith's pretty broken up about it."

"I don't get it." It was hard to imagine Gideon's monotone stepdad feeling much emotion about anything—let alone Gideon. Perhaps I didn't know the guy as well as I thought. "But why is Gideon grounded at all, then?"

"It's called assault and battery, Jonah," Mom said, going legal for the moment. "I'd say a few days of Disney+ is a pretty lenient sentence. His mom's a lot nicer than I am."

Even so, Gideon was out for the count, and it was all because he'd stuck his neck out for me. I turned back to the Crew and narrowed my eyes.

"Listen, guys. In two days, Senator Bud is coming to Carbon Hill." I switched off the TV. "Sure, we lost the U.S.A. And, yeah, maybe we're down one Crew member. But I'm a long way from giving up. Gideon wouldn't quit. So I say we cook up one last plan, one final mission, and we do it in Gideon's honor."

Paco covered his mouth to conceal a grin. Rashi chuckled. "So what you're saying is, we should, like, *dedicate* this operation to Gideon?"

They all looked deviously amused, like I had a sticker on my forehead and nobody wanted to tell me. Not the reaction I'd been expecting. "What's the problem?"

"Sorry," Rashi said. "It's just that Sunny gave, like, the exact same speech a couple hours ago."

She raised the composition book she'd been filling out and showed me the title:

"OPERATION GIDEON"

PLAN D:

DISRUPTION

STEP 1:

HIT RECORD

Saturday, October 29

2 days until Operation Gideon

"My name is Jonah Kaminski. Last time I posted a video, it felt like a darker world. As for today . . ."

I flipped the screen to show the golden sunrise from Martic Pinnacle.

"Even after yesterday's disaster at Creekside Middle, this community's looking a lot more hopeful than it did a few weeks ago." I flipped my phone back to selfie mode. "There's one person I'd like to thank for that hope: United States Senator Jim Budley. Thank you, Senator Bud, for listening to our young voices. We're ready to talk about how we can all 'Win-Win' as Americans. If there's time, I would be honored to show my support onstage at Monday's WWG rally."

I pulled the phone way back to reveal the bright blue *I LIKE BUD* pin on my sweatshirt.

"No matter what happens, we'll still like you."

I gave a firm thumbs-up, hit *upload*, and dropped to the ground in laughter. I'm not sure I'd ever had to bottle up a laugh against such incredible temptation. I wasn't alone, either—the Crew was in stitches all around me.

"I think take five's a keeper," Mom said.

"Yep." Paco edited my title and description before handing the phone back to Mom. "That's the best we're gonna get."

"I blame the script," I said. "You didn't have to make it so hilarious."

Paco gave a big, toothy smile. "The corny thumbs-up was all you."

"It's the perfect trap," Rashi said. "For a politician like Bud, there's no bait more attractive than flattery. If he won't support World War G, we'll trick him into *accidentally* supporting it."

"After that, he'll have to own it." Sunny flipped to a sketch in Rashi's composition book showing a stick version of me and Senator Bud, shaking hands onstage. The crowd before us hoisted signs with *#WorldWarG* and *Bud for Senate*. She grinned. "Sometimes all you need is the perfect photo."

I smiled back at her, thinking of her family. If we could make those graves disappear, Sunny would get a perfect photo of her own.

Paco leaned in and squinted at the drawing. "So, we've gotta get Jonah onstage at Bud's greenwashing rally *and* get the whole audience to play along?"

Everybody nodded.

"Sounds like a long shot," he said.

"You're talking to the long-shot queen." Sunny waved him off. "All things are possible."

Mom's phone rang. She shushed us and answered. "This is Cassandra . . . Of course . . . I couldn't agree more . . . Okay . . . Buh-bye."

She hung up and looked over to the expectant Crew.

"That was Senator Bud's assistant." Mom raised her eyebrows

archly. "We're in."

The Crew exploded. The five of us—Mom included—all hopped around on Martic Pinnacle like we'd just won the Powerball. Sunny gave Mom her signature hug.

"Alright." Rashi set her watch. "We have a ton to do and forty-eight hours to do it."

She rattled off tasks for me, Mom, and Paco. Everyone had a role, all except for one of us.

"It's a beautiful plan . . ." Sunny's voice trailed off as her eyes shifted away. "Too bad I won't be there to see it."

"What are you talking about?" I asked.

"It's too risky now," she said, surely thinking of those two relentless grown-ups from the future. "They'll see me."

"No, they won't," I said, a tiny sunrise glowing inside my chest. I finally understood the feeling that made Sunny bow her head and place her trust in something bigger than herself. I had tried and failed to save the world alone so many times already. But this time it wasn't gonna be Jonah who saved the world; it was gonna be *us*. All of us.

"You'll be there. But you won't be seen." I gripped the same American flag Sunny had planted on the night she'd saved my life. "You got here as a pink astronaut, Sunny, and that's exactly how you're going home."

STEP 2:

KEEP A STRAIGHT FACE

Monday, October 31

26 minutes until Operation Gideon

The Monday sun crept up over smokestacks. It seemed unusually bright, warm for October 31. Mom, Sunny, and I climbed out of our run-down Prius and made our way past a legion of cable news trucks. It was time for Senator Bud's "Win-Win Green" rally. Mom looked unusually fancy in her U.S.A.-colored sundress. Sunny and I had dressed up for Halloween, me as a disappointingly G-rated zombie (thanks, Mom) and Sunny as a pink astronaut from the future. Turns out Halloween is always the perfect day for a time-traveler to hide her face.

In the shadow of the plant, I found the United Students of America, nearly a hundred of them, mingled in with the dozens of Senator Bud fans who had come for the forum. Rashi's handmade *I LIKE BUD* signs were everywhere, held high by a host of skeletons and superheroes and DJs. Chewbagoats, too. We had about seven of those.

In less than half an hour, I would take the stage with Senator Bud and unleash our master plan: Operation Gideon. With so many cameras rolling, Senator Bud would have no choice but to play along.

If Sunny's logic held up, this action could make Senator Bud change the world *just enough* to keep global temperatures down *just enough* to reduce global rainfall *just enough* to keep that dam from breaking in 2099. Only three things could possibly threaten our success: the Soda Jerks, the Allisters, and any of Richard's G-Force cronies.

Unfortunately, Threat #1 had parked their battered ice-cream truck right next to the crowd of locals. The Soda Jerks stood guard beside it. Their white suits and paper hats were ragged and stained, looking years older than when I'd first spotted them outside of Gideon's yard. The short mustached guy looked more like a zombie than I did. The tall woman didn't look much better, clutching her gas pump–looking contraption like the deadly weapon it was. One shot from that device would send Sunny or me or even Mom straight into the toxic future those Jerks had been fighting so hard to keep in place.

Sunny gave my arm a squeeze. "Trust," she murmured through the pink helmet. "They won't spot us. Just stay calm."

We strolled right past them for the building's entrance. I even managed a realistic enough smile. The Soda Jerks were so busy searching the rowdy throng that they searched right past us. So many kids and so many wrists, but not a wristwatch in sight. Their thief could be anywhere.

I winked at the students of the undercover U.S.A., the ones that Paco and Rashi had rounded up over the past forty-eight hours. Many of them winked right back. Sunny raised a fist and chanted "I LIKE BUD! I LIKE BUD!" until the crowd joined in. Even the old folks, the actual fans of Senator Bud, got in on the action.

"I LIKE BUD! I LIKE BUD! I! LIKE! BUD!"

A hand gripped my shoulder from behind.

"Alexander Hamilton," a voice crooned behind me.

I whipped around to find Rashi dressed like a man from the 1700s—royal blue coat, rows of brass buttons, and a white ruffled shirt. "My name is Alexander Hamilton," she sang on, somewhat in tune while unsheathing a plastic sword.

"Nerd alert," Paco said. He'd dressed up, too, but not for Halloween. Just a white button-down with a pair of glasses I'd never seen him wear before. "Let me guess." He inspected my gray hoodie and low-key zombie makeup. "Rocky Balboa, right?"

I shot Mom a glare. She'd made me go easy on the gore.

Mom folded her arms. "No apologies. I know you need to cover for Sunny, but I am not letting you go up there looking like a corpse."

"But a zombie *is* a corpse, Mom." I turned to Paco. "Didn't we all agree to come in costume?"

"I did!" Paco pointed to his glasses, then undid a couple buttons to show us the Superman tee underneath. "I'm Clark Kent."

"Hidden superpowers." I recalled all the times we'd pushed Paco to show the world his voice. "Very poetic."

"Any word from Gideon?" Paco asked.

"I talked to Danielle this morning," Mom answered. "He's binge-watching *Star Wars* today. Still perma-grounded."

A security envoy rushed in from the side of the building and swarmed around the Crew. I almost panicked and made a run for it, but Mom threw an arm out to block my escape.

"Cass," the biggest guy said. "We're short. Any chance you could help out until we find a replacement?"

Mom gestured at the star-spangled sundress she'd bought just for the occasion. "Looking like this?"

"It's the monitor room. Nobody'll see you." He handed Mom a security badge. "Thirty minutes max."

Mom checked the time. "I'll give you twenty." She turned to Sunny and me. "We're good?"

"Golden." As long as I had the pink astronaut at my side, I was ready to take on the world.

Mom followed the envoy, but one of the guards hung back. "I'm supposed to walk you in," he grumbled to me, as if this wasn't his job.

"I'll see you on the other side," Rashi said.

The guard escorted me toward the building—along with Sunny, who'd stuck with me.

He paused, apparently bothered by the pink astronaut tagging along. "You wanna explain this?"

"Oh, well, she's um—ha, she's my—" Something told me Best Future-Friend wouldn't be the most productive answer.

"Sister," Sunny interjected through her mirrored helmet.

The guy peered over his sunglasses for a second, and I noticed a bruise around his eye. Compliments of Gideon, I assumed.

"Tough week?" Sunny asked through the visor.

The guy shrugged. "Whatever, kid. They don't pay me enough."

STEP 3:

SPEAK OF THE DEVIL

16 minutes until Operation Gideon

The security guy left us at the VIP room door. The pink astronaut and I could finally relax—at least for a few minutes. Since we'd passed the Soda Jerks without a hitch, all we had to do was chill out on the other side of that door until it was time to take the stage with Senator Bud.

"Hiya, fakers," Bacon said as we entered the room.

I gagged on the smell of body spray and gawked at the sight of a fully loaded G-Force, minus Lindsay Allister. Of course they were VIPs. This was Allister territory.

"Nice to smell ya," Sunny quipped through her helmet.

Bacon let out a huge mock-laugh, which seemed to confuse the rest of the G-Force. One of them laughed reflexively, too, until somebody elbowed him for it.

Bacon looked me up and down. "An Eagles fan," he said, observing my white, gray, and green face paint. "Nice costume."

"I'm a zombie," I muttered back, but Bacon wasn't listening.

"Who's your secret girlfriend?" He leered at his own reflection in Sunny's tinted visor.

"You don't need to know my name," she said.

Bacon laughed again. "But I *want* to know. Pretty please." He clapped for a pass, and the shortest G-Force member swiped Sunny's backpack—Sunny's *mother's* backpack, the only scrap of Sunny's family to survive the floodwaters in 2099. The smirking boy tossed it straight into Bacon's hands.

In that moment, I discovered yet another thing Gideon and I have in common: picking on me is one thing, but pick on my friends and it's so long, Bruce Banner, hello, Hulk.

I charged, but another G-Force member intercepted and knocked me onto my butt. The eighth grader's meaty hands clutched my shoulders to keep me down.

"Let's see." Bacon unzipped the bag's front pocket. He pulled out Sunny's precious photo and made a show of squinting at the picture. "What kinda name is 'Monday'?"

I couldn't take it. From my spot on the ground at his knees, I threw out my hands and gave Bacon's green gym shorts a swift downward tug. They dropped all the way to his Air Force 1s. This was the first and last time I ever saw G-Force-branded underwear.

Bacon dove for his ankles and toppled over along the way. To assist their fearless leader, the entire G-Force dropped everything—including me. I snatched the picture back and shoved it into my pocket. Sunny grabbed her backpack, and the two of us raced for the door.

"APOLOGIZE!" Bacon's voice cracked, reverberating through the concrete hallway. "Come back here and APOLOGIZE!"

We fled the sound of Bacon's fury, hoping to find our way to the building's main atrium and the stage I'd have to occupy in ten minutes' time.

I took us down a long hallway that led to a bright yellow industrial door. Promising. But the door was locked. We could hear the G-Force scuffing the floors—closer now. They were catching up.

"In here." Sunny tugged me through a smaller door, the only other choice in that narrow hallway. Some kind of supply closet, maybe? It reeked of cigarettes, but at least it was dark. Sunny popped off her space helmet, and together we listened. Feet shuffled and squeaked outside the closet, hurrying toward the other door at the end of the hall. A fist drummed against it.

"Fakers! You can't lock yourselves out there forever!" Bacon must have assumed that we'd made it through. We heard the gong-strike of his foot against that heavy-duty door and then his babyish grunts. "Ow-ow-ow-ow. My toe!"

Sunny struggled to contain her laughter. I struggled to keep from coughing as my lungs burned with the rancid closet air.

When the hallway outside went quiet, I took a good puff from my inhaler, and Sunny said, "Let's go."

The two of us moved for the closet door—only to be tugged straight back by each of our collars.

"That kid's a joke," a thin voice scraped behind us, "but at least he respects his elders."

I spun to find Richard Allister, his face lit by the embers of a glowing cigarette. For reasons I didn't care to know, the fossil fuel millionaire had been chain-smoking in the shadows of this dank supply closet, which looked quite a bit larger than I'd guessed before my eyes had time to adjust.

"I was just thinking of you two." Richard blew out a long stream of smoke. He pointed to a couple of chairs barely illuminated by the crack under the door. "Have a seat."

We obeyed. It's one thing to defy adults in general, but when you're face-to-face with Richard Allister in full-blown boss-battle mode? Different story.

Sunny and I sat on the rusty metal chairs in front of a rusty metal desk, Sunny's pink helmet resting neatly on her lap. Allister pulled a string, and a single hanging bulb flickered to life. This was no closet, I realized. It was an office. An old, unkempt office now packed with cleaning supplies and tools.

The man pointed at my gray hoodie with his cigarette. "That kid from *E.T.*, right? I get the reference."

"I'm. A. Zombie," I informed him through gritted teeth.

"I. Don't. Care." When he got angry, Richard's thin, gravelly voice sounded like a bucketful of coals grinding together. He sat behind the desk and took another puff. "You'll never believe it, but this room used to be my office."

With his perfectly pressed suit, his gold watch, and his trim red beard, Richard Allister looked entirely out of place among the mop buckets and paper towels.

"My old man offered me the company right out of college." His putrid smoke snaked around us. "But I wouldn't let him retire until I'd worked my way from the bottom up. I started right down here, literally in the basement, and it took me only two years to reach the company's highest-ranking executive title. I *earned* it."

"Yeah," Sunny grumbled, rolling her eyes so hard you could almost hear them. "Your daddy had *nothing* to do with it, I'm sure."

Richard smooshed his cigarette into an old coffee mug. "I'm going to show you something."

He stood up, dug into his pocket, and pulled out a rock. The shriveled black stone was practically a pebble, but Richard Allister displayed it between his thumb and forefinger as if appraising some precious gem.

"Do you know what this is?" he wheezed.

"A turd," I said.

He pretended not to hear me. "It's the first shard of anthracite coal ever found in this part of Pennsylvania. The man who found it was my great-great-great-grandfather. He dug it up. Bought the land. Built an empire." He held the coal closer and closer to my face as he spoke. "This is the very source of Carbon Hill. Jobs, homes, prosperity—all of it grew up from this tiny seed."

"I wouldn't call it a seed." Sunny looked as indignant as I'd ever seen her. "More like a weapon of mass destruction."

Richard closed a fist over the shard and shoved it back into his pocket. "Tell me: What if I woke up one day and decided that *I* wanted to go on strike? Any idea what would happen?" He shrugged with an air of thinly suppressed rage. "No more jobs. No more money. No more power when you flip on the switch. I keep the *planet* running, boys and girls. Is it getting a little warmer? Maybe. A few more storms? Fine. That's what the prosperity is for. If things get bad, you can stay inside and run the AC, and it's all because you *know* that Allister Energy will keep the power on. Men like me are the life force of this world, and look at the thanks we get!"

He lit another cigarette and began strutting in circles around the tiny office.

"You know," Sunny said, "I'm not from around here. But the 'life force' I believe in says that the *meek* shall inherit the earth."

At this, Richard Allister laughed the biggest, fakest, emptiest laugh in the history of the human race.

"The meek?" He flicked his cigarette onto the floor. "This earth belongs to the men who know what's theirs. The *meek* are the ones who get locked in a closet at five minutes till showtime."

With that, Richard Allister burst into the hallway and slammed the closet door behind him.

STEP 4:

PLOT YOUR ESCAPE

5 minutes until Operation Gideon

I leapt for the door. Locked. We'd been trapped by that fake-skating wannabe celebrity.

"Only five minutes to go." Sunny checked her watch. "He was stalling you!"

Desperate, we scoured every inch of the room for a key, a vent—any chance of escape. We found nothing.

I snapped my fingers: an idea. "Your watch. Just pop us back a few minutes, before Richard was here."

Sunny shook her head. "We don't know when that was. Plus, we could bump into our past selves. Not to mention the Jerks." She pounded on the door. Kicked it. Nothing.

She dropped back into a chair and pulled off her pink glasses. I melted back onto the chair beside her, hyperventilating into my hands. How could I come so close just to get locked out again?

"Breathe, Jonah." Sunny put a hand on my back. "We'll find a way out."

"It's not just that," I told her. "He knows. Richard Allister knows *exactly* what he's doing to the world." The secondhand smoke took over my lungs. My airway tightened.

"I told you as much," Sunny said. "On the very first day we met. The greed is so much worse than you think. The history books tell us that people like Richard knew what was happening to the world long before you were born." She sighed, looking more exhausted than angry. "Richard Allister believes the science with all his heart. He knows what's happening. But a 'life force' guy like Richard can't even look at the end of the world without seeing another way to get rich."

I pulled out my inhaler. "So that's it, then? Allister Energy will always be around."

Sunny unfastened the chunky gunmetal timepiece from her wrist. "Let's just leave it at this." She flipped over the device and showed me the logo etched onto its back: *Allister Defense.*

"Once Allister Energy is done melting the earth," Sunny said, "they'll be good and ready to sell us the lifeboats. And the walls. And the weapons."

"That's who you stole from?" I asked.

Sunny nodded.

"And the Soda Jerks?"

"Employed by the Allister family business."

I buried my face in my hands. The Allister family business gave us the apocalypse. The Allister family business gave us the Soda Jerks. The Allister family business gave us the timepiece itself.

"Why does everything have to come back to the Allisters?" I grumbled into my palms.

The words caught me off guard just as they bounced back. *The Allisters.* Plural. There was more to the Allisters than Richard.

There was Lindsay.

A wave of memories came flooding back to me, a dozen awkward moments I'd picked up with my super-sensitive awkwardness detector. I remembered Lindsay's anger toward Bacon when he'd taunted me in the rain. I remembered the heartbroken look she'd carried onstage at the assembly, when they'd forced her to put on a G-Force uniform. And most of all, I remembered the strange words she'd uttered from the auditorium stage:

"I could've done so much more. Not just open a door for you."

A door. Could it be that we'd already tipped Lindsay off but didn't know it yet? Perhaps, four days earlier, I'd been witnessing the results of a time-jump that we hadn't yet taken.

"Future Fact!" I shouted. "I wanna use a Future Fact."

Sunny clapped her hands to speed me along. "About what?"

"Lindsay Allister! Why were you always so sure that she was 'okay'? What was it about Lindsay's future that you wouldn't tell me?"

Sunny's eyes flashed, like she'd just solved the entire riddle on her own. She pulled the Lesson Planner from her rugged pink backpack to double-check before answering. "Future Fact #4: About ten years from now, Lindsay will become one of the world's most famous climate activists."

"Then why in the world didn't you recruit her?" I asked.

Sunny twisted her mouth. "I considered it. But all the bullying you got from her friends . . . it made me think she wasn't ready."

"Well, I think she's ready after all," I said, the pieces still arranging themselves in my head. "Sunny, what happens if we go back a few weeks?"

She shrugged. "If we're lucky, this door's unlocked. But if we try to change anything about those days, it might disrupt the timeline, remix the present, even compromise the mission."

I nodded impatiently. "Thought you might say that. But what if we go back and change just one thing, one tiny thing that won't make a difference until today?"

"I suppose it's possible."

"Then set your watch for Monday, September twenty-sixth."

"The first day of the teachers' strike?" Sunny asked.

"Not just the strike," I said. "The day we recruited Lindsay Allister."

STEP 5:

Monday, September 26

35 days until Operation Gideon

Lucky for my lungs, the supply closet air was 100 percent smoke-free on the morning of September 26. Luckily for Operation Gideon, the door was unlocked.

Sunny and I slipped out of the plant and reached the Murder House well before past-Lindsay and her friends did. The two of us crouched on the porch behind an abandoned sofa. Soon, the gang assembled around the stoop, too absorbed in themselves to catch us spying from the shadows nearby. Some of them, Bacon especially, were mimicking the teachers' chant in baby voices. Lindsay stayed quiet. I watched as past-Me wandered toward the school, staring awkwardly at the picketing teachers.

"BETTER FUNDING! FAIR PAY! SHOULD'VE HAD 'EM YESTERDAY!"

"Hey, Jonah!" Past-Lindsay called to my past-Me, who looked in every possible direction before looking at Lindsay and snailing his way across the street. "I saw your video."

The scene felt different now than it had when I'd lived it the first time. How had I missed this? Lindsay was not making fun of me. For all I knew, she liked the video. It was Bacon who had interrupted with his relentless teasing.

We watched as past-Me called him a phone head and stomped away. Now that was one moment I'd rather not relive.

"Phone head," Sunny snickered. "The clapback king."

After past-Me was gone, Bacon went on dominating the conversation. Lindsay stayed glued to her phone, like she was just waiting for the gang to leave. A minute later, the eighth graders started hitting her up for money.

"Come on, Lindsay," Bacon whined. "We can't chill at the mall without buying anything. They'll kick us out."

Lindsay rolled her eyes, unsnapped a pocket on the back of her phone case, and forked over a small wad of bills. The gang went wild with appreciation. Girls hugged her. Boys clapped.

Seconds later, they were gone.

Lindsay tucked her phone away and stared at the striking teachers across the road. It was a lonely sight, the way she hunched on the stoop of the Murder House. For years, I'd mistaken that cluster of hangers-on as her friends. But clearly they only cared about Lindsay Allister the money machine, not Lindsay Allister the human being.

"Hey, Lindsay," I stepped into view at the edge of the porch. Sunny followed. "Can we talk?"

"Um. Sure?" Lindsay seemed puzzled to see us popping up out of nowhere, but not exactly suspicious.

"We're about to ask you the weirdest favor of all time," I began. "So . . . buckle up, or whatever."

"First things first." Sunny joined her on the stoop. "Last summer, while your dad was shooting his secret *PunkWork* episode, your grandparents took you scuba diving along the Great Barrier Reef."

Lindsay furrowed her brow. Nobody was supposed to know about her dad's TV disaster. (This was weeks before Sunny would stream it onto every phone in school.)

Sunny continued, "The scuba instructor told you how climate change was causing the oceans to acidify, which was eating away at the reef. She told you that the whole thing might be gone by the time you're as old as your dad."

Lindsay's eyes widened. "Is this a prank?"

"Later that day, while you swam around that dying reef, you got to thinking about how much your family's wealth was costing the world. And right there, deep underwater off the coast of Queensland, you made a decision."

Lindsay sat back, tears forming at the rims of her eyes. "You can't—It's not—How could you possibly know that?"

Sunny was smiling. "Why don't you tell Jonah what that decision was."

"I—" Lindsay looked to me. "I swore I'd spend my life undoing all the destruction my family's caused." She covered her face. "But how could you know all that? I've never told anybody."

Sunny put an arm around her. "Because you're *the* Lindsay Allister. It's all in your autobiography."

Sunny knew Lindsay's story inside and out. But that story was about to change—if only a little. We were going to give the great Lindsay Allister an early start, and all she had to do was open a door.

I sat down on Lindsay's left. "I know firsthand how weird this is gonna sound. But we're from the future, Lindsay. And we need you."

STEP 6:

Don't Be Late

Monday, October 31

3 minutes until Operation Gideon

We'd hurried back to the plant, back to the basement exit, back to the closet, and back to the morning of October 31. Now my ears popped, and the lights came up. Richard Allister's secondhand smoke rushed back into my nostrils. We were right back where we'd left off, trapped in a toxic closet with all of Operation Gideon depending on us.

BAM!

The locked door shook with a smashing blow. Then another. Something was beating furiously against it from the hallway side.

I gripped my inhaler, just in case the Soda Jerks were here to drag me off to their smog-ridden 2100. The door gave way, bursting open in a swirl of dust and cigarette smoke.

Through the haze of her father's pollution, I watched the long-haired figure of Lindsay Allister emerge triumphant through the open doorway.

"Am I late?" she asked between panting breaths. A long-handled sledgehammer hung from her grip.

Sunny shook her head with a big, proud grin. "You came right on time."

"Ever heard of a key?" I said between coughs.

"I had one job." Lindsay raised the hammer in a Mighty Thor power pose. "Might as well do it in style."

Lindsay ditched the hammer and led us at Olympic speed through a concrete maze of old hallways and stairs. "Grandpa let me play around in here when I was little," she panted. "These were offices like a million years ago, but most of them are empty now. Take a left up here."

We followed her up a short flight of steps and landed in a bank of ancient-looking elevator doors. Lindsay slapped a button, and we waited for the next ride up. "This'll get us near the stage."

Her phone blasted out a cluster of notifications. She smiled at the screen. "I assume you've been following the news?"

"I don't have a phone," I said, catching my breath.

"It's never exactly *news* to me," Sunny added.

Lindsay showed us her screen. "This is Philly." The Rocky stairs were mobbed with students in red, white, and blue. "Harrisburg." She swiped to a photo of the state capitol packed with students, then kept on swiping: "Pittsburgh, Bethlehem, Scranton, Lancaster, York, Erie—there are like twenty strikes across the state of Pennsylvania. They're all asking Bud for World War G."

"Twenty new chapters of the U.S.A.," I said. "But how?"

Then I spotted the grin on Sunny's face. Only one person in the world could possibly assemble so many people in such an impossibly short time.

"This was you?!" Lindsay held back a chuckle. "Everyone upstairs is in cardiac arrest right now, especially Bud, from what I hear."

I gaped at Sunny. "When did you manage to do all this?"

"Friday," Sunny said. "But you and the U.S.A. did more to recruit those schools than I ever could. All those stories you collected, Jonah, the ones that Creekside kids told in front of the news cameras—that's what inspired these recruits all over the state. I just gave them a little push."

"*Sunny.*" I wasn't about to take humility for an answer. "You organized twenty different schools across Pennsylvania in just one day?"

She shrugged and pointed to the timepiece. "One day. On loop. I might be fourteen now, by the way. Not entirely sure."

I used my hand to compare heights. She really had grown a few inches.

Ding.

An elevator had finally landed. The rusty doors slid open—revealing a pair of white, sooty uniforms, each with a crinkled paper hat.

The Soda Jerks.

I backed up slowly and clenched my fists. My heart raced. Then I saw the truth in their sweaty, nervous faces. They were the scared ones.

"Jerks," I said.

"Caterers, actually," the tall woman croaked. Under the fluorescent elevator light, they both looked older, grayer, more worn out. A side effect, I assumed, of one too many trips in their good-for-nothing time machine.

"You make a good vampire." The exhausted man sneered at my costume.

"I'm. A. *Zombie!*" I shoved him back into his elevator. The man pushed me back, charging his way out and knocking me against the concrete wall. In my pocket, something cracked on impact.

I raged against the man like I was Gideon with friends on the line, but Sunny dragged me away. We fell backward, cornered now, with the Soda Jerks looming above us, hungrily eyeing Sunny's timepiece, the object they'd risked everything to reclaim. Lindsay tried to pull them away while holding the elevator, but the Jerks wouldn't budge.

"It was a fatal mistake, you know," the woman said. "We would never have found you here if you hadn't taken that last jump. But you slummers just had to keep *thieving* your way through history."

They both dove for Sunny's wrist. I fought to pry them back, and Sunny flailed between them, giving her all to fight them off.

"The only thing I took," Sunny grunted, kicking them back just long enough to unfasten the timepiece, "was a future that belongs to all of us."

The man snorted. "That *future*"—he reached out to collect his prize—"is the property of Allister Defense."

Sunny snapped it back and grinned. "Then I suppose this belongs to her!"

She flung the watch—hard—over the tall woman's shoulder, and it slapped straight into the raised hand of Lindsay Allister.

"Meet me upstairs!" Sunny shouted as Lindsay sprinted off into the subterranean labyrinth of hallways beneath the Allister Energy Plant. Both Soda Jerks took off behind her, leaving Sunny and me free. Those so-called inventors had eyes only for the timepiece, that precious device they could never have completed without hiring some underpaid math teacher in the 2090s. To them, the watch was theirs and theirs alone.

"Come on." Sunny dragged me into the old elevator and slapped the ground floor button.

I hesitated. "Don't you need that watch to get home?"

"Sure do." Sunny folded her arms with confidence as the door slid shut. "But I'll bet Lindsay knows these halls better than the original architects did. She'll lose the Jerks in no time."

"But what if she can't?"

"It's called trust." Sunny's smile shone with a faith so absolute that I couldn't help but smile, too. "Don't forget, Jonah: saving the world is a team sport."

STEP 7:

TAKE THE STAGE

Monday, October 31

Operation Gideon

The moment the elevator doors slid open, I could hear the amplified voice of Senator Bud ringing through the cavernous hall: *"I'd like to welcome Mr. Jonah Kaminski!"*

I had an appointment with history, and I was late.

"Jonah?" Bud's voice reverberated back into the elevator bank.

Before I could take off, Sunny grabbed me by the arm and handed me her photo. "Go show them who really owns the future."

The voice of Senator Bud resounded awkwardly from the stage: *"Jonah couldn't make it?"*

"Quick!" Sunny sent me hurtling out into the meeting hall.

Even though my chest was burning, I ran like the future of the world depended on it, stumbling up to the side of the stage. There I saw Richard Allister, who spat out his tea and broke into a coughing fit, and Bacon, who reclined on a metal folding chair with one foot on ice. Smash Kelly was there, too, looking more exhausted than ever. He didn't even look up from his phone as I jogged up the steps.

At long last, I overtook the stage.

When I met the searing lights, a hundred young voices broke

into cheers. It was the undercover U.S.A., still disguised as a mob of Senator Bud superfans. It looked like every TV channel in the world had a camera posted in the crowd.

My lungs tightened. For the first time ever, I beheld Senator Bud in the flesh. He was old, much older than I'd expected. And I don't mean retirement-old. More like end-of-life-Steve-Rogers-old. Skeleton-old. His green flannel looked a size too big, and his green hard hat looked a size too small.

"The man of the hour!" Bud flashed a bleach-white smile and threw me a handshake as I approached center stage. "I hear this boy's got something to say."

I pulled Paco's speech from my hoodie pocket and spread it over the podium. Sunny's grave-site photo went right beside it, a reminder that her entire family depended on what I did right here and right now.

My lungs tightened up a little more.

A young voice from the crowd screamed, "WE LOVE YOU, BUD!"

Everyone broke into a rousing chant of "I LIKE BUD!"

The senator stepped away from the podium and whispered into my ear. "It's all yours now, kiddo. Just keep things positive, okay?"

He slapped me on the back as I leaned up to the mic. My hands were sweating through Paco's speech. I had to start reading.

The speech began with a touch of shameless flattery: "I want to thank Allister Energy for letting us do this here today, and the G-Force for showing us there's more than one way to change the world." Breathe. "And, of course, I would like to thank Senator Bud for bringing our divided community"—I stopped for another wheezing breath—"together."

I could still taste the secondhand smoke. My lungs were on fire. I glanced at Sunny's grave-site photo, then scanned the crowd for Mom's reassuring face. But she wasn't there. She must've been stuck subbing at the monitor room.

"Today," I resumed through labored breaths, "as we remember . . . the ruins . . . of our own beloved school . . . not many of us feel included"—I sucked up a little more air—"in your so-called nation of winners."

Bud's white grin receded. My face was hot. The Jonah Kaminski Nerve-Machine rolled into motion, that same old feedback loop of anxiety and asthma. It used to be fear that turned the ignition. But this was different. I'd never felt braver. The heart rate, the dry mouth, the sweat—this time the whole chain reaction seemed to be starting in my lungs. A quick puff could shut it down. I dug one hand into my pocket, feeling for the silver inhaler, gasping for the sweet release of oxygen it promised. I pulled it out, and my stomach dropped.

The same inhaler Sunny had used to save my life on Martic Pinnacle was now a small pile of silver shards. I suddenly remembered the Soda Jerk shoving me away from the elevator. The crunch in my pocket when I hit that wall of concrete.

Time slowed to a crawl.

I could see it all in front of me now, the entire future of the world. Every Sunday, Monday, Vera, and George Turner of every generation to come—all of them depended on these next few minutes. On me. My asthma would take over if I didn't slow down, but you can't take a breather when history's on the line.

My thoughts rewound to something Sunny had told me after

our first day together: "*We need you to save the world, Jonah.*" But that wasn't all she said. "*. . . you'll never be able to do it alone.*"

I'd found the answer. The only way I could buy myself enough time to breathe.

"I can't do this. Not without my friends." I took a deep breath. "Sunday Turner . . . come on up."

A pink astronaut took the stage, and the crowd applauded my futuristic friend for what felt like a solid minute. I breathed slowly, mindfully, just like the nurses had taught me after my first attack. I still wasn't ready for the crowd to settle, so I bought myself another minute by calling up another friend.

"Our campaign manager," I said. "Rashi Kapoor."

Hamilton-Rashi, the American Revolutionary herself, strode onstage to the roaring applause of the U.S.A. After that, I called up 'Paco' Francisco Mercado Baez, the Superman logo showing faintly through his Clark Kent dress shirt. With him came a few more precious seconds of breathing time.

Sunny pulled the whole Crew into a tight group hug, right beside Senator Bud, who looked like he had no clue what to do with himself.

"My inhaler broke," I whispered into the huddle. My chest had settled, but not completely.

"He needs to breathe," Sunny said. "Someone's gotta step up."

"I'll do it." To my disbelief and the shock of a slack-jawed Crew, it was Paco who volunteered.

He took a step back from the huddle and unbuttoned his white shirt, revealing the Superman tee underneath.

"Hidden superpowers," Rashi marveled as Paco tossed her the button-down. He approached the mic and took off his plastic glasses. The rest of us stood arm in arm behind him.

Paco picked up the speech he'd written and balled it up. He squared his shoulders and leaned in toward the mic.

"My name is Francisco Mercado Baez," he began, "but my friends call me Paco. I was born on an island that feels very far away from here, but it's not. The world is not so big. Just look at us." He gestured back to the Crew. "Our families are from Carbon Hill, Puerto Rico, New Delhi. We are superheroes, revolutionaries, and astronauts."

I looked at Sunny, who smiled back in her glitter-pink suit.

"Every one of us is different. But if there's one thing that brings us together, one thing that forces us to make friends, it's that we all share the same little world. The same future. We only get one, so we have no choice but to fight for it." Paco surveyed the crowd. "Who stood with us last week?"

Every costumed hand went up.

"If you marched with the U.S.A., if you took a stand with us at the ruins of Creekside Middle, I'd like you to stand with us now. Come on up."

A few grown-up gasps shot through the crowd. Richard Allister scream-whispered from stage right. Security rushed in front of the steps, but the senator waved them down when he spotted all the *I LIKE BUD* signs those kids were waving.

"Oh, let 'em on up here!" Bud chuckled with a wink. "I like you guys, too."

Student by student, the stage filled with Chewbagoats and Avengers and DJs. Perhaps the best costume of all was the "student"-activist who'd come disguised as a teacher—a couple of kids had forced Mr. Dan to join them onstage.

Last of all, a panting, sweaty kid arrived onstage and shoved her way toward me and Sunny. With all that red hair hidden under an *I LIKE BUD* ballcap, it was easy to miss Lindsay Allister in the ranks of the U.S.A. Sunny offered her wrist, and Lindsay fastened the watch right where it belonged. She'd brought it back, and all without a Soda Jerk in sight.

My lungs had powered up to a full charge. I gave Paco a nod, and he pulled me over to the podium.

"Bring it home," he said. "Just pretend it's YouTube."

I grinned all the way to the mic.

"When Senator Bud talks about 'winning' the future together," I began. "He's not wrong. We'll never save the future alone. We can do it as one united country. But not just united for the fun of it. Not just united to win campaigns. Let's unite and actually *do* something for a change. Not in fifty years. Not in thirty. But in *ten* years we can cut our emissions in half."

Behind me came the sound of a hundred hands tearing the *I LIKE BUD* wrapping paper off their poster board signs. Just as Rashi had planned, the U.S.A. now uncovered its hidden message. Half of the signs shouted *TEN YEARS TO TURN THE TIDE*. The other half said *#WorldWarG*. Every phone in the crowd popped up to capture the moment. A stage once flooded with young Bud supporters had blossomed into the United Students of America.

I turned to face Senator Bud and his now-wilted expression.

"You can call it 'saving the future' or 'Win-Win Green' or whatever you like," I said, "but you know what we're asking for. And you know what we call it."

Our recruits picked up the chant from there:

"WORLD WAR G! WORLD WAR G! WORLD WAR G!"

Everything had gone according to plan. Better, in fact. We'd put our union on display and put this grown-up on the spot. Any second now, Senator Bud would join his voice with the U.S.A. and demand a war-sized effort to fight the climate apocalypse. If he did, it just might be enough to save Sunny's whole future.

Bud smiled. Then frowned. Then smiled again. The poor guy looked like he had blown a gasket.

Rough hands shoved me aside. Richard Allister covered up the microphone to hide his voice from the crowd. "Bud, you let me pull these kids off my stage, or I'll have to kick your senator butt all the way across it."

The senator flashed his winning smile and leaned away from the podium. "Make it quick," he said through his teeth.

The audience gasped. Unfortunately for Senator Bud, Richard Allister's wiry hand may not have been the best way to muffle a mic.

Allister whistled to his security team, and a dozen brutes rushed onto the stage. Rashi threw up a peace sign, and the U.S.A. dropped into a sitting position. Allister security would have to carry us away one student at a time. Nobody fought back, but we didn't stop asking for "WORLD WAR G! WORLD WAR G! WORLD WAR G!"

I checked Sunny's photo. Still no change. What was it going to take?

A young lady with a campaign pin skittered across the stage and whispered something to the senator. His face went pale before he lurched back up to the hot mic. The world had heard what he'd said to Richard Allister, and he was just now finding out.

"C'mon, folks!" Bud called to the security team. "This isn't necessary."

But no Allister employee was taking orders from Bud. Sunny and I were the first to get pulled. A guard the size of a small elephant hoisted us up to our feet, but not before I managed to swipe Sunny's photo from the podium. The news cameras shifted to capture the image of us kids getting dragged away for demanding a decent future. It was an outrage.

Mr. Dan couldn't take it. He stood up and made a run for Richard Allister while shouting quite a few words that you can't say on television. Unfortunately, the guards dragged him back.

The elephant carted me and Sunny to the elevator bank along with Rashi and Paco. Running low on hope, I handed the picture back to Sunny. Not one gravestone had faded.

"Don't quit now," she said with a sad-but-hopeful smile, staring deep into the photograph. "It's only ten fifteen. The whole future's on the table."

Sunday Turner didn't know it at the time, but 10:15 a.m. was precisely when that table would turn. We'd now meet the new future, the one thing that nobody, not even Sunny herself, had counted on. It came as a blaze of red, white, and blue. Raging fast from the back of the hall to the edge of the stage.

"JAMES LYNDON BUDLEY!" she shouted.

I knew that voice. It was the voice of crayoned wallpaper, of broken figurines, of accidental $20 App Store purchases. Nothing shot me through with the fear of God like this voice. One thing I knew Senator James Lyndon Budley was about to learn firsthand: when my mother lit up on your full legal name, you were a dead man walking.

"It's Cass," one of the guards marveled. "She looks like an American flag." He caught an elbow from the elephant-guard, who was trying to pay attention.

Mom tugged the microphone off the podium while laser blasting Senator Bud with a look of righteous fury.

"Sorry I'm late," she said, now amplifying that deadly voice through a dozen high-powered speakers. "The monitor-room *door* was having some technical difficulties. You can bill me for the damage."

She tossed Richard Allister a busted door hinge. Apparently, I wasn't the only one he'd tried to lock out of today's event.

"You know, Senator, it's a real shame." Mom pointed a finger at Bud. "About a hundred kids are getting carted off like criminals right now, all because their senator won't do what it takes to protect their future. You had no problem sending my generation off to war"—she gestured to her prosthetic foot—"but now our children are asking for a fight that *really* matters, a fight that isn't gonna swallow up thousands of lives, and you're telling them that's too much to ask? Man up, Senator. Do your job. Or maybe someone else will."

Mom dropped the mic and bounded off the stage. She made a beeline for Sunny and me, but a swarm of reporters stopped her at the foot of the stairs. They all wanted a comment from Cass Kaminski, the thirty-five-year-old Carbon Hill security guard. The Purple Heart Iraq War vet. The third-year law student. The Mom.

They all assumed she was running for office.

STEP 8:

GO HOME

"Jonah!" Sunny cried. "This is it!"

I spun back to find Sunny on her knees, watching all three gravestones fade out like time-lapse clouds giving way to the sun. The costumed Crew had gathered around her to watch the picture fade out entirely. With a trembling hand, Sunny punched a new date into her timepiece: *October 31, 2100*. Her work here was done. But she paused, not jumping off just yet.

"She's not going to start Peter-Parkering out now or something, right?" Paco did a Thanos snap for emphasis.

I shook my head. "She's got this." I knelt to join her on the floor. "You did it."

Sunny smiled, proud. "But not alone." She looked across our faces, then back down to the watch. "I never did tell you," she whispered like a prayer, "about the math teacher."

"The one who finished the timepiece?"

"Yes." Sunny pulled out the Lesson Planner one last time. "Her. The real inventor. The same one who worked out this whole plan but died too soon to save the world herself."

She turned the inside cover for all of us to see:

If lost, please return to: Vera Turner

"Your mother's backpack." I gulped to hold back the tears.

"Waterproof." Sunny gave the bag a loving pat. She kissed the Lesson Planner then stowed it safely away. "I guess we've got another thing in common now, don't we, Jonah?"

"Historic moms," I answered. Both of us laughed before her smile went bittersweet.

"Rashi." Sunny pulled out the tiny hourglass from the campaign manager's home office. "Remember to make time."

"Count on it," Rashi said, tearfully tucking it into her blue Hamilton jacket.

"Paco." Sunny tapped on his Superman *S*. "Remember your power."

"I will," Paco said with his chin up and the truth in his eyes.

"And Jonah," Sunny whispered. "Number Five."

One Future Fact remained. I could have asked her anything I wanted. My mind raced through the possibilities, the opportunities, the dangers, and the fears. But I couldn't think of one future event that might not already be altered by the three people huddled around me. Soon, I thought, my Best Future-Friend would be sitting in some twenty-second-century diner, sharing waffles with Monday, Vera, and George. That was the only Future Fact I needed, and I already believed it with all my heart.

"Keep it," I told her, looking back at Rashi and Paco and thinking of Gideon's song. "The future isn't facts. It's people. And I've got the future right here."

Sunny threw her arms around me for a final and unexpected hug. I'm no hugger, but I'll always make exceptions for world-saving pink astronauts from the future.

"Look at the time," she said, rising up tall and checking the timepiece once more. "I'd better be getting home."

With that, Sunday Turner—the girl who came out of nowhere, who raged at the darkness and smiled like the sun, who put the whole future on the table and prayed for every meal, who looked at a lonely, dying boy and saw a chance to save the world—took one giant leap back to the future she'd saved.

"Is she gone?" Lindsay Allister asked, having only just caught up with the Crew.

"Not gone," I said. "Just home."

"Well." Lindsay hit the elevator button. "Speaking of gone, I can get us out of here."

"Then welcome to the Crew," Rashi said.

All four of us shuffled into the elevator: Lindsay hit B to take us out through the old basement wing. But before the sliding doors made a move, the elevator bank darkened with two haggard shadows.

Not again.

"Back off!" Lindsay blocked the door as those sweaty, scarred wannabe inventors stumbled toward the remaining Crew.

The woman gave a sigh of relief, her eyes still hungry and wide. "For every action, there is an equal and opposite reaction. It's basic physics."

"A scientist!" I shot back. "Why don't you try *inventing* something?"

"Let's put it on their reading level," the man wheezed, jingling a key chain that looked like an ice-cream cone. "Time to face the consequences of your actions."

It might've been enough to scare me, but it wasn't my turn to be scared. The man froze in horror as the key chain faded into nothing, just like Sunny's grave-site photo. The woman froze, too, now inspecting her transparent hands in the dim industrial light. With barely a whimper, the two of them were gone. Whether they'd somehow drifted back to their proper place in history or faded into nothing, I couldn't say. But I got the feeling this was the last we'd see of them on this side of the twenty-first century.

"Please tell me I wasn't the only one who saw that," Paco said, reprising his Thanos snap.

Before any one of us could answer, a man stormed into the elevator bank in place of the Soda Jerks. He stopped the sliding door with his hand.

"I am so getting fired," Mr. Dan panted, hopping into the box with the rest of us.

"Room for one more?" another familiar voice said. It was Mom, sweating through her now-legendary American sundress. She stepped into a little space between me and Mr. Dan as the doors slid shut.

"Rough day at the office?" I said.

Mom nodded and blew the curls out of her face. "I don't wanna speak too soon," she said, "but I think I just got fired."

"Awesome!" Mr. Dan said. "We can trade unemployment tips."

Mom laughed unusually hard.

"I dunno," she said, resting her hand on my shoulder. "I think a new position just opened up."

THE END OF THE WORLD AS WE KNOW IT

15 minutes until detonation

"We are running out of time," I groaned, gritting my teeth at the unbearable stress of it all. The summer sky was nearly black. Big problem.

"Dude, I'm moving as fast as I can," Gideon said. "It's not my fault Principal Rivera's yard is like ninety percent rock. Here." He passed me the mallet and held the stake evenly against the grass.

I pounded the sign into our principal's front lawn: *CASS for Senate.*

Gideon flipped his hair back and rose to appraise our work. After Mom had announced her run last winter, he'd sworn not to cut his hair until after the primary election. Something told me he wouldn't be cutting it even after she'd won. It made him look like the rock star he'd always been.

"It's a yard sign, man, not a van Gogh," I said. "We're late for the rendezvous."

"But we've got a few deliveries left." He pointed to the signs strapped onto my back.

"We've got tomorrow," I said.

We hopped onto our SLYSR Model-Zs and made for Martic Pinnacle.

Everyone had gathered not far from Sunny's flag. Two hundred eighty-two days had passed since she'd planted the star-spangled banner, dressed up in that pink astronaut suit of hers. Just the look of it made me sad, how the last sign of Sunny had flapped itself ragged, already fading with time.

Rashi greeted us with hugs and rushed back to the portable command center she'd made out of a card table, a camping chair, and her wireless laptop. "I have news," she sang. "Has anyone heard from Paco?"

"Not me." Lindsay had just arrived with a stack of Maroni's pizza. "What's the news?"

Rashi zipped her lips. "Not without Paco. I want the whole Crew to hear this."

Paco zoomed up the trail on the SLYSR he'd inherited from Sunny. "The CASS account just hit one hundred thousand followers!" He slid to a dusty stop.

Rashi applauded teasingly. "Now just multiply that by ten, and we'll almost match Paco's *personal* followers! Almost." As always, Rashi had the numbers right. Paco's words had attracted quite a following after his televised speech went live to the world. His superpower was no longer Carbon Hill's best-kept secret.

"We're all here now," I said, still waiting for the news. "Don't leave us hanging."

Rashi folded her hands. "So, we just got final numbers from our chapters around the state."

"And?" We said it all at once.

"Check your phone." Rashi twinkled a few words into her laptop and smacked the *enter* key. My pocket buzzed. We all checked our phones to find the same notification from Mom's social account.

WE CANVASSED 200,000 VOTERS IN ONE DAY!!!

In the second I took to read it, the post had already racked up twenty likes from our volunteers all over the state.

A mud-spattered pickup truck crunched up the wide, well-worn path and parked near the pinnacle's edge. The door burst open with a blast of tumbling fur. Einstein, the time-traveling labradoodle, barreled toward my best friend and attacked him with sniffs and kisses. Back on Halloween morning, just as the Soda Jerks had faded out of the twenty-first century, Einstein had faded right back in. Was it Sunny's doing or some mystery of spacetime mechanics? I'd never know. But I did know one thing for sure: Einstein had sworn off car-chasing for good.

Mrs. Smith hopped down from the driver's seat of the great big pickup. "Did I miss it?"

"You're right on time," Lindsay said.

"I told ya, Mom." Gideon slapped the hood of the truck. "If there's one thing this tank is good for, it's off-roading." After Zero Hour, Gideon's stepdad had started lending his truck for any and all U.S.A. business. It was never perfectly polished anymore, but Mr. Smith didn't seem to mind.

Gideon reached into the truck bed and pulled out a long, black instrument case. He still hadn't removed the shipping label since the gift was delivered to his home on the day after Halloween:

To: Gideon

From: Sunny

Make a joyful noise.

The delivery was postmarked on October 28, the day Gideon performed his first song.

Two more adults climbed out of the truck: a bearded man with a *CASS for Senate* T-shirt and Cass herself—my mom.

"When are you gonna shave that thing?" Lindsay pointed with her pizza plate.

Mr. Dan proudly stroked his salt-and-pepper scruff. "This is my unemployment beard."

"You are literally employed by the campaign," Rashi said.

He shrugged. "My boss likes it."

"Shave and you're fired." Mom patted his cheek.

"Ew," Lindsay said. "Your mom is flirting with your teacher."

I shrugged it off. "Not my teacher anymore."

I set my chair next to Gideon, who had just popped open his instrument case, revealing a banjo. Sunny had carefully hand-lettered a ring of words to frame its five strings, just like the photoprint in Gideon's room. Except this banjo said something new, something Sunny wanted all of us to remember:

THIS MACHINE IS THE END OF THE WORLD AS WE KNOW IT.

"I still don't get it," I said. "Sounds pretty dark for Sunny."

"Not dark at all." Gideon slung on the instrument and plucked out a few happy notes. "It says 'the end of the world *as we know it*'—not 'the end of the world *period*.'"

"It's like the apocalypse." Rashi pulled her camping chair up next to mine. "You know, in the original Greek, that word means revealing, uncovering, opening up."

"Starting something new." Paco took a seat on the grass in front of us.

I shrugged. "I get the 'new' part, but how do you know that our new future is gonna be a good one?" I observed the tattered state of Sunny's American flag. "How do you know that we can win?"

"Well, that part's easy," Gideon answered. "We've got friends now."

He strummed a little faster as the sky before us exploded into flares of red, white, and blue. Gideon started singing "This Land Is Your Land," and the whole Crew sang along.

But not me. I sat back and inhaled the Fourth of July breeze—not fast, like I was out of breath, but slowly, like I was taking a drink. I watched the fireworks unfold behind the bright stars and broad stripes of Sunny's waving banner.

Her flag was still there.

SECRET WEAPON

An Emergency Transmission from the Author

I wrote a lot of this book while covered in sweat, running circles around my neighborhood at five o'clock in the morning. That's because, once I had the idea for *We the Future,* it seemed only fair to write it like Sunny or Jonah would—with urgency. So, I wrote this book early in the morning and late at night. I wrote it over lunch. I wrote it on vacation. I even found a way to write this book by voice-texting the words into my phone during my daily jog.

Why the drama? Two reasons:

1. I am nothing if not dramatic.
2. The subject of this book could not be more serious.

The climate emergency is big, it's bad, and it's well worth fighting. But all too often I see people treating their climate fight like a solo mission to use less energy and shrink their own "carbon footprint." Sadly, though, in a world where a small number of companies produce the vast majority of greenhouse gas emissions, these personal changes won't come close to solving the problem.

Nobody saves the world alone—just ask the Avengers.

Saving the world starts when people like you begin assembling teams and demanding big changes to the destructive systems that threaten the future of life on Earth. Our roads and power grids were built for a destructive, fossil fuel–powered modern world. But a modern world doesn't have to be destructive, and it doesn't have to run on coal and gas. With enough of you teaming up, you can force the adults in charge to start building a future that's less apocalyptic and more, well, futuristic.

This kind of teaming up is often called "political organizing." You can do it through canvassing like the Crew did, or making phone calls, or even texting. To get started, I'd suggest getting hooked up with an organization that's already doing this work—and having your friends join, too. If you visit **heycliffIewis.com/start**, I'll point you to a few groups that were designed for youth climate activists like you.

And even if you're feeling like Jonah did when the story began, not quite ready to start teaming up, there's still one secret weapon you can help unleash. You're holding it in your hands right now. Rather than storing *We the Future* on a shelf, try giving this book to someone else—maybe someone who would make a good Sunny, Gideon, Rashi, or Paco. And who knows? Maybe *they'll* be the one to recruit *you*.

After all, only you can save the world, but you'll never do it alone.

SHOUT-OUTS

The People Behind the Book

It's honestly hilarious how much help I had in writing *We the Future.* This book simply wouldn't exist without every last one of these wonderful people:

Jen Nadol and **the Unter Agency**, for championing this story even when I'd started losing faith;

Meg Gaertner and the team at **Jolly Fish Press**, for supercharging this book and launching it into the world;

Sean Easley, for seeing some weird potential in a first-draft manuscript I'd mostly written while jogging, and choosing me as your Pitch Wars mentee;

The activists in **the Sunrise Movement**, especially **Julia Epstein** and **Bre Macpherson-Rice**, for demonstrating the community and dedication it takes to fight for good jobs and a livable future;

Sophie Xiong, **Sav Thorpe**, **Allison Troy**, **Eliot Stone**, and others for proving that making friends is perhaps the very best side effect of local political organizing;

Becca Rast, **Nick Martin**, **Jonathan Smucker**, **Eliza Booth**, **Jules Berkman-Hill**, **Zak Gregg**, **P.D. Gantert**, **Izzy Smith-Wade-El**, **Jess King**, and all the organizers and leaders who have helped turn Lancaster, Pennsylvania, into the epicenter of an organizing revolution;

Eugene Johnson, who penned an epic social post after we'd lost a local election and inspired one of my favorite lines in this book

("We've got friends now");

Adam Perry, for becoming my very first IRL author-friend, inspiring me to write middle grade, and providing so many on-point critiques;

Carl Pearce, for a cover illustration that makes the Crew look just as fierce and historic as I'd imagined them;

Scott Trobaugh, for helping me play armchair art director without making a complete fool of myself;

And, saving the bestie for last, **Jenn Lewis**, for reading *We the Future* more times than anyone else on Planet Earth, myself included. Everything good in this book is just me trying to make you smile.

About the Author

Cliff Lewis is a time-traveler from the 1990s, presently parked in the 2020s. He's a professional writer, a hometown story-slam winner, and a keynote speaker living in Pennsylvania with his wife, their two kids, and a little dog named Pippin. In his spare time, Cliff volunteers for local progressive organizations, which once led to a crew of young climate activists devouring all of his family's traditional election-day chili.

Learn more at **www.heycliffewis.com**

Follow **@heycliffewis** on Instagram, Twitter, and TikTok

Write a letter to **heycliffewis@gmail.com**